BLAME RANE

RANE

Rene' O'Shea

Cover art by Donald Wooten @ www.hollagraphics.com
ISBN 978-0-9740082-5-7
First Edition

G.O.O.S.E. God's On Our Side Enterprises
GOOSE Publishing™ is a subsidiary of Nichole Holdings, LLC

FOR

EVA FULP MARTIN

&

CYLLANA NICHOLE

"I am an American... Indigenous to the Americas. Nowhere else could I, this so-called Black person—African, European, Indio— exist. ... Only here; *only here*, she said..." ~ **Alice Walker**

TABLE OF CONTENTS

INTRODUCTION

Blame Rane is a Black woman, according to the **one drop rule***; born and raised in the American South. Like most African Americans, she is actually of mixed heritage. There exists in her ancestry: an African American woman, named Tuppie, who died and became a crow; a Caucasian American woman, named Gwendolyn, who died and became a pigeon; and a Native American woman, named WindRider, who died and became a cardinal. These are their *her*stories.

* "The **one-drop rule** is a historical colloquial term in the United States for the social classification as black of individuals with any African ancestry; literally, it means that any person with one-drop of black blood in them is considered a black person." ~ Wikipedia.org

PREFACE

FIRE AND ICE

But what of black women? ... I most sincerely doubt if any other race of women could have brought its fineness up through so devilish a fire. ~ **W. E. B Du Bois**

ENDINGS

Ethel Rane dreamt of fire, as her house burned down. Nightmares *always* plagued her sleep, so this was nothing new. In fact, considering her shamefully adulterous day, the nightmare was warranted, as well as expected.

There was an eerie, too surreal quality to this dream. Ethel could hear the faint tick tock of her solid gold watch, from inside the antique armoire, and she definitely smelled smoke…neither of which should be possible, in a dream. There was also some problem with her lungs in this dream. Even as she slept, she seemed to be suffocating, desperately needing air.

Thick clouds of acrid soot rolled quietly through the house, turning ordinary darkness completely black. Dainty dancing ceramic figurines, the crystal candy dish and gold gilded vanity mirror, all exploded—sounding like the 4th of July. Lethal ruinous flame leapt from baseboard to ceiling tile, incinerating everything in its path, including her husband Sherman, who lay beside her, roasting. The walls, from roof to shaky foundation, became crisp as burnt bacon, and crumbled, like twin towers, back to dust.

Ethel wanted to scream, the way you do in dreams, but could not. She needed to wake up, but the die was cast, and she would not. The moment she felt she might open her eyes, and end the hellish nightmare, was the same moment she felt the blistering heat. Reverie gave way to reality, and Ethel understood, *completely*, that this was no dream.

Fire, in all its magnificent glory, buckled the headboard and seized the coveted locks of her silky hair. It sizzled down Ethel's pretty face, boiling her eyeballs in their sockets. Flames flashed across her creamy brown shoulders, frying skin and sinew alike; while hot blaze broiled her vocal cords, choking out the intended warning for her daughter, Blame.

The flesh of her arms and legs melted right off the bone...the bone was reduced to smoldering ash. There were sirens in the distance. Ethel could hear them as she lay burning...her breasts and womb turning to butter.

In the fleeting seconds before life ended, so many things became clear, like the true meanings of despair and retribution. But what she understood most, with the last feeble bit of her scorching brain, was the long wide difference between right and wrong, and the priceless value of precious life. As Ethel prayed, too late, for mercy and more time, her heart, like the vanity mirror, burst into a thousand smoking pieces of hot glass.

CLOUDS GROW ON THE VINE

October 27, 1989

Dead is dead, Mrs. Douthit rationalized. She waited for the RA to fetch Blame from her dorm room, and considered what to say. Unable to invent good words for bad news, she thought instead about the girl, Blame. Strange name. Always made Mrs. Douthit wonder who was at fault. Anyhow, she concurred, dead is dead...nothing else to it.

The Resident Advisor rapped lightly on the dorm room door. "You have a phone call, Blame. And a message, too," she bellowed; then continued down the hall. Blame peeped out into the empty corridor and made her way to the phone, dangling ominously from its chord. She paused, recognizing her name on a post-it-note. Blame peeled the note off the cinderblock wall and snatched up the hanging receiver.

"Hello, this is Blame," the timid teenager whispered.

"Thank goodness, I finally got you. Is that you, Blame?"

"*Mrs. Douthit?*" Blame hadn't fully registered who she was talking to; still, the fine hairs on her neck stood at attention and her able knees went weak.

"You need to come on home, Blame. I...uhm... well...I don't know no other way than to just tell you." Never envied for her tact, Mrs. Douthit took a deep breath and dove right in, shattering the calm surface and shallow depth of Blame's placid world. "Your mamma and daddy's dead." Another deep breath, then, "I'm sorry to say, they burnt up in a fire, night for last." And, as an afterthought, "Well...you have my condolences Blame. Blame? Blame Rane?"

A frightful scream leapt to the edge of Blame's throat but wouldn't escape her mouth; it clamored and banged inside her head. The silent scream rattled her frame crashing into vital organs, causing something to shake and crack inside her lithe

7

body. An invisible, debilitating force clutched her windpipe, squeezed her chest, and liquefied her legs. Blame suddenly understood why people fainted. As her compassionate brain locked down whole regions of itself—to absorb and deflect the pain—she suffered temporary blindness, temporary paralysis and temporary insanity.

When she could breathe again, Blame dropped the phone in its cradle, and managed, somehow, the few difficult steps back to her dorm room. She passed long, terrifying hours crouched under the desk, like a frightened kitten, deciphering Mrs. Douthit's impossible message. She knew her old neighbor was not a liar; but, "*mamma, daddy, and dead*" all in the same damned sentence could **NOT** be true...not in Blame's universe.

She concentrated on breathing and waited patiently for her father to call. Surely he would call, and set things aright...like her bicycle and left knee, when the training wheels had to come off. Daddy, Blame thought, will fix this, too.

She examined the note swimming in her sweaty palm, turning it over and over for clarity. It was a message from...a *fire* department? Blame wanted to return the call—put an end to the absurdity—but the routine logistics of securing a landline, and dialing a number, escaped her. Besides, she convinced herself, as she folded and ate the post-it note, it simply wasn't true. Just as clouds did not grow on the vine, her parents, *both of them, absolutely could **not**, have mercy, **be dead***.

632 ROSE LANE

At daybreak and on autopilot, Blame packed a quick bag and took a series of buses from her dorm room on the campus of Broward University in Washington, DC, to her childhood home in the military town of Norfolk, Virginia. She sprinted from the bus stop to 632 Rose Lane—her feet somehow knowing the way. She rounded the corner and froze, gaping in horror, at an ominous pile of charred brick, burnt wood and black soot. Mrs. Douthit said she needed to come home; but there was no such place on earth anymore for Blame Rane.

Nineteen year-old Blame felt the very earth shift beneath her feet. The wretched scream lodged in her body, ripped from her lungs, finally pushing its way past her vocal chords. A great flood gate burst open, releasing a ready swell of hot tears. Blame collapsed in the street, and pressed her weight firmly against the pavement, trying desperately to keep the earth on its axis.

Awakened from nap by the pure pain outside her front door, Mrs. Douthit braced herself and prayed for strength and right words, to help bridge the gap between naked grief and letting go. The old woman ambled across the street on her walker, and slowly, but surely, silenced the horrific sounds of misery absolute. She coaxed Blame to her feet, and they trudged back across Rose Lane, both leaning on the walker for support.

WindRider, the Indian-red cardinal, could not process the fact that Rose Lane was not a village. She shook her head and wailed for Blame, not understanding why she was left so alone by the tribe. Why weren't the women rushing out from their homes to console her? Did Rose Lane have a chief? And where was the shaman with his bag of medicines? She wanted to stroke the thick tangle of brown hair resting on Blame's back. Lacking hands, she instead, twirled, stomped and chanted what little she remembered of the funeral dance...her leather skirts slapping in the wind.

Tuppie Rane, the Black African crow, sat shivering amidst the charred beams and rafters of Sherman and Ethel

Rane's burnt-down house. She reflected quietly; dead now, but still wanting to understand why suffering, misery and death were the plight of her people. Again, she asked God, "Why?" Again, there was no answer—no rhyme, nor reason—for her family's despair throughout the centuries. She pulled her threadbare rags tighter around her thin, but ample frame, and rose up from the soot—looking more like Phoenix than crow.

Gwendolyn Rainier, the White European pigeon, not having any other place to be, perched atop the streetlight and noted the neat little bungalow Mrs. Douthit and Blame were moving toward. She straightened her satin bonnet, and hoped this Mrs. Douthit could find some way to keep the girl. She wished that Andrew, a wealthy great nephew, now living in Florida, might somehow find out about this Blame "Rane", and come to her rescue.

Tuppie Rane glowered at Mrs. Rainier with seething contempt. Gwendolyn shot back an equally nasty scowl. WindRider TwoSquirrels, now finished her funeral dance, looked at them both with disinterest...wondering again, why they were there.

Anyone watching would tell you: a wounded girl fell down in the street. Three little birds came to watch her. The black crow settled among the ashes of ruin; the red cardinal pranced and chirped upon the trunk of a Buick; and a fat white pigeon, preferring to be called a rock dove, alit atop the lamppost. After an old woman, with heavenly words, helped the girl to her feet (because the wound was not fatal); the three little birds, differently hued, flew away in different directions. The black one went with the flock, or the "storytelling" of crows.

Mrs. Douthit settled Blame in the seldom used guest bedroom, with a plastic storage container—no bigger than a boot box—housing the handful of debris salvaged from 632 Rose Lane. Blame was alarmed the remnants of her world could fit in such a compact package. As a quiet continuous stream of snot, tears and grief ran down her face, curled under her chin and saturated her neck, she bit the back of her hand to muffle her miserable moans.

Scenes of a life danced across Blame's memory. Not the birthdays, holidays or vacations, but the once mundane details of everyday existence. She saw Sherman's contemplative, furrowed brow, wire-rimmed spectacles resting haphazardly on the narrow bridge of his nose, studying a large stack of bills. Heard Ethel's coveted voice rising and falling in the laundry room, where she folded silk linen, and hummed a gospel hymn. Blame wished she knew the words to her mother's song.

When Blame emerged from the bedroom, Mrs. Douthit sat her before a platter of tuna melts and sweet pickles, and pushed a legal pad and several envelopes across her old Formica-topped table. "This here's the business you need to tend to," the childless woman explained, crunching into a crisp sweet pickle. "From what I can tell, your daddy had some insurance, but he had two mortgages, too. Humph, such a shame, black folks don't never own nothing outright. And goodness child, your mamma had more credit card debt than there's gold at Fort Knox!"

The forlorn teenager choked down a bland bite of tuna melt stuck in her palette, wiped fallen tears away from the green Formica table, with a flowery paper napkin, and tried to focus on the bright yellow legal pad.

Mrs. Douthit continued, filling the empty space between them with a barrage of important questions. "Ain't you got no family or friends you can call on in this troubled time, Blame? And what about college? Your daddy would've wanted you to finish. You know you got to get your folks buried proper...nobody else to see to it. Where you gone live? What you gone do girl? Blame Rane?"

She wanted to press the uprooted girl to her bosom, and squeeze the pain away, but Mrs. Douthit wasn't the touchy feely type, and wasn't quite sure how to unfold her thick arms. The urge, along with the opportunity, passed them by. "If it's any consolation to you Blame," the old woman ventured, offering her best at compassion, by patting the girl's trembling hand, "the Fire Marshal said the smoke got to 'em long for the fire ever did, so they didn't hurt none. You fix it in your mind like that, you hear? Sherman and Ethel went to sleep as usual, and 'stead of waking up, they went on off to heaven." They sat that way for a while, both women thinking of burning flesh.

Mrs. Douthit searched for a bright spot in the darkness. "Oh! I almost forgot," she exclaimed, forcing a smile on her weathered face, and pulling a set of keys from her sweater pocket. "Fire didn't touch the Buick. Least you got that....and God. You always got God when you ain't got nothing else, Blame." Then she retired to her bedroom leaving Blame alone to sort out her life; knowing full well the only family was an uncle far removed, somewhere in Carolina. Mrs. Douthit also knew Blame didn't have any friends. Her exotic looks, especially her eyes, made the neighborhood girls distrust her; and made the boys to assume she was out of their league. All the child had was a Buick and a box of half burnt memories. It was a sad set of circumstances, but the old woman knew there was no time for tears. She soaked her dentures and aching feet and said another prayer for Blame.

Later, the distressed teenager lay in Mrs. Douthit's guest bedroom, terrorized by haunting images of her family on fire, mourning her great loss. She considered the sweet release of death, and thought *seriously* about joining her mamma and daddy. One night the pain and grief seemed insurmountable; the orphan got up to see if there was anything Mrs. Douthit's medicine cabinet strong enough to do the trick. A trio of differently feathered birds chirped and flapped hysterically at the window, drawing the lonely girl away from such fatal thoughts.

Eventually, the grief became manageable, as grief does; and Blame finished what the fire started, having Sherman and Ethel cremated. There was a 21-gun salute, honoring Sherman's service during the Korean War, with only Blame and Mrs. Douthit in attendance. Two cheap urns and an American flag were added to the plastic tub of memories.

A week later, the homeless teen rolled up the highway in her father's immaculate 1982 Buick Regal, with its broken heater. Her belly and gas tank were full, courtesy of Mrs. Douthit. She checked her purse, again, for the $70.00 Mrs. Douthit had also given her. (Blame was developing a quick habit of checking to make sure things were where they should be.) Mrs. Douthit promised to watch the mail for the insurance check; and because winter was at the door, she gave Blame a hand-knitted woolen cap.

In the solitude of her dorm room, the sophomore mapped out a plan for survival; considering first her assets— shelter (the dorm), food (a meal card), clothing (she was Ethel's daughter), and transportation (her daddy's Buick). Her first priority was getting the one thing she didn't have—money; so while her peers headed to morning classes, Blame set out to find a job. The economy had taken a recent downturn, but she eventually snagged a fulltime, low-paying, 2nd shift gig. Sewing in a textile factory wouldn't have been a dream come true three weeks earlier; but in her present plight, it was more than she'd hoped for. Hope was still a long way off for Blame Rane.

The girl took her meals in the school cafeteria, parked her car off campus, and dodged the Resident Advisor for the rest of the semester. She saved what she earned from her minimum wage job; but at $3.35 an hour, it wasn't very much at all. She slept when she could and cried less and less for her dead parents as the weeks went by. The tears were now stingily shed more for Blame.

Blame returned to 632 Rose Lane to close her parents' estate and repay Mrs. Douthit her kindness. There were no funds to collect from the insurance proceeds. Debtors claimed their portion—the total sum—and many lofty balances were still due. This was disappointing to Blame, who was counting on that money to make a fresh start in life.

When the Dean of Students caught up with Blame, just before winter break, she knew the jig was up. He informed her she'd failed all her courses, had a zero account balance, and needed to vacate the premises, *immediately*. The bashful teen who rarely spoke up or out, breathlessly related her catastrophe to the Dean, between sobs and shudders. The Dean sympathized, but reminded Blame that a University was not a charity organization. He gave her a handful of Kleenex, a list of aid agencies, and called someone from maintenance to help remove her things. Blame loaded her pittance of belongings into the freezing Buick and set off down the road...with no particular destination in mind.

TUPPIE RANE

Fire a bad way to go. Yo death stay witcha, you know... ya birth do too. When it all over and you waitin fo de Judgment,

14

like me; you memba evuhthang—joy and regret, de womb n de grave, alike.

I likes to recolleck on my own birth day—that li'l bit o close time wit my mamma. I sees huh face, I hears huh voice. I even know the rhythm of huh heart and the swayin of huh hips. But I never knowed huh name. I wont nursed by my true mammy but bout seben munfs. Das when I's sold to Massah Rainier. Whad dey wanna buy a baby fo? Well, I reckon dey bought me causen dey could. White folks is sumphin else.

Anyhow, 19 years a heap lot longer to knowd yo mammy den seben munfs was. So I reckon li'l Blame be awright. I bleeve I just stick roun a bit and see fo mysef tho; easy to do now, bein a crow. Ole fat Missy Rainier, she be a pigeon now...shoulda been a rattle snake, she so mean and nasty. Don't know the Injun...pretty l'il cardinal tho. A rare bird she is...carryin round a eyeball!

Oh dear, I beg your pardon. You probably haven't understood a word I've said. I am bilingual now, in death, and I subconsciously lapse back into my native tongue from time to time. You may call it Plantation Pidgin, Niggerlish, Ebonics. It's the peculiar language pieced together by millions of African slaves, from different tongues and tribes. Our Caucasian captors would only bark short commands at us, never speaking in complete sentences. With no formal education in America, and a full scale attack at keeping us ignorant, I'd say we did a pretty remarkable job learning to communicate!

Well...maybe not a remarkable job; but we did the best we could, considering. And so will Blame. With so much ingenuity in the blood...dat chile bound to be awright. Les see...

BUICK BLUES

Blame pulled her father's cold, blue Buick into the last agency's parking lot. The other charities turned her away, citing: she didn't have a permanent address, there were no minor children involved, contact the Norfolk office, or, she already had a job. Blame mustered up some confidence and marched into the rundown storefront, decorated with Christmas cheer. She hoped the festive holiday season might bode well in her favor.

Ironically, Blame was greeted by a fellow classmate. Lindsey Gessler—an average, all-American blond, with poor exam scores and mediocre grades—was a 5th year junior on a free ride to the HBCU, courtesy of a minority grant. Upon graduation, she would assume her rightful place in the family business.

Lindsey immediately recognized Blame from an Economics class. She remembered Blame being smart; she also recalled her standoffish, unapproachable attitude—really just a severe case of shyness—and she didn't care very much for Blame Rane. As an unpaid intern, Lindsey wasn't qualified to make decisions regarding assistance; but she was bored, the staff was in a meeting, and she wanted to have a little fun with Blame. "May I help you?" she asked, peering over the top of her designer frames, with a slight smirk on her face.

Blames heart sank. Her usual shroud of insecurity quickly replaced her revved up confidence, as she looked wistfully to the floor and recited her miserable tale. Lindsey poked and probed during the interview, wanting to make Blame as uncomfortable as possible; delighting in the light sheen of sweat on Blame's forehead and the near-to-tears crackling of her voice as she recited her pitiful tale. After much posturing, Lindsey informed Blame the Agency could offer *no* assistance. She politely dismissed the broken girl...her smirk having grown to a full-toothed smile.

Blame bolted ran from the Agency, embarrassed and more hopeless than ever. She sought refuge from the cold in a Burger King, where she washed up, ordered a coffee, and waited for her shift at the textile mill to start. Blame watched and wept as merry holiday shoppers flooded the busy streets and a quiet snow dusted the picturesque scene. The depressed trauma victim scoffed and released an uncontrollable cackle at the very notion of Christmas.

After work, Blame crashed a 24-hour Laundromat to do her laundry, and keep warm in the process. When the establishment emptied of its patrons, the hungry girl retrieved her mother's crochet hook from the "memory box", and fished a bag of chips from the vending machine. She combed the classifieds for a place to rent; but her weekly pay was only $134.00; it would take months to get enough money to move out her daddy's car. Discouraged, Blame dozed off wondering instead, how much it might cost to fix the Buick's broken heater.

Meanwhile, back on Rose Lane, Mrs. Douthit bolted upright in her bed, plagued by a terrible feeling her bashful neighbor, Blame Rane, was in dire danger. It bothered her so, that she slid out of bed, and dropped down on her old sore knees to say a prayer for the girl.

Blame woke up in the Laundromat, startled and petrified to find two gruesome homeless men hovering over her, salivating. One guy, covered with scabies, flashed a rusty pocketknife in her face. The other, with snaggleteeth and greasy hair, pinned her down in the chair. Blame scanned the empty Laundromat for help. The scabies covered assailant snapped her bra loose with his blade and groped her breasts underneath her sweater. Snaggletooth ran his slimy tongue across her face, whispering filth in her ears; he unzipped his pants and stroked himself. Mr. Scabies' abrasive, sandpapery hands moved from her breasts and down her trembling body. His fingers dug into the nap of Blame's pubic hair, inching toward her vagina. Blame let out a bloodcurdling scream just before a dirty hand clamped down across her mouth.

A wayward group of teenaged boys was lurking about the streets that night, when they should have been home in bed. They heard Blame's cry (or possibly a prayer) and burst through the Laundromat doors, rushing the would-be rapists. Blame kicked past the crowd and lit out the building, leaving her laundry of warm sweaters. She peeled out of the parking lot, jumped a curve and sped up the snow-packed road shivering…a little colder now because she'd pissed her pants, her heart racing a hundred miles a second.

Conscious of the wasted gas, she pulled into a rest stop. Blame couldn't seem to wash away the grimy nastiness of her attackers. She changed clothes, trashing the ones she had on, and tried to put the disgusting image of her attempted rapists out her mind. Blame screamed and cursed her parents, again, for dying broke and leaving her in such fucked up condition.

Blame cried and tried her best to stay awake, listening to Gospel music on the car radio. She finally dozed off at dawn to the sounds of The Georgia Mass Choir, singing "Somebody Prayed for Me".

From that night forward, Blame slept on the back seat of the freezing Buick. Even with her comforter, all the clothes she had in the world, and her father's American flag piled on top of her; it was still too damned cold to sleep. She ate cheap fast food, washed up in gas station bathrooms, and developed a fast addiction for coffee and cigarettes (caffeine to keep warm and stay alert, nicotine to stave off hunger).

That January, the entire eastern seaboard was covered in a solid sheet of ice. Frigid winds blew in off the Potomac with D.C. boasting its lowest temperatures in recorded history. Fire claimed her family; but frost quickly became her number one nemesis. Staying warm was her biggest challenge and every night Blame prayed she wouldn't freeze to death before dawn. She stopped crying altogether; the icy tears were too cold on her freezing face. Her teeth chattered so much that her jaw ached. Her toes and fingers grew numb, and slightly blue. But worse than the subarctic temperatures, was the biting, much colder, loneliness she endured.

Mrs. Gwendolyn Rainier, the fat pigeon, was there, worrying nonstop—because that was her nature—clutching her silk handkerchief and wringing her winged "hands" over and over. WindRider, the cardinal, sensitive to all things—even the suffrage of hewn down trees in the forest—felt as if a thousand daggers were upon her flesh. Tuppie was steadfast with the knowledge of what was there in Blame's bloodline—namely, herself. Tuppie the crow knew, even if Blame did not, that she would surely survive.

Blame dreamt of warmth and comfort, coveting the smoke curling from chimneys. She daydreamed about the clever ladies cruising up the highways, with all their shit seemingly together, and wished she knew their secrets. She tried but failed to remember anything useful her parents might have told her about making a way in life. Blame grew bitter and cursed her parents every night; and wondered—like she had one night at Mrs. Douthit's house—if life was worth living at all.

When the homeless, hungry teen was truly at the end of her rope, suicidal and in serious jeopardy of developing hypothermia, she overheard a co-worker in the break room mention she needed a roommate. Blame was not one to talk to strangers, but she nearly leapt over the tiny tables to introduce herself to Toria Black. She still didn't have enough money to move out of the freezing Buick; but she could definitely go Dutch with someone. Toria eyed the musty smelling girl suspiciously, thinking anybody who wore a hand-knitted wool cap 24-hours a day probably had some serious mental issues. But, considering how badly she needed a roommate, Blame Rane would have to do.

For the rest of her life, Blame was haunted by an inner chill, close to the bone, even in summer. She didn't use the air-conditioner, refused to eat popsicles, and never took ice in her drinks. She permanently lost all feeling in her left pinky toe. When she bathed or washed dishes, she didn't bother with cold water at all. She developed an irrational fear of Laundromats, a peculiar fetish for heavy quilts, and an absolute loathing for the entire month of January...ironically, her birth month.

There wasn't to be any grief counseling for the nineteen year-old orphaned daughter of Sherman and Ethel Rane...not even a shoulder to cry on, or kind words of comfort and solace. Nor were any white knights coming to save the day. She was ill-prepared to negotiate the rapid waters of life; but she'd been forced into the torrent just the same. The ground kept shifting and Blame kept wobbling. She soon discovered she couldn't press down on the fast-spinning world to make it stop, or even slow down. The only real option, Blame decided, was to simply spin with it. And before long, Blame Rane was spinning out of control.

PART I

BLAME RANE

"She didn't read books so she didn't know that she was the
world and the heaven's boiled down to a drop."
~ **Zora Neale Hurston,** *Their Eyes Were Watching God*

Love is rife with risk for a motherless child. ~ **Paige Tangney**

CHAPTER 1
BALTIMORE WEEKEND

July 1990

"Where the blunt, Blame?" Toria asked. Then kicked off her shoes and flopped down on the cheap gray sectional, in their shared walkup apartment...still bopping her head to the thumping go-go music, playing in the street below.

Blame popped the top on a 40 ounce of Private Stock, which they would also share, and pulled two dollar dinners from the freezer. "Should be one in the smoke box," Blame responded, rinsing out two glasses, like hot water could really destroy roach germs.

"Oh yeah, it's one in here. Damn girl! We ain't got but a blunt worth of weed left." Toria shouted from the larger back bedroom. "Time to find that niggah, Ronnie; you know how a bitch hate to run out!" Blame laughed at her funny roommate, poured their cocktails and slid the cardboard box dinners into the warming oven. Toria rolled a blunt and flipped through the channels of stolen cable on their little "hot" tv.

Toria, 21, was originally from Detroit. She'd gotten into some kind of trouble she refused to talk about, and moved to DC to stay with her Aunt Linda. Toria got kicked out of her Aunt's house one month after Blame was booted from the University. The girls became necessary roommates and fast friends.

Blame dreaded the solitary, mundane life she'd always lived, and worked hard to fit in with Toria. She pretended to have the same experiences Toria had growing up; creatively matching the jaw-dropping stories her friend regaled her with. She lied about smoking weed and cigarettes and drinking liquor since 9th grade. She'd actually only tried such vices once, at the

Senior Day picnic, and that experience had been a *huge* embarrassment.

Blame exaggerated about having high school boyfriends and college-girl flings. She'd truly lost her virginity during her freshman year—finally out of sight of her father's prying eye— to a boy whose name did not even matter. She simply wanted to shake the social stigma of being a virgin. Knowing at least the anatomy involved, she could fake the back and forth banter she and Toria shared during late night girl chats.

Blame pretended as if talking loud and talking shit, blasting radios, watching Jerry Springer, and being quick to fuck any boy with a decent rap, were the norm. When, considering her quiet, isolated upbringing, such distasteful behavior couldn't be further from the truth.

Now 20 years old, Blame was beginning to learn the world was big and mean. Because she'd been homeless, more than a month, she knew for fact it was bitterly, miserably cold. Blame thought a girl like Toria could probably teach her some things she would need to know...things her mother, who hadn't disclosed any useful information, failed to instruct her about.

Needless to say, Mrs. Gwendolyn Rainier, the fat White pigeon, was mildly appalled. But really, she hadn't expected much more from Blame. Blame was after all, and much to Gwendolyn's regret, one of the niggers.

Toria blew weed smoke at the fat pigeon lounging on the fire escape landing, and shooed it away. She passed the blunt to Blame, stuffed her mouth with the meager meal, and washed it down with warm malt liquor. "If that bitch Tan in QC send anotha one of my batches back, I'ma have to see bout that ho," warned Toria, picking up the conversation where they'd left off.

"Bitch just be hating cause ain't nobody jocking her busted ass. I think she like Tyrone."

"Oh Toria, everybody in the mill know Tyrone be checking for you," Blame responded.

"Girl please, I ain't hardly studied in no niggah making the same money I make. Cause we both know the mill ain't paying SHIT!" They both laughed at the shared knowledge. Blame made a mental note: a man should make more money than a woman.

Toria continued, "That bum can check all he want, shit I'm tryna holla at one of them niggahs down on the block by the Chinese spot. They be selling rock, girl. Niggahs stay with they neck fulla gold, bumping in them Beemers and Benzes, and shit. I got my eye on the big dog down there, Drake. You know his boy, Ricco, be asking me about you, Blame. And that niggah is FOIN!"

Blame giggled and blushed, knowing very well who Toria was talking about. Anytime she went on his block, Ricco made it his business to drop what he was doing and walk her to her destination...be it the Laundromat, the Grille, the rent office... Blame knew he had money because he made a point of showing off his wad often, picking up her tabs and paying her bills all over the neighborhood. She liked the attention and conversation, not to mention the cash she saved on everyday things. Still she rebuffed Toria, countering, "that whole crew headed straight for the pen. I can't be getting caught up with a niggah gone be trapped off in the joint for twenty to life." They both laughed, with Blame wondering if her street lingo was legit.

"So, what happened with that team leader position you applied for?" Toria asked, changing the subject to bring Blame down a notch or two.

"They gave it to Amanda," Blame answered, sullenly.

"What?! You mean to tell me they gave it to the white chic? But you trained her Blame! She only been there what, like two months, and you got hired back in December, right? Plus you already knew how to sew. That heifer don't know a damn thing about how to do that job. And ain't she a high school drop out anyway? Wow! That's some real bullshit, man." Toria stuffed a soup cracker into her mouth to stifle a laugh.

"Tell me about it. I think she got a GED; but I've been to college. I can't figure out what they based the decision on." Blame, not understanding the rules of the game, seriously thought there was opportunity for growth at the mill. Now it seemed she might be stuck at minimum wage until retirement age. She couldn't fathom how people lived their whole lives on so little money.

"Humph, maybe she sucked the right dick," Toria joked, just to see if she could get a rise out of Blame. Blame didn't respond, but wondered if that was really how all the ladies who cruised up the highways to their comfortable, warm houses made ends meet. She quickly put the thought out her mind.

"Well, later for you scrub," Toria said, tossing the dish towel to Blame. "Some of us is old enough to get in the club, rootie poot. Don't wait up for me," she added with a wink. She went to the bathroom to shower and change, and was out.

Blame went to draw her bath, pushing aside Toria's battery of vaginal washes and douches, perfumes and powders—which was always a hassle. But Blame figured the collection of coochie supplies must be necessary, considering all the random fucking Toria did. She ran the hot water, and got in. Blame liked it hot—hot as fire; having once been so dreadfully cold.

In her bedroom, Blame rummaged through the plastic storage bin of broken dreams. Her favorite item in the memory box was a singed photo of her beautiful mother. She enjoyed the idea of being able to possess her mother whenever she wanted...something she hadn't been able to do before the fire.

Ethel beamed in the photo, holding up an imitation Tiffany lamp she'd been *so* proud of. Blame considered all the stuff her mother had—the many material items destroyed in the fire—and wondered how she would ever obtain such finery, when she could barely pay her bills in a dead end dump. She assumed ceaseless shopping was an important part of womanhood because it was her mother's one true passion. Blame was unaware of the things that truly defined a woman, and was beginning to consider herself quite the failure. She lingered over the photograph nearly an hour, wondering how people escaped poverty, before drifting off to sleep. She dreamt of extremities—fire of course, and now frost, as well.

Toria made it home a little after nine the next morning, too geeked up to sleep. She whisked into Blame's room, raised the dust encrusted blinds and forced the jammed window up as far as it would go. A cardinal landed on the ledge.

"Rise and shine girl! Get up; we going shopping. Get up Blame!" Blame pulled the covers over her head and rolled over, knowing she couldn't shop without money. "Hey, who's this?" Toria asked, pointing to the picture of Ethel Rane, resting on the night stand.

Blame quickly flipped back the covers, feeling suddenly protective of her dead mother's photo. She snatched it up so Toria wouldn't touch it. "My mother," she responded, defensively.

"Dang, let me see it. Oh, she pretty Blame. Y'all got some Indian in y'all family don't you?" The cardinal, on the ledge, cringed at the word "Indian" but stuck its breast out a little, just the same. "Why you don't never talk about your family? I mean you told me how they died, but that's it. And you was a only child *too*. I know yo butt was *spoiled*. Tell me bout yo daddy." Toria asked casually, as if she wasn't prying.

"Ain't much to tell," Blame admitted, while wondering if she had been spoiled. She looked at the picture of her mother and also wondered where the Native American features came from. But Ethel seldom talked to Blame, so that would remain a mystery. "They was just ordinary people," she added, dragging herself out of bed and putting away the photograph. Blame smiled at the cardinal strutting on the windowsill, with a stone in its talon, as she moved about the room picking out her clothes for the day. Toria lay across the foot of the used single bed and waited for Blame to open up. Toria liked to have as much information as possible about a person...never knew what might come in handy someday.

"Let's see...my daddy was in the Navy. He was born in Ohio, but his folks were from some town in North Carolina. He met my mamma when he was stationed in Orange, Texas. He used to joke about mamma's mean old grandmamma Sue...swore he rescued mamma from a life of boredom in Orange. But if he took her to some excitement in Virginia, the party was over fore I came along. Daddy's last station was in Norfolk, that's where I was born. He worked at the shipyard when he got out the military. Mamma worked off and on, here and there. They were quiet people. Daddy was a homebody and mamma *stayed* in the malls. Daddy made hisself sick smoking cigarettes. I think that's what started the fire. Mamma...well, mamma was... different..."

Toria wiped away the tears wetting Blame's cheeks. Blame hadn't realized she was crying, and was immediately

27

embarrassed. She wanted to be "hard" like Toria; thinking assimilation was required to keep her necessary roommate and first real "friend".

"Oh it's alright, girl. I know if something happened to my mamma I would just throw myself right on over in the grave with her. Okay!" Toria changed the subject (because it wasn't the kind of scoop she was looking for). "Enough of that sad shit, girl. You blowing my high! I'ma change up, be ready in twenty minutes. We got brunch dates!"

Blame looked in the mirror, tracing the reflections of her mother and father. Ethel's deep ruddy complexion was nearly as red as the little cardinal still preening on the ledge. Sherman was the soft, warm, light brown of fresh baked bread. Blame was a reddish-brown mix of the two—the color of cinnamon, or Carolina clay. They were of average height, and so was she, 5'6", for a woman. While Ethel and Sherman both shared eyes of brown, Blames' had always been a curious mystery. Hers' were an odd mix of gray and brown, more gray than brown, with little flecks of copper here and there.

Sherman made jokes about his sandy-brown, half-breed hair, swearing it had a mind of its own—curly one day straight the next, wild some days, tame on others. Ethel, on the other hand, had long black hair, straight as a pony's tail and fine as a spider's web. Blame's locks were a marriage of the two...brown like her daddy's, long like her mamma's, naturally curly, but permed straight, with brassy copper highlights that matched the flecks in her eyes. She had the body of a dancer, svelte and taut with curves in all the right places, and her beautiful hands could have easily belonged to a master pianist. Blame had no idea she was what most people, in America, considered beautiful.

Blame got herself together and threw a kiss to the redbird, roosting on the ledge. She'd heard that was supposed to bring good luck. Then she did a double take. *Was* that a stone in the little bird's talon...a marble, maybe? ...And hadn't she seen that bird before?

WindRider, the cardinal, celebrated Blame's memory of Ethel...and she exhilarated over the mention of sweet Sue.

When the two young ladies were refreshed and dressed, they ran down the steps, taking them two at a time, to find a chromed out BMW 735i waiting at the curb. Blame stopped cold in her tracks...her father's warning about "getting in cars with boys", echoed in her mind. Toria grabbed her by the wrist and nearly drug her toward the open back door, while she herself hopped into the front passenger seat. Ice Cube's "Rolling Wit' The Lench Mob" was blasting through the open windows, along with an aromatic cloud of marijuana smoke. Ricco was in the backseat, and Drake, who was damn near a D.C. celebrity, was pushing the whip. "Girl, get in the damn car!" Toria sternly commanded. Blame did as instructed, and off they went.

"You looking fresh today, Miss Blame it on the Rain," Ricco yelled over the bumping base, "but I bet I can make you fresher."

"Whatever," Blame retorted as she sparked the newly rolled blunt he handed her, thinking to herself: fuck it, it's a Saturday in July, I'm off work, and Toria ain't gone let nothing crazy happen to me...I might as well roll with it.

The crack game was in full effect, and Drake and Ricco were on top. Their first stop was an upscale steakhouse in Georgetown off Pennsylvania, where they ordered T-bones, lobster tails and a bevy of mixed drinks Blame never even knew existed. Then they were off to the Union Station Mall on

Massachusetts Ave. Toria raced through the shops like Flo Jo, piling clothes in both their sizes on the counters. "Fuck a dressing room, they fit," she slurred, still tipsy from the drinks. Drake and Ricco didn't flinch at the totals; they pulled out their wads, paid, and kept it moving. Blame didn't say a word, but felt oddly like she was stealing something...the image of Ethel in the faded photograph hung precariously in her mind.

The next stop was a Korean joint, where the girls were dropped off to get their nails done. The men, meanwhile, had to run and take care of some business elsewhere. Later, they all crossed the Woodrow Wilson Bridge and bounced to Baltimore, where yet more "business" had to be handled...blunts in the air, conversation flowing, and drinks toasting the whole way. After the business was in order, they made their way to the Harbor for a dinner of fresh seafood and ice cold beer. Two blocks over from the Harbor, Drake circled into the parking lot of the Hyatt Regency, as a flock of crows circled overhead. He and Ricco jumped out the flashy whip, keeping the engine running.

Pigeons on stoops and cardinals on ledges, occasionally ...but the great flock of crows was ever present...hovering much, much higher.

"Ahm, Toria...what the ef are we doing at a hotel?"
"What the fuck you *think* we doin at a hotel Blame? I don't know if you was paying attention, but bitch you done ate a hundred dollars' worth of food, and them bags in the trunk got more than a G worth of shit in 'em! That's fucking Drake and Ricco! Do you know how many bitches would kill to be sitting where we sitting right now. You better just chill and roll wit it. 'Cause you damn shole bet not even *think* about fucking my shit up right now. Be damned if I'm gone put in 40 years at the

fuckin mill!" The Detroit in Toria was on full blast. She fluttered her new acrylic nails in Blame's face and added, "Bitch I'm trying to get some rings on these, stop trippin. And anyway, ya sitting on a damn goldmine Blame. Pussy ain't just for peeing!"

"This is some bullshit. I didn't ask for none of that shit. Come on Toria, what the fuck? Oh so what, we prostitutes now?! "

"Bitch please, you didn't say 'no' to none of it either. And trust, ain't no run of the mill hos getting it like this. And anyway, what's the big deal Blame? You know you like Ricco. And he been trying to holla at you for a *long* time now. Don't make the shit more serious than it need to be. It's just dick, Blame. Ain't ya first, won't be ya last. Anyway, what the fuck dem li'l bum niggahs up at Broward give you besides a wet ass? Bitch you betta get yours 'cause I'm damn shole gone get minz!" She lowered her voice to a whisper, "Shut up. Here they come," then to an even lower, clinched-teeth growl, "you bet not fuck this up Blame."

"Ay," Ricco said, tapping on the tinted glass of Blame's window, "how bout you come put on a little fashion show for me upstairs? We can order some room service and chill...maybe check out a nice little after hours spot I know bout later on. Let me get somebody to carry your bags baby, 'cause you too damn fly to be toting shit." Drake and Ricco walked around to retrieve the girls' booty from the trunk.

In the eight months they'd known each other, Toria knew for a fact that Blame hadn't dated anyone, let alone slept with anyone. She had serious reservations about the sexual escapades Blame spun during their late night chats. But where she came from, there weren't any virgins over the age of 12, so in her estimation, Blame had to at least be fucking. Hell the bitch was grown and she didn't act like no dyke, Toria thought.

31

Toria had known all along how this day was going to end, but she sure as hell wasn't going to share that info with Blame. Ricco was Drake's boy. They did everything together. And Blame was just the bait Toria needed to hook a big phat Drake fish.

"Get the fuck out the car Blame!" Toria growled.

CHAPTER 2
FILLING HOLES
ETHEL RANE

I shake my head in disgust, cover my face in shame, and commiserate on her pitifulness. She's doing drugs, partying with thugs, and living in squalor! What has become of our Blame? I would love to be able to tell you, "She wasn't raised that way." But the more I think about it; she wasn't raised any kind of way. She was just there, in the house we lived in. Grandma Sue used to say, "If you don't put nothing in; you can't get nothing out." Hard to say what'll become of Blame; I don't recall putting anything in. But really, what did I know?

I was raised by my great-grandmother, Sue Dusty. She fed me and clothed me, and as long as she had a place to live, so did I. I was brought up to be thankful and grateful; so I guess I appreciated GranSue covering the basics. Still, I was missing something. She was my *great grandmother*, for goodness sake! She lived during slavery! And I wasn't born until 1937. She talked non-stop, always preaching...but really, what was GranSue going to tell me about middle century America—the 1940's-60's? I mean really...that foolish old woman had a damn bird for a best friend.

I did enjoy listening to some of GranSue's stories though, especially the ones her own mother told her about her grandparents. Gran did not remember their names; only that her African-Creole grandfather was named from the Bible. Her Cherokee Indian grandmother was named Hurricane or Breeze, something like the Wind. Sitting at her feet listening to those stories, I used to think, WOW, my heritage is the Bible and the Wind, how great I must be.

Gee, I never told Blame those stories. Perhaps I should have. I never took her to church either, which had been the foundation of my own rearing. My husband, Sherman, was a good man, just not the church-going type. And since I no longer *had* to go, what was the point? Did I shortchange Blame? Well, if I did, it wasn't my fault; I had no training for the job. Nobody showed *me* the ways of motherhood.

My own mother, Philomena, did not want me. She left me with GranSue not long after I was born. Gran was 87 years old by then—already crippled and half blind. Oh, Philomena came back, from time to time. She came back to eat our food, sleep in our beds, raid Gran's little tithing fund, and help herself to my clothes. Philomena came back for loans (which were never repaid), a lamp she could use...a picture frame she just had to have. And though I was on my best behavior when she came to hustle us—accommodating her in every way—Philomena never came back for me. *sigh*

I hated our unpainted, shotgun, clapboard house. All I wanted was for my mamma to take me home with her. It made no sense to me that she wouldn't; because people were always saying how pretty I was; and Philomena loved pretty things. Philomena moved a lot, but she always lived in the prettiest places. Nothing special on the outside, but inside, they were magnificent! When I was little girl, I went to her houses five times. When I got older, she said I was too big and blossomy to be coming round her man friends.

Philomena wore nylons, shiny ear baubles, and bright red lipstick. She drank hooch and laughed a lot, and played "race records" by Cootie Williams and Eddie "Clean Head" Vinson, on her Victrola. When she danced, she looked like something liquid—shimmying and shaking so; I used to wonder if she had any bones at all.

And *Ohhh*, the beautiful things she had in her houses—
silk curtains, embroidered pillows, little glass ladies with
parasols in a cabinet she called an étagère. Ain't that a *pretty*
word—étagère? Crystal candleholders and decorative perfume
bottles, why Philomena even had dishes with pictures painted
on them, that she called china. I wanted some of that china.
When GranSue and I ate beans—always beans and vegetables,
hardly ever any meat—off our pitiful tin plates, I pretended we
were dining off Philomena's fine china.

GranSue said Philomena needed *things*, to fill up the
hole in her heart. Gran said everybody had a hole. That old
woman said the craziest things. I took that one to heart though,
thinking it would be a good trick if I could learn how to find and
fill people's holes, starting with my momma, Philomena.

We didn't have no Victrola in our flimsy, three-room
shack. The only music I ever heard was the blasted church
organ. If I wasn't at home or school, GranSue and I could be
found at Greater Ebenezer Baptist Church. *God*, I hated that
place! But since I had to go, I tried to make the most of it. I
pretended to catch the Holy Ghost a lot, just so I could dance
and move my hips like Philomena. I liked to upstage the girls
with my pretty hairdos and snazzy dresses, too! (That was as
close as I could get to Philomena's shine).

GranSue made my dresses. She used to say, "I can't teach
you nothing bout book learnin, Ethel. Alls I know how to do is
work wit my hands. So I'll learn you that." GranSue could turn
any piece of plain material into a work of art. She told me when
she was young woman, all the rich white folks in Orange wanted
her to do their sewing. "They didn't hardly never pay me
nothing," she would say, "but sewing kept a roof over my head.
And you gone learn it too Ethel, so's you don't have to get yo
pennies doing what yo mammy do."

35

I didn't know, then, what Philomena "did". I suspected it was something ungodly, by the way GranSue screwed up her face when she talked about it, like she did when turnips gave her gas. Whatever it was, it took its toll on Philomena. Over the years, I watched my mamma get shabbier and shabbier. I wasn't allowed in her houses anymore, so I don't know how her finery fared. Of course GranSue blamed it on the devil, like everything else concerning Philomena.

When I got grown, I started helping myself to some of GranSue's church money too, and sneaking out to juke joints. I met a boy named Dave, down to Wild Willy's, who told me he would buy me anything I wanted if I slept with him. Well, I wanted a pair of lace gloves with little pearls sewn in around the wrists—like the kind Philomena wore in a picture she sent to GranSue. Dave got them for me. We exchanged our gifts at the train yard, in an empty box car. I got a splinter in my behind, but I sure *loved* those gloves.

Dave had him a girlfriend named Glo. She was a big old ugly girl, coal-colored with nappy hair; so she didn't like me. One night, me and Dave was dancing close and nasty to a Lavern Baker song; and Glo told me—after she slapped me halfway cross Wild Willy's—I was whore, just like my mamma. I ran home crying, not because my cheek hurt, but because I believed Glo was telling the truth, about Philomena being a whore.

The next time I saw Philomena, in winter, she was walking downtown, wearing a mohair coat, still looking shabby though—bloated and worn out. I stopped her on the street and asked her how she got that coat. She laughed in my face, her breath smelling like bourbon, and pulled me down on a bench, saying to me, "I got this and everythang else what's mine by laying on my back. You's a woman now, Etty (that's what she called me, Etty), and pretty too. It'd be real easy for a looker like you to get some nice things from a man with some money. You betta think on it, lessen you wanna stay stuck in that shack wit old GranSue, til it's too late. You betta learn how to get you some stuff for you get too old, Etty."

I started asking around town about Philomena, and a fairly large consensus of the population of Orange confirmed she was indeed a whore. She may have had a big red ruby ring, which I wanted *real real bad,* but she had a terrible reputation, too. Church folks wouldn't let her in their homes, and she was starting to look like something the cat drug in. I figured there had to be another way to get the things I wanted—some middle ground; and I decided to wait until I found me some.

While I was waiting, for middle ground, Philomena died. I cried and cried. Folks said she had cirrhosis of the liver. But I think her hole ate her...that's why I kept mine full.

I waited a pretty long time for Sherman Rane. He was a military man, wined and dined me from the very start. He gave me presents all the time, too, things I pointed out when we went window shopping, then pouted and whined about for a week. I found out his hole was "good" hair. Even though I liked the bob style, I started growing my hair out. When I laid on my back, like Philomena; I'd fan my hair out across the pillow. Sherman liked that. I liked the nice hotels we did it in, soft beds, and no splinters in my butt. Being in the Navy, he didn't have to pay for his own upkeep; and before long he was spending every penny of his pay on me (and my good hair). Sherman was good middle ground.

Time passed, and Sherman was being reassigned to a base in Virginia, clear across the country. He promised to write. But I didn't need no damn letters. I needed a vacuum cleaner, and that fancy pair of pink spectator pumps I'd seen on sale. So

37

I lied, twirling a ringlet of hair around my finger, and told him I was pregnant. I told him I loved him too, because it sounded like a good hole-filler.

So Sherman Rane married me. My GranSue died on my wedding day, in 1965, but I was too happy to be sad. With nothing holding me in Texas, I moved to Virginia with my new husband. Three months later, when he caught me in the bathroom, wringing out my monthly cycle rags, I cried and cried about having a miscarriage—I put on quite a show, too.

Sherman kept on pestering me, so five years later, I had him a baby. He fussed, but I named her Blame. I didn't have any more babies for him, though. Roe v. Wade came along right on time for me! I was glad Blame was born so pretty, it made her daddy happy. He even bought me my own car! As a matter of fact, in the 70's, he bought me three cars! When I sold the last one in 1980 to buy that Queen Anne furniture and an antique armoire... and to pay on my secret debts; he flat out refused to get me another one. Bills, bills, bills—got so that's all I heard from that man.

Blame was alright—nice and quiet...stayed in her room most of the time, doing what, I don't know. There were some things I didn't like about her, though...her eyes for instance. They should have been mine. Maybe then I could have done better than Sherman...got me a man with some real money. And the irritating way she wanted to sit up under me, always trying to talk to me or ask me something or another. I didn't have no time for that. Those five times I went to Philomena's house, I sat quiet in the corner—pretended like I was invisible. I don't know why Blame couldn't learn to do the same. Got so I had to lock myself away in the bedroom just to get some peace.

Well, at least I loved Blame...I guess. I mean, I never left her on the front porch, promising to come back for her, and failing forever to return. Philomena never made *any* attempt at loving me. Blame knows I loved her. I don't recall outright telling her so—but she had a Easy-Bake oven, and a gold add-a-bead necklace when they were in vogue, too. I'm sure she knew. I *am* her mother, after all.

She's not turning out the way I'd hoped, though. But then again, had I ever even hoped? Well, water over the dam now...I guess Blame will be okay. Her roommate seems a bit too much like Philomena, but boy, can that girl shop! And somebody else picking up the tab, too...sounds like my kind of party. Wish I could have been there.

I like it when somebody else is paying. Which is why I liked Noel Jones—a fellow I met at the butcher shop. He was 71 when I was 52. He was real ugly too, nasty black, like Glo from back home. But he could still do it; and he wanted to do it with me...said he'd get me a car. I could almost sit on my hair by then, but that didn't faze Sherman anymore. He wouldn't budge off a penny. So I did like my mamma taught me. I was going to pick up the Pontiac Noel Jones got me, the day after the fire. I sure wish I coulda drove that pretty car.

I do a lot of wishing now, and wondering, if I missed anything in life...being so busy, filling my own inherited hole. *Ohhh* but you should have seen my home before it burned down. I had *so many* pretty things; prettier than *anything* I'd seen at Philomena's houses...those five times.

Still, I lived for 52 years and I never rode a Ferris wheel or ate a dish I could not recognize. I was always too busy to make any friends or learn anything new. I didn't visit a zoo or swim in an ocean—and I grew up on the Gulf of Mexico, died in walking distance of the Atlantic! I never loved my dearly departed husband. I didn't teach my daughter anything about anything—she picked up on some cooking and sewing, though...always stuck up under me.

I was never as courageous or honest as the Bible or the Wind. And the fire marshal—speculating to Cathy Douthit about smoke inhalation being the cause of my death—erred in his assessment. I felt the flames...still do.

CHAPTER 3
JUAN RICARDO MURDOCH

"Oh yeah, that's real nice. Turn around. Um hum...*real nice*," Ricco commented on the second dress he'd purchased for Blame. She smiled, because it *was* nice and she really liked the way she looked in it. She liked the clothes Toria picked out for her at the mall. The classy cuts were outstanding (like something her mother might have worn); they gave her slim body such definition, making her look and feel glamorous.

Blame sashayed over to the couch to pass the lit blunt back to Ricco, and he pulled her down next him, clutching her wrists a little too tight for comfort. She wished she had just turned around and gone back in the bathroom to try on the rest of her new gear. "I'm just getting started, Ricco. Don't you want to see the rest of them?"

"Shit fine as you is, you look good in a pair of baseball socks, ma. Nah, I done seen all the clothes I need to see you in tonight." Since she didn't respond to the obvious, Ricco tried another approach. "Well...I finally got you to spend some time with me. Did you enjoy yourself? Told you when we picked y'all up I was gone make you fresher than you already was," he laughed. Then added, seriously, "On the real though Blame, I just wanted you to have a good time. You know how I feel about you." And having escorted her around the sleazier side of the nation's capital for a number of months now, he truly had grown to care for her...in a possessive sort of way.

Blame blushed, and got up to inspect the wet bar and find the remote control. Thinking one more drink might be just what she needed to get with it; Ricco obliged her, releasing his grip on her slender wrists. She turned the television to BET, which was ironically playing Salt n Pepa's "Let's Talk about Sex", and made two gin and tonics. She'd never made them before, and was too heavy-handed with the gin. Ricco failed to correct the error. By the time the blunt was ashes and their glasses were empty, Blame was relaxed and receptive to everything Ricco was kicking. After the third round of drinks, Blame was officially drunk.

Blame woke up to find herself pressed against Ricco's chest, nestled under his strong arm. She was drunk but not comatose, and though the evening was a blur, she clearly remembered Ricco took her on the ride of her life. Kissing, stroking, licking, sucking and fucking. She discovered she had a clitoris, a g spot and the ability to have multiple orgasms. She couldn't suck a dick yet, but it didn't stop her from trying. She recalled being on top, being on the bottom, being on her side, bent over the sofa, up against the wall...her pussy was sore and still dripping wet. She peeled herself off of him and tiptoed quietly to the bathroom—legs still trembling from the workout.

She turned the shower water on very hot and let it run over her. She felt a hand press into the small of her back. Ricco was on his knees behind her. He raised her left leg and licked her from her clit to her asshole. He continued until her body shuddered and her sweet cum filled up his mouth. He stood up and pressed himself into her from behind, the shower running over them like a waterfall. She came again, and again. Then Ricco exploded and slumped to the floor of the shower. He closed the drain, turned off the shower, and let the tub fill up with piping hot water. Blame lay down beside him and they both drifted off to sleep in the soothing bath.

On her second waking, Blame, who had been dreaming of fire, was in a panic! Where the hell was she? She flailed around feeling heat on her skin. Ricco held on to her tightly. Water!

She connected the dots in her groggy head and fell against his chest. Water and Ricco. He kissed her forehead as she relaxed in his muscular arms.

"You okay?" he asked, stroking the wet brown curls that lay on her cheek.

"What time is it?" she asked.

"Who the fuck cares? We ain't got nowhere to be."

"Easy for you to say. I gotta go to work. Forget about what time it is...what *day* is it?"

Ricco laughed, "It's Sunday. You hungry?"

"Famished."

"Order us some room service," he instructed, stepping out of the tub, and wrapping himself in one of the heavy white robes provided by the hotel. "I need to run next door and check on my man. Order us some toothbrushes and shit, too. This high ass mutha got to have concierge service. And we gonna have a talk about that 'going to work' shit when I get back."

Blame held her breath and slid under the water, wondering, first of all, what concierge service was, and secondly, what the hell had she done? But her body felt like silk under Ricco's caresses, and the pitter patter of her contented heart was something totally new to Blame. It felt like a rosebush was blossoming in her groin, and she wanted to give herself to Ricco—please him in any way he saw fit—so whatever she was feeling at that moment, would never end.

She bathed, ordered combs, brushes, toothbrushes, socks, underwear, Texas omelets, cheesecake and juice; charging it all to the room. As she applied her lotion, she realized Ricco had touched every single inch of her body. She pulled her hair back in a ponytail, slipped on one of her sharp new dresses—crisp linen with tortoise shell buttons. Blame admired her new clothes, and for a very brief instant, she wondered if spending time with Ricco might be an easy way to escape poverty. The thought only lasted a split second, but it was enough time for a tiny seed to be sewn.

Blame sat on the comfortable sofa, waiting for her man to return. Though their coming together had only been a 24-hour ordeal, she now thought of Ricco as her man. Twenty year old Blame Rane thought she was officially in love. (She was dick whipped at best.) But, never having been in a relationship, and touched only once previously, by a boy, naïve Blame had no measuring stick with which to gauge.

Ricco returned in time to tip the service...excellent timing, because Blame hadn't thought of that detail. "So," he started, unfolding his napkin and placing it in his lap, "they say 'a drunk man speak a sober mind'. Is that true for women, too?"

Blame savored the delicious food, detecting real cream in the cheesecake. "I don't follow," she answered, now fearful of what her drunk mouth might have said during last night's sexfest.

Ricco pushed himself away from the table and looked closely at Blame, checking for the telltale signs of a liar. His business dealings had given him a keen insight into the hearts of people. "What did you say your last boyfriend's name was?"

Blame gulped her juice down and dropped her fork. She didn't know what to say. She wasn't sure what she'd already said, and she couldn't remember any details of the stories she'd made up for Toria. The only thing she was sure about at that moment was the passion stirring in her for Ricco. A feeling so warm, it made her never want to tell him a lie. "I've never had a boyfriend," she answered, sheepishly.

"Um hum...and before last night, how many times have you had sex?" he continued, making her feel like she was on trial.

"Once. But we weren't in a relationship or anything. He was just a guy at school...just sex."

"I see. And where's your mamma?" He continued grilling her.

"Dead. She died in a fire." She held her breath and fought back the haunting image of devouring flames.

"Well...that's what you said last night. I thought you was bullshitting. Yeah...I knew you was something special the first time I laid eyes on you." He finished his omelet never taking his eyes off of her. She sat motionless, still feeling like she was in the witness chair, as her eggs grew cold. "What you want Blame?"

"Huhn?"

"What you want? You feel like I took advantage of you last night? You want it to be a one-time, wild, Baltimore weekend, or you want to see where it go? I mean you green as hell, but you ain't no baby. You got to know what you want."

The timidity she had known all her life started covering her. The shroud of self-consciousness was slowly wrapping itself around her. She felt small, insignificant and unsure. She wanted to hide under the table, like she'd hid under the dorm room desk when her parent's died. But she decided to continue on the track she'd started on...to hell with shame and fear, she would just tell the truth. Her plush surroundings egged her on as she weighed her pitiful existence against the security Ricco represented. She cleared her throat and stated the facts as plainly and clearly as possible. "I just want to be with you, Ricco. I'm sure you do stuff like this all the time. I guess me and Toria are just two more girls who wound up in a hotel with you and Drake. But if you're asking me what I want. All I know is; I want to be with you. I like the way you treat me, and I want to *always* feel like I'm feeling right now."

The interrogating DA was replaced by a young man feeling mutually thrilled (at finally conquering a too-long pursuit). A grin spread across Ricco's handsome, ebony face. He picked up Blame's delicate hand and kissed it. "Alright baby. Alright; you want it, you got it. You gone be my girl. 100 percent though, no bullshit. And this ain't got shit to do with Drake, or your girl Toria. You need to dead that ho anyway. This about me and you. Come on, take a ride with me."

Drake and Toria were "sleeping in", so Ricco had to make a few quick runs to a barbershop, smoke shop and somebody's basement on the grittier end of Baltimore. He lifted the BMW's hood and returned to the car with a bag, a box and a gun. Blame gasped.

"Oh wow, now don't tell me you thought I was a shoeshine boy," he chuckled.

"What exactly *do* you do, Ricco?" She queried, trying to compose herself, and stay cool. The supple leather seats of the expensive car aided in calming her down. She could just picture herself being one of the smart people she daydreamed about, cruising up the highway in style.

"Let's just say I'm a traveling salesman, pharmaceutical rep. Trust me, the less you know, the safer you'll be."

"What's in the box?" she queried.

"My wares."

"And the bag?"

"My business." He turned the radio on to the sounds of Digital Underground, and they both humpty-danced, laughing, in their seats. "*Blame Rane*. You the real thing girl. But, what the hell kinda name is Blame?"

"The kind my mamma gave me. And you don't look Spanish, what kind of name is Ricco?"

46

Juan Ricardo...Murdoch, but keep that to yourself. And my father was Dominican. Least that's what my moms say. I ain't never met the dude so don't get me to lying. You got a daddy?"

"I had a daddy. I ain't got nobody now."

"Correction, you got me now. And I ain't going nowhere!" he laughed. He adjusted the radio volume then asked, "So, what was you taking up at Broward?"

"Accounting."

"Numbers cruncher, huhn? That's cool. I knew you was one of them high IQ chics. Shit, you had a daddy growing up and everything. You ain't never messed with none of my boys. You almost too damn good to be true. And look at these pretty l'il hands; you ain't never done no real work, either. I'ma keep 'em pretty, too. You can forget about going back to that mill. You heard?"

"I already told you what I want to do, Ricco. I just want to be with you." Blame responded. The tiny seed of a better life nestled itself in her warming bosom.

"Well that's what's up, Miss Blame it on the Rain. And that mill shit is dead. My girl ain't working in no damn mill. I mean you can work if you want to, get yourself a little part time gig or something. Shit, go back to school if you want. I'm saying, I got ya back; I got ya bills. I'ma just need for you to keep doing it like you did it last night. Keep my shit tight, keep the house clean, and be where I tell you be. Don't question me about what I do, and don't sweat me with bullshit, 'cause certain bitches is just part of my business. But you my girl, though. Stay fly and keep your mouth shut. Fuck the police, and stay outta other niggahs' faces. You gone have to find some new friends, too. Ya girl Toria making a bad name for herself in the streets. Oh yeah, and we got to work on your head game. I'm definitely gone

need my dick sucked on the regular. Can you handle that?" he
chuckled, completely full of himself by then.

Blame was appalled. Dick sucked on the reg? He ain't no
fucking pimp, what's this shit about other girls? Be where he
tell me to be and keep my mouth shut? *And* he wants to choose
my friends, too? *Please.* He ain't my daddy. My daddy dead.
Humph...maybe he's just testing me, she thought, trying to see
if I'm down (something Toria once said was very important).
Plus, I can really get with that part about not working in the mill.
A little part time gig at the mall is more my style anyway, she
thought. And maybe this *is* the best way to get the things my
mamma had, and get the hell out the ghetto, she speculated.
Blame just nodded her head in silent agreement, but the look
on Ricco's face said that wasn't enough. So she said, "okay,
yeah...whatever." And the tiny seed took root.

Ricco couldn't believe so much of his bullshit was floating.
He wondered if there was something wrong with Blame. It was
almost like she didn't know how banging she was. Then he
thought, maybe she was just that stupid, and continued with his
list of demands. "You cut your hair I'ma fuck you up, yo. And
you *gots* to get rid of them freaky ass colored contacts, too.
Them shits make me nervous. Can you cook, girl?"

"Of course I can cook, my mamma was from Texas. And
these my eyes, fool."

CHAPTER 4
MISTRESS GWENDOLYN RAINIER

Actually, they're *my* eyes. My nose too, for that matter. And that is the truth. I'll tell you what else is true...

The ship sank. Luckily, close enough to harbor. Granddaddy made it ashore, indentured to service with his life, but alive nonetheless. He was just a boy when he sailed to the New Country, still full of the hopes and dreams the virgin land promised. Grandmother was a bondwoman, too. They belonged to the same "generous" Jew who purchased them from a debtor's prison in Ireland. Their mutual crime? Being homeless waifs born to Irish whores; who incidentally stole bread to stay alive.

Granddaddy worked very hard, never allowing his clubbed foot to hinder his progress. Grandmother had a large groove in her forehead, extending an inch beyond her flaming red hairline. It was a permanent fixture; created by the carrying of baskets on her head...baskets filled with laundry, wood, produce...the heavy stones that formed her master's wall.

My grandparents were never married—their status made marriage illegal. They stole little moments of time together, when their brutal master wasn't watching. Quick and hushed fumbling in the dark was the only pleasure their weak, deprived bodies ever knew. That was the extent of their union. But there had been enough stolen time to produce daddy.

Daddy settled the family debt, in his twenty-third year of life. His parents, though much too young, were both deceased by then; worked to the death, they were. Once free, Daddy struck out across the Mountain, with the rifle and rations he was promised. He kept the papers declaring his freedom, (which he couldn't read), in his breast pocket, close to his heart.

Daddy said Granddaddy loved Ireland. Daddy said that was only on account that Granddaddy was never a free man in this country. Daddy would know—being able to bear witness to both sides of the coin—bound and free. Daddy said it's better to be free. So he loved the place he found on the other side of the mountain, as a free white man. He adored the parcel of land his rifle helped him keep, the house his own hands built, the fields he alone plowed, and the traps he alone set. Father knows best. So, I did not reserve any affection for the emerald-green isle of Erin, either. I fell in love with the land of my birth—and I was born in Tennessee.

Mother grew up behind the walls of the fort. In those days, outposts of military were most necessary to make war with the savage natives still milling about the new land. Daddy, on his rare visits to the fort, had the pleasure of watching mother grow up, over the years. When she was old enough, fourteen to be exact, he made her his wife. She had four brothers and Daddy thought she could produce the sons he needed to survive off the land. He was right; there were seven of us children in all. I have six older brothers...somewhere in Tennessee.

Ours' was a backbreaking life, in a crude home, filled with an overflowing abundance of quiet love. Daddy loved, and so mother always made, sweet pecan pies. Mother loved, and so daddy always caught, fresh trout. My hunting, fishing, trapping and farming brothers were a comfort to us all. Their favorite pastime was keeping the murderous Indians at bay. Mother sewed my dresses with affection and daddy played his whittled flute for me often. He reminded us daily that, though we were poor, we were so fortunate, so blessed by our Maker, to be free.

...

Master Charles P. Rainier of Rainier Estates, Baylorton, North Carolina, crossed the Appalachians as well—twice in his lifetime. His first visit was official business, meeting with the politicians and military men of the then-frontier. He had some information regarding the expulsion of natives and the proper way to break African slaves. When he wasn't in the meeting houses, he roamed the Tennessee countryside, hills and hollers, always seeking new farming methods.

He stumbled upon a quaint little place carved out of the hillside, and was quite taken, swept away in fact, by the only daughter of a very poor man, who farmed and trapped to eke out his paltry living. A wretched, lowly little man, who had been born slave and was now free. Master Rainier was most enchanted by the farmer's daughter, Gwendolyn—particularly her sparkling gray-brown eyes, with bright flecks of copper here and there. Her severe shyness and quietude was especially pleasing to him. It wasn't hard for a man like Charles Rainier, who regularly bought and sold human beings, to notice the clear evidence of servitude in her father's humble demeanor. He literally purchased the young girl from the needy farmer.

With his business settled, Master Rainier returned to the Eastern side of the mountain, North Carolina, with his young, auburn-haired bride, riding atop a buckboard wagon. He spent the entire journey counseling her on the finer things of life, teaching simple points of etiquette, and ravaging her young, tender body.

...

I must say the Carolina estate and all its trappings were well above my station. The distance between the two, in prestige, was nearly as vast as the great difference in our ages—Master Charles being 28 years my senior. I was determined to fit right in; and I knew from day one I would not be moved!

I overheard the stories he told our visitors—elevating the status of my Tennessee origins. I memorized the yarn that was supposed to be my history, repeating it to myself daily. I played the part from the very beginning, quite adept at my new role. I began reciting the fable to our social peers as well, embellishing further our fabrication. The deceit eventually lived long enough and grew large enough, to become true, even in my own mind.

Our niggers, therefore, bothered me irrationally. Our brood of slaves sickened me with their frightened speech, inhuman existence, and jittery eyes, ever examining the floor. I especially hated the little nigger boy who chopped our firewood—knowing that was daddy's occupation when he was another man's property. The flattened foreheads of the African women made me shiver, and think about my grandmother. They might as well have been animals. Oh how I despised their very existence. But worse than my hatred of the slaves, was the calculated and cultivated erasure of all existence of my dear Tennessee family. My part in that bitter annihilation is what made me cringe at my reflection in the looking glass.

Silly to think now, but I truly believed all the slaves knew my dirty little secret. I thought they could see evidence of a bondwoman grandmother in my gait, pick up traces of trash in my laughter. Did I hold my chin in the fashion of someone that could be owned by another person? Was the stitch in my embroidery dead giveaway of a girl spawned from slaves? Were there telltale signs in my posture that screamed "her lineage is no better than that of a filthy auction-bought African!"?

I believed the niggers whispered about it, down in the pathetic rundown shanties where we housed them. I was certain they snickered about it in the kitchen, when rolling out dough for my breakfast biscuits. Oh, how I dreaded the idea of someday being exposed as a charlatan. Since I believed the slaves had the knowledge and power to dethrone me; I totally, unequivocally, HATED those niggers!

In fact, I was known to be the most brutal Mistress in the county—taking indescribable pleasure in whipping the slaves myself. Why the ladies of adjoining plantations even counseled with me to learn the practices I employed on my obedient niggers. I beat my property, spat on them, kicked and slapped them for any little trifle. It was my way, you see, of creating space. Every blow I struck distanced me that much further from my shameful slave-for-a-father past.

Damned bondwoman grandmother—child of a whore! I grew to detest the lame and rotten scoundrel who made it ashore when the ship sank...my so-called grandfather, filthy vermin died in bondage. And Gwendolyn Rainier was the second-generation product of their wretched union? Oh contraire! I was American aristocracy...damn near royalty, depending on my audience!

I worked very diligently at positioning myself just so on the settee, for hours at a time, eating and lounging...imagining how a refined, sixth-generation, white woman of leisure might pass the day. I even pretended the brand new jewels my husband gifted to me were time-worn family heirlooms— scratching the bands and stones with granite to add the character time and wear produce. Under no circumstance would I wear cotton, only silk and satin, fine wool and linen, sable and lace for me. I absolutely reeked of pedigree! I fed the

53

lie to bursting, and in time, the truth became a lie, and a lie was the unmitigated truth!

Master Rainier, my dear husband, journeyed across the mountain to Tennessee on only one other occasion, in our lifetimes. My folks, I suppose, were still living at the time. I suppose. He invited me to accompany him...thought I might want to lay eyes on my dear old mother and father again...my brothers perhaps. I respectfully declined, thinking to myself, who on earth could he be talking about? What mother? Which father? Whose brothers?

Why I was the wife of a wealthy plantation owner. I was mother to a son who would inherit acres upon acres of land and nearly two hundred slaves. I would have been hard pressed to even recall my true maiden name in those days. The lie of my history had breath and a heartbeat of its own by then. For heaven's sake, I thought, why in the world should I care to see ghosts? How could I demean myself by speaking, with reverence and adoration, to a dirt poor farmer, who was once himself, the very lowest thing on earth—an insignificant slave?! He had been property—like a pig, a row of corn, or a hairbrush. Return to rubbish? Never! Lest the lie should begin to unravel.

I will tell you this final truth...refusing to visit the place of my birth, to see the faces of my parents, who loved me so; is surely one of the things I regret most in my life. Of course, I now realize the treasure that is family, no matter its origins. Now I spend every inch of time, as a lowly pigeon, seeking out the last bit of blood I have left on this planet. Her gray-brown and copper eyes, which are mine (and were also my mother's, by the way) are a comfort to me. The up and down heave of her breasts when she sleeps, is my very breath, lingering on in the world. I look at the wretchedness of her life, and wonder, like Mrs. Douthit, who is to Blame?

CHAPTER 5
TORIA'S TAKE

September 1998

This shit is too damn funny for words. Oh now I'll admit wasn't a damn thing funny in the beginning; I was bout ready to murder that funky bitch. I swear I wanted to scratch dem damn cat eyes right out her fucking skull. But *now*...I'm bout to piss on myself laughing at Blame Rane, this shit is *sooo* fucking hilarious! See girl, what had happened was...

We got home from our weekend of flossin' with Drake and Ricco. I'm all happy, like Blame, I could just kiss you for not fucking up my game plan. I didn't think she was gone be down with partying solo with Ricco, but by the time we crossed back over the bridge to D.C., I was giving her much props for being a shonuff ride or die chic.

We got back to our walkup, and didn't go sleep 'til four in the morning. We stayed up filling each other in on what went down in our hotel rooms. I thought I made a pretty good impression on Drake. Girl, you know I was suckin' nuts and everything. The way I put it down, I *knew* he was gone try to hook up with me again. Blame was tripping though; silly bitch thought she was in love. And I don't know what kind of lines that niggah Ricco was dropping on her dumb ass, but she really thought he loved her too. Clown!

So for the next two weeks, this niggah Ricco laid up in our apartment like his name on the damn lease, and this fool bitch, Blame, done started laying out of work. I kept trying to school her about these slick ass street thugs, but she just kept saying, "You'll see."

Well, see, I did. One day when it's getting close to the time for us to go to the mill, she tells me she ain't working there no more. Five minutes later, Ricco knocking on the door. I open the door; he talking about, "get your shit, I got you a new spot," dangling a set of keys in her face. Then he drops a fat knot of dough on the counter, talking bout, "I'ma be out of a town for a few days, so you gone have to do the decorating yourself." Then, "Hey, what's up Toria?"

I'm like, what the fuck? What's up Toria? Like he didn't even realize I was in the room. Niggah *I'm* what's up! How in the hell was this country bitch from fucking Norfolk getting it better than me? Hell I'm a redbone with the fattest ass and titties around this piece. Bitches in D.C. wasn't even rockin no bamboo earrings and isometric haircuts 'til *I* showed em how. I got Detroit flava, a topnotch head game, and niggahs know I'm down for whatever. Somebody slap me, 'cause I *know* this shit ain't going down like this. Well...if it was, then Drake *must* be on his way up here to move me outta this rattrap any day now. The fact that I hadn't heard from him in two weeks didn't really mean nothing; he *was* a busy man, and whatnot.

But this here what takes the cake! I been carrying this bitch, right. Teaching her how to roll blunts, wiping her fucking tears when she boohooing bout her dead ass mammy, introducing her to the right people and shit. Do you know she ran in her room, flung some clothes in some damned garbage bags, snatched up that raggedy ass plastic bin and hollered over her shoulder, "I'll be back for the rest of my stuff later." Now remember, this the same bitch didn't even want to go in the hotel in Baltimore. Bitch ain't say bye, kiss my ass, nothing...just bounced. Fuck half a month's rent and everything. And how the fuck was I s'posed to get to work?

Least she coulda done was let me rock the Buick, 'til I got on my feet. Ungrateful bitch!

Well, all I can say is: what goes around comes around. Now I ain't gone front, I was pissed like you would not believe...but she who laughs last, laughs loudest. And bet I'm laughing my black ass off right about now. Girl, let me tell you how this shit played out.

After I got over my initial rage, I started getting worried about the girl. Real talk. Ain't nobody seen Blame. I'm talking like two, three months. I can't ask Drake what's up because after that Baltimore weekend, his punk ass acted like he wasn't feeling me no more. Anyway, later for that li'l dick niggah. So I'm on the bus one day going to hook up with ole dude, Tyrone from the job, right? Cause a bitch gotta eat. And who do I see on the boulevard getting out at the Dominican hair spot? This bitch Blame, flossing in a motherfucking *Range*! I pulled that damn bell so fucking hard I thought I stopped the bus my damn self. So I hops off the bus, check out the ride...license plate say SUAV-A. That's Ricco's lame ass handle. Oh okay, it's like that? I goes in the shop and plop my fly, phat ass right down in the seat beside her. Bitches staring cause what I'm doing in the salon when my wig already tight as hell, right.

I say, "What's up strange bitch?"

And she all like, "Ohhh Toria! Girl I miss you! It's *so* good to see you," trying to give me a hug and shit. But I can tell her punk ass scared, 'cause she don't know how I'm coming at her, see.

So I backs her ass up. "You know where the fuck I stay, you ain't miss me *that* much." Then her cell phone ring. I can tell from the convo, she talking to Ricco, and its real obvious he got her ass on lock. She telling him where she been, where she at now, how long she gone be...then she tell him she bumped into me...I'm in the salon right now. Strange look come across her face and she try to turn her volume down and talk in code and shit. Then she say, "but Ricco, she my friend." I roll my eyes at that news. I don't know what the fuck he say, but then she say, "you trippin, why you need to hear me tell her that?" He say something else I can't hear. And she flinch, then she say, "Well, you tell her then." And would you believe this bold bitch put the damn phone on speaker?!

"Toria, can you hear me?" this mothafucker ask.

"Yeah. What's up Ricco?" Fucking hair stylists shushing up they customers and shit, so everybody in the shop can hear what's going down.

He say, "I done tole my girl I don't want her fucking with you no more. You ain't been in DC a hot year, and you done already fucked half the team. You can't be fucking up my girl rep. You bad news T, and you need to get lost. Now don't let me catch you stalking my wifey no more, ya heard? You do, I'ma have to send some real live bitches to come see bout your trifling ass. Oh yeah, and Drake said ya pussy stink. Beat it bitch!"

Now they ain't have to do me like that. I mean you don't do a damn dog like that; and all out in public to boot. Bitches turning up they nose like they can smell my pussy across the room and shit. I wanted to crawl up under the counter. Blame cold ass sitting there with her cell phone stuck up in the air; bitch face look like stone. You know I coulda threw her fake ass threw that damn plate glass window; but I know them niggahs Drake and Ricco is the truth, so I tuck my tail and run. I'll live to fight another day. I promise myself though, I don't give a fuck how long it take, I'ma get that devil-eyed bitch. That shit hurt me so bad I ain't never even been back on the block where that salon at. And she was supposed to be my friend. Shit she wouldna even hooked up with Ricco if it wasn't for me.

But anyway girl, time goes by. I see Blame and Ricco at the club, VIP with the rappers, champagne poppin off and shit. I see Blame and Ricco, Drake and some stanking Puerto Rican tramp, everywhere, looking like DC's finest all over town...Blame rocking the latest everything, from designer shoes to jewels to fur fucking coats. They little set is straight ballin' and shot callin'. Ain't nothing else to it. So you know a bitch is bout truly ready to blow a fuse. Grapevine saying they rest in the same condos the fucking Congress people stay at. And I'm still up in the roach-infested dive she left me in...done got fired from the mill, lights bout to get cut off and shit. You know, my Aunt Linda said she knew that bitch was sneaky from the jump. I shoulda listened. And I'm just praying for the day this fake bitch fall the fuck off.

Okay so it's a coupla years later, like '92, back when they let dem police go that whooped Rodney King ass, and niggahs set LA on fire! And next time I see Blame, bitch big as a fucking tick. She got to be bout 8...9 months pregnant. Now I *know* it's just a matter of time before her shit go south. I'm from Detroit, and I done seen this shit a million times. A baby *always* change the game, and never for the better. So I just watches and waits. Then...break out the cigars! It's a boy! I heard she named him J'Rick...country ass bitch. What the fuck kinda name is J'Rick? Little niggah stay fly though, I got to give it to Ricco. That's who the fuck I shoulda got with from the get go. It was starting to look like they was gone be UP forever.

But finally, some mo time go by and bitch ain't looking so fly no more. I seen her when I was at the music store, copping Nas', "Illmatic" joint. So it had to be bout '94, right?

Her skinny ass got the nerve to start losing weight. It ain't hard to tell she done got a little coke habit. *Plus*, that niggah done started going upside her head! But I knew way back when she fronted on me in the Dominican hair spot: you give a niggah that kind of control; expect to start getting yo ass whipped when the honeymoon's over. Bitch act like she ain't see me, girl. Running around in dark shades and wearing a pound of makeup, but she couldn't hide that black eye or them purple ass bruises on her l'il bony arms. Shit starting to get funny, right? Told you it was gone be trip. Her momma named her right, cause Blame be lame. Ha Ha Ha Ha! But that ain't even the half; bitch, check this out...

A l'il time pass, and I'm coming up in the world now, right. Told you these motherfuckers can't keep a good bitch down. So I'm chilling with some really real niggahs now...dope boys from NY. King of the set is this niggah named Brown—grimy Brooklyn cat. And guess who his bottom bitch is? You guessed it! Yours truly—ka ching ching! So we at the dope spot chillin, and who do I see copping a bundle of boy? Mr. Suav-a himself! Girl, I bout broke my neck running downstairs to ask Brown, my new niggah, "Was that Ricco? He a dope fiend?"

Suspicions confirmed! Niggah been hitting the heroin for some months now. Probably started out like most clowns, trying to keep the dope dick, so they can fuck they bitch right. Cause heroin keep your dick hard for days, and you need that li'l boost when you hittin the powder too hard; cause, on the flip side, too much cocaine *will* fuck up your dick game. So like most niggahs, Ricco probably thought he was just playin around with the dope, doin a little balancing act so he could fuck like he used to. But that damn monkey jump on your back when you ain't looking, and that's all she wrote...you's a fucking junkie for you know what hit you! And honey I know bout me some dope

60

dick. Brown got a little table habit hisself, and he be wearing the pussy out. But I ain't new to it, I'm true to it; and this bitch can definitely keep up. I mean I know he got other bitches, but I swear I got this niggah sprung.

Oh, Oh! And I ain't tell you, bout this same time…let's see it was '95…yeah, I remember cause that's the year Eazy E died from AIDS. And the government was shut down back then too. Girl D.C. was off the chain when that shit happened! So word, it was definitely '95, and I finds out dumb ass Blame pregnant again! Well pop the *motherfucking* champagne! It's a Girl! Puhahahaha! I'm hollering by now…shit is just too damn funny to me. Bitch having babies for a damn junkie and getting her ass beat at the same time! Say what? Oh, she named her Carla, Karma…some shit like that…but listen though…

Then I hear Ricco and his boy Drake ain't sniffing dope no more…they *main lining!* Straight banging diesel with the dirty needles, whole 9, right. And chile you *know* some niggah's nodding out on a dope high damn shole can't run no proper business. Drake gets popped and Ricco go on the run. Heard he had his whole family running with him. But you know how it go…a junkie ain't gone get too far.

Honey I was at the trial in '97 when both of them bum ass niggahs got served up on fed time for conspiracy and e'rthang. And you know that fed shit is day for day. I'm talking bout niggahs ain't coming home 'til they at least 40! What Prince say? Party over oops outta time! Ha Haaaa! Tables turned now fa sho, and I couldn't wait to see that phony ho, Blame, in the street somewhere. I swear I dream about dragging her punk ass.

Okay so last night, I'm sitting in my man, Brown, Benz, right. We double parked in the projects 'cause he need to straighten some workers out. Well who the fuck do I see getting out a damn gypsy cab, dragging two little nappy headed chaps up the tenement steps?! Bingo! Dumb ass, busted ass, shouldn'tna-never-tried-to-play-me, Blame broke-the-fuck-down Rane!

They say revenge is a dish best served cold. Well this shit was straight out the motherfucking freezer. And make it so bad; I ain't neven have to do nothing. Stupid ho did it to her damn self. My mama always used to say, "Time is a motherfucker...sit back and watch what it do." Mama was right. Eight little years, and this bitch done straight crashed and *burned*.

Girl! You know I made it my damn business to be right out there in front of her building the next afternoon. I had to let Brown put it in my ass so he would let me hold the Benz by myself for a coupla hours, though. But it's all good; it's give and take out here in these streets. He tried to rip me a new shithole, but I ain't mad at him. I did get to floss and flex...for a day.

So anyway, bout two o'clock, this raggedy heifer come walking out the project roach motel, a far cry from them condos uptown, I'm thinking. Check it out now...I'm parlaying in the whip, bumping Jay-Z's "Hard Knock Life", and when she get right beside the Benz, which she jocking hard as hell, by the way, I slide the tinted window down so she can see who the fuck it is...and BAM!

I say, "What's up Blame?!" Bitch look like she seen a ghost. "*Um hum*...what goes up must come down, ho. And I see you done hit rock fucking bottom. Oh this my niggah Brown whip. I know you heard of him. Ya dope fiend boyfriend used to cop smack from him fore he got knocked. Anyway, holla at us if you need some work or something...shole hate to see them rugrats go hungry. Oh yeah bitch, we buy food stamps too...case you fall on harder times and need to make a li'l change for some pampers or something. But hell, from the looks of things, yo shit can get no more raggedier than it is. Well, gotta go. Bye bum bitch!"

Bwahahahahah! Now tell me if that ain't the saddest damn ghetto story you ever heard in your life. I told you the shit was gone be *pure d damn* hilarious! Chile, I laughed all the way to the drugstore to get me some Preparation H for my hemorrhoids, and something for this little cold I can't seem to shake. Had to hurry up and get that Benz back, too. You know Brown got the tendency to get a little bit physical his damn self. But that's just 'cause he under so much stress. I get finished blowing that niggah dick; he'll be ah'ight. Bitch, pass the blunt!

"Damn. Damn. Damn." The little birds cried.

CHAPTER 6
DOTSUA: CHEROKEE FOR REDBIRD

Look at what life has done to Ethel's daughter, poor Blame.
Watching her, even from this distance, hurts too badly. The
Great Spirit chose me to feel the anguish of all things, great and
small. Since there was nothing I could do to help her, and I
could no longer bear to watch; I flew back to Texas for a while,
riding the high, wide wind. I am thankful to the Great Spirit for
making me dotsua, a redbird, for this time after life. Flying from
the East Coast to Texas is so much better than walking; I assure
you. Memories of the walking time still give me great pain.

My name is WindRider TwoSquirrels. My wise pappa
named me WindRider during the first year of my birth, in 1824.
He must have known the Great Spirit would make me a redbird
in this second part of my being. I never rode the wind in the
first part of my life; unless you count my nights with Aaron.
Have you ever seen a redbird blush? Thinking of those nights
with Aaron still makes me blush. Ah, my dear, brave Aaron...
One squirrel is a very good kill for little Cherokee boys. I
went hunting with my brothers, when I should have been
planting with my mother. I did not fear retribution, because I
came back to the village with not one, but *two* squirrels...a most
amazing feat for a child my age...and unheard of for a *girl*! So
outstanding was this accomplishment, my pappa completed my
naming. That very night, by ceremonial fire, he added
TwoSquirrels to my identity.
So I am WindRider TwoSquirrels and I was born at Uweyv,
which is what my Cherokee people called the River. Because
our village was on Uweyv, our lives were very easy. I lived on
Uweyv, the river, when the devil was still very young in our land.

64

Oh, have you never seen the devil? His skin is white, like the fishes belly. His eyes are like the water. His hair can be like corn, or fire...dirt or midnight. He has two words for everything. He says this, but means that. He means this, but says that. We do not understand the devil. But the Great Spirit told us he was coming. So we were not surprised when he arrived.

By the time I lived fourteen years, when the year was 1838, the devil had turned my great Cherokee people into cattle—herding us into pens. He said he wanted our homes... our homes would be his home now. (This would later include the whole world—he does not stop). He said he found a new home for us. He was taking us there, on foot, at gunpoint. Have you never seen a gun? Well if you've never seen the devil, then I suppose you have never seen a gun either. It is something he made; something only the devil could fashion. It has fire and metal. It has many arrows and can kill many men, women and children, from very far away. If you knew the power of the devil's gun, you would understand how we became like cattle, and why we walked away from our homes.

We walked many days and many nights, through changing landscapes and changing seasons. We walked across great mountains, through low valleys, over wide rivers. We walked on dirt, grass, snow and stones. We slept and ate very little. The young ones and the old ones were first to die. The devil's gun said we had no time for burial, so we carried the ones who fell dead. We would bury them at our new home, if ever we got there. People came out of their houses to watch us walk by. The people cried when they saw us carrying our dead; and so the Trail we took was named Tears. But the crying people did not try to help us.

I wanted to be one of the dead ones. I could feel all the misery of my great people and I could not bear it. We finally came to a place where the earth turned red. There were no trees to relieve us from the sun's heat, and the dust flew like it had wings. I could not bear the pain of my suffering people one more day. I prayed and prayed for the Great Spirit to put me with the dead. When we lay down at night, so the devil could rest his horses, the red dust flew strong. It was so strong we could not see each other and we could barely breathe. I knew the Great Spirit was making a way for me to live; so I turned left and ran away. The Great Spirit hid me under the red dust cloud and I did not hear the horses' hooves pursuing me.

I ran for many days. I ran until I could no longer feel the suffering of my great Cherokee people. I pretended to be Uweyv, the river, and just kept running. The season and the landscape changed again. And finally there were forests where I could hide and hunt. I slept in the trees by daylight. I ran and ate what I could at night. When I was very tired, and very lonely and very near starvation—I became aware of a tracker. I don't know how I knew this, but someone was following me. Perhaps the devil has found me, I thought.

I tried to stay awake to see if the devil was indeed upon me. Maybe I could catch and kill him, and take suffering out of the world. But I fell asleep. When I woke up, there was a sack of food in the tree. I knew it was a trick, bait to trap me...but hunger made me eat it. When I finished, there was no rope around my neck, no net over my head, no gun at my back—so I kept running.

This happened for three days and three nights. On the fourth day, I pretended to be asleep and I saw the tracker who left the bags of food in the trees for me. He saw my open eyes;

and though I did not understand his tongue, I knew he was telling me to come down out of the tree.

He was not of my people. I was crimson in color; he was the same brown color of roasted pecans...or burnished brass. His hair was like the lamb's wool; mine is like the horse's tail. I did not know if he was a good man or a bad man. But his skin was not white like the fishes belly, so I did not think he was a devil. His shiny black eyes laughed and spoke to me. They said he was sent by the Great Spirit to watch over and protect me. I was very lonely. So I came down from the tree.

I did not run anymore. We walked on together, until the land ran out. I now know we were in the Gulf Coast town of Orange, Texas. We made a home there and we were very happy. We remained there all the days of our short lives— Aaron and I. And he never brought me pain.

His father was French creole—his mother, Ivory Coast African. I have learned all these things as dotsua, the redbird. These are not things I knew as a woman. I have even flown across the big water and seen the African village of Aaron's mother. It was just as our village on Uweyv had been, alike in every way. I was not surprised to discover this. I have learned, by riding the wind, all the people of the world live in much the same way. Only the devil is different and confused. The devil used his gun and forced his ways upon the world. So now the world is confused. There is no more peace like our living at Uweyv; there is almost no more love.

Aaron and I had a very great love. There is still living fruit from the tree of our love—Blame Rane, daughter of Ethel, who was also our fruit, (but she will never know that). She lives on the river called Potomac, but she has no peace. J'Rick is as handsome as Aaron and little Karma loves the dotsua, redbird, which sings outside her window. I will miss this fruit of our union; but I cannot bear the suffering. Besides, others whom I do not know, watch over them—the crow and the pigeon. So I am flying on home. Orange, Texas is my home. Because Uweyv seems like a dream to me now; and I wonder if such peace ever really existed at all.

CHAPTER 7
THE LEAN YEARS

November 1999

Blame tickled Karma and adjusted her ball cap. She checked the big clock on the wall, checked the number on her ticket, and waited. It was going to be another long day at Social Services. She had better things to do, like gossiping with Lish across the hall, drinking 40 ounces and watching Maury do DNA. But it was time for recertification, and without WIC, food stamps and an AFDC check; she might as well roll over and die. At least she didn't have to sit up in Housing too. The beneficent government said Blame could live in her raggedy, decrepit project apartment for the rest of life.

Karma squirmed in her seat, anxious to play with the snotty-nosed kids across the room; but Blame could see the dirt on their faces, necks and hands a mile away. To avert Karma's attention from the motley crew, she reached into her bag of goodies and produced a sandwich bag stuffed with animal crackers and a juice box. Blame was fast becoming a welfare mama veteran; she knew a day at Social Services required a whole battalion of ammunition, and knew that tactic would keep her daughter busy for another 20 minutes or so.

With Karma preoccupied, Blame fished in her bag for the latest piece of jail mail she'd received from Ricco. It arrived three days ago and she hadn't even bothered to open it. She already knew what it said: he loves her and the kids so much and he's so sorry things turned out the way they did; he admits now he had a problem with drugs; he didn't mean to stray, but she should still take the kids to visit their other sister Monique; his lawyer's working on an appeal so he might be coming home sooner; he'll never do anything to hurt her again; did she ever catch up with Brian because he was holding some money for him...find that niggah and put some money on his commissary. Blah, blah, blah... Blame retrieved a pen and notebook from her bag and responded in kind.

> *Dear Ricco,*
>
> *I talked to Brian, and he told me to get lost. I should've been the one holding OUR money; because Brian, whoever the fuck he is, ain't studied in your "wife" and kids. But that's what you get for trusting everybody over me. And you know what kind of shape you left us in, so don't be expecting NOTHING on your commissary unless that bitch, Keisha, put it there. And speaking of the bitch, Keisha, you must be out of your damned mind if you think we're going to start acting like one big happy family. Until you get a DNA my kids don't have any sister named Monique. And is Keisha on Brian's stoop begging for crumbs, or am I the only fool in this picture? Anyway...*
>
> *J'Rick and Karma are doing fine and asking about you every day. I hope that appeal comes through. I'm sitting at Social Services right now and this shit ain't cutting it. I hope you're serious about leaving that dope alone when you get out. You know you made a lot of promises to me, Ricco. And I did everything you asked me to do. EVERYTHING. So I hope you do get to come home soon so you can make good on your word. I still love you, but you already know that. Me and the kids won't be to visit for a while because I can't afford the bus fare. But know that we're thinking about you and we love you very much! Keep your head up.*
>
> *Love, Your Wifey,*
> *Blame Rane "Murdoch"*

Karma finished her snack and grew restless. Blame checked the number on her ticket again, and decided a trip to the restroom would kill some time. When they returned to their post, Blame took out one of Karma's books and read to her daughter. A few of the other welfare mothers cut and rolled their eyes at her. One was even foolish enough to say, "Oh that bitch think she fancy...reading books and shit." Blame shot them a screw face, and continued reading "The Little Engine That Could". Before long, the dirty kids across the room gathered in to listen to the story, too.

70

Her number was finally called. She gathered up her daughter and supplies and went to office No. 2 for the usual. Only she found out it was not going to be the usual. There was something new going on in the world of welfare; and for Blame to continue receiving her benefits, she would have to enroll in the Work First Program. It would pay for daycare while she looked for a job. Going forward, she would have to go to the unemployment office every day, enroll in work ready programs, and maybe even pick up garbage off the highway to earn her keep. Blame just answered with the usual "yes ma'ams", took the literature she was being handed and signed her name to everything Ms. Crenshaw put in front of her. She glanced over the schedule of places she was expected to be, stuffed the daycare and bus vouchers in her purse, and headed out the office.

On the bus ride back to the projects, Blame took a moment to process what Ms. Crenshaw was actually saying. It appeared that in order to keep that joke of a welfare check and some lousy food stamps, she was damn near going to be required to work a fulltime job. So, she thought, she might as well just get a damn job. She was visited by the memory of sitting in her lonely dorm room—the last time she deduced fulltime employment was her very best option in life.

Wow, she thought, that was nine years ago, and what the fuck have I accomplished? Hell, instead of going forward, she realized, with her project housing existence plus the added responsibility of two kids and no support, she had hustled backwards. She didn't even have transportation. Blame kicked herself again for letting the Buick get towed for parking tickets, and then not bothering to claim it because, *Ricco*, who had just bought a Range Rover, told her to forget about it. She noticed, once again, all the sleek, dark cars cruising up the highway, steered by women who seemed to be on the right track in life...probably going to warm comfortable houses, she thought. Oh what she'd give for a car right now!

Blame fingered the letter from Ricco, looked at Karma sleeping on her lap, then turned to face the window so the other passengers wouldn't see her crying. She noticed the birds again, the black ones. She cried silently and started to become conscious of the fact that black birds always seemed to be present in her life. Why had she not noticed this before? Thinking back now, they were always there—not front and center of course—but there still, in the corners and fringes of her life. It had to be a sign—and *black birds*? Whatever the omen was, it couldn't be good, she thought.

She looked closer at the flock. Their oily black bodies were the color of the burnt, charred remains of 632 Rose Lane. She imagined fire roasting her father's furrowed brow, erasing her mother's long, shiny hair. She closed her eyes tight against the images and tried to concentrate on something else. Mrs. Douthit's tuna melt came to mind, and she laughed. She wiped her face and made a mental note to call, or least write to Mrs. Douthit...check on her wellbeing.

" Momma, me and Karma want some cereal and it ain't no milk!"

"J'Rick please, can't you see I'm busy? Make y'all some pop tarts, then."

"You ain't busy. You just curling your hair. I'ma tell my daddy you got a boyfriend when we go see him," threatened the mature, seven-year-old.

"Boy! If you don't get out my damn face. And fuck yo sorry ass inmate daddy. For your information, Mr. Crown ain't my boyfriend; he's just a friend. And he paying for your camp, so

72

you betta act like you got some damn sense when he get here. Now get in there and make Karma a pop tart. And pick up y'alls toys out the living room. Hurry up, boy!"

Carl Crown was an older man, forty-eight. He was a regular sugar daddy to random women about the same age as Blame, who was then twenty-nine. By trade, he was a slum lord, with a plethora of raggedy row houses all over Baltimore and Washington D.C. Blame loathed his rough, calloused hands on her body, but he kept a little weed and powder on him at all times. Plus he was always good for a light bill, clothes for the kids, hair and nail money. He was also married.

Blame finished her hair and looked around the dump she was raising her children in. She broke down in tears because depression is painful. She was sick and tired of being poor...tired of being hungry...tired of nightmares about snaggleteeth and scabies, nightmares about fire and frost...tired of the world spinning out of control...and tired of feeling so damned sorry for herself.

She wanted Ricco home. She would rather a fist across her jaw and some sense of security, than this desperate scraping by. She thought about her parents again, and realized maybe she'd been so accepting of Ricco's bullshit because she didn't want him to disappear overnight...the way her mamma and daddy had. Anyway, fuck them, she screamed, cursing her parents once again, for dying in debt. The more she cried, the more she understood, no matter how many times she checked for his clothes in the closet, just like Sherman and Ethel, Ricco was gone.

As quickly as she'd begun to cry, she stopped. She leapt off the unmade bed, and smashed the picture frame, housing Ricco's photo. She dumped a drawer full of his prison letters in the floor and ripped them into a hundred pieces. She flung open the closet, drug out the suitcase storing his gear, and tore his dated clothes to shreds. Ricco wasn't coming home. Hell, she was in the fucking projects, where daddies weren't allowed. He didn't even have a home to come to.

And to hell with black eyes and busted lips, she thought, as her emotions flew all over the place. I don't need that niggah, Keisha can have him! He ain't got shit no way...bastard lost everything getting high! I don't have to live like this. I don't care what it takes. If the world doesn't end on Y2K; I'm getting the fuck out of Washington, D.C.!

Suddenly, there was a loud BOOM! Blame and everyone else in the project building knew what it meant. There had been an off and on problem in the boiler room for weeks now. Down in the sooty bowels of the aging high rise, the antiquated furnace had finally stopped working. Blame almost lost it. At one point in her life, Blame had been homeless and cold. She could feel the frost coming...knew it would include her children this time. She also knew she was powerless to do anything about it. She fumbled with the thermostat, out of habit, knowing full well it was caput. She wondered how she was going to keep her children warm through the night...and maybe the weeks, until the heat was fixed. Blame looked in the mirror and vowed to herself, "over my dead body!"

Once again, without any therapy or medication or even a Sunday visit to the corner church, Blame determined to pull herself together and find a way out of her wretched condition. She came from a "good home" and she was going to provide her children with the same...a home that, at the very least, would be warm and safe. But she didn't take the time to think, reflect, or plan. She tried to imagine what her own mother, Ethel, might do in this same predicament. But as had been the case through the years, she could find no trace of wisdom, nor glean any ready answers, from the memory of her dead distant mother. Blame decided to do *whatever* needed to be done, to do it quickly and, like Malcolm X said, to do it "by any means necessary"...starting with a car to cruise up the highway in, followed by a warm, comfortable home.

The corny rat-a-tat-a-tat on the steel door signaled Carl's arrival. Blame wiped her face; then scurried around the tiny apartment, kicking toys under the sofa, throwing a pile of dirty clothes in the coat closet, sweeping crumbs off the coffee table into her palm, and depositing them into a dying potted plant. She opened the heavy, rusty door and was greeted by a smiling Carl Crown, carrying a greasy bag of Chinese food and a bottle of cheap wine. The hungry children smelled the food and came, tumbling out of the kitchen. They filled up on chicken wings, lo Mein, and shrimp fried rice; then the children were sent to their shared bedroom to watch 24-hour cartoons.

Carl tossed Blame a pill bottle and a pack of rolling papers...being older, he preferred joints to blunts. The pill bottle contained a dime bag of weed, a half gram of coke, and a piece of a drinking straw, cut on an angle. Blame took a quick one-and-one, hitting both nostrils with a little coke. Then she rolled two coke-laced joints, put on *Baduizm*, and poured the wine. Carl was busy talking about his favorite subject, himself; so Blame wasn't really paying attention. She was trying to think of the best way to let him know what she really needed. Then something Toria once told here came to mind.

After they fucked on the couch (because her bedroom was a wreck), she flushed the spent condom and wiped her pussy off with a damp, mildewed washcloth. She returned to the living room to find him sucking down the last of the lo Mein. She ignored her own growling stomach, and got into beg mode. "Look Carl, you really ain't doing enough to keep thinking you can just fall up in here and get some ass whenever you want it."

"Oh shit, here we go. I brought y'all dinner, I brought the party with me," he said motioning to the drugs on the plastic coffee table. "And I told you I'll take care of that camp for your kids," he added in his defense. "What else you want from me?"

"I need a job, Carl. But ain't no decent gigs round here. All the good jobs is in Maryland. But I ain't got no way to get out there every day." She glanced at him quickly to see if he was following her. Then she pouted and batted her eyelashes, remembering that's what Ricco liked. Fuck it, she thought, then continued, "I'ma just make it plain. I need a car. I mean when I get a job, I can pay you back. I just need transportation, right now...a little springboard to get on my feet."

"A *car*?! A whole damn *car*?! Shit I don't even come around but bout once a week, and even then, we don't always do it. Now you asking me for a *car*? What? You think I'm made out of money or something? Girl you tripping. I don't jingle like that." He packed up his party supplies, grabbed his keys and jacket, and headed for the front door, shaking his head in disbelief.

Desperate, Blame raced around the coffee table, with the duct-taped leg, and cut him off at the pass. She stood between him and the rusty steel door, and looked directly into his eyes. She'd also learned from Ricco, that her wild eyes made men uneasy. Since begging wasn't going to work, she decided to try plan B—head. Blame dropped down to her knees and unzipped Carl's slacks, keeping her eyes glued to his the whole time. She reached into his boxers, pulled out his flaccid Johnson and sucked him off right in about three minutes flat.

She had never given him a blowjob before. Ricco had made her practice over and over until she learned to do it right. When she'd mastered it, he required at least two a day. Anything less resulted in her wearing an icepack on her lip or eye. She knew she was good at it too...probably the best. Hell she'd done it for Ricco so many times; she could probably blow a dick, fry chicken and polish her toenails without missing a beat. Fuck Ricco!

Carl Crown was blown away. Black men in his generation just weren't used to getting their knobs polished...and never looking into eyes as hypnotizing as Blame's. "If you do right, you can get that every day," she smiled up at him, wiping his cum from her chin. "When your toes finish uncurling, we can talk about that car." She got up and went to the bathroom to vomit, gargle and brush her teeth.

She returned to the living room to find Carl grinning ear to ear, Cheshire-cat style. The satisfied man was even humming some old school tune. "Every day?" He asked, eagerly.

Blame lit a cigarette and responded, "I need something good on gas, Carl. Clean, not too many miles on it...big enough for my kids to ride comfortable, too. Now I done told you how my baby daddy used to put it down before he went away. It can't be nothing wack. And yes, every damn day of the week...*if* you do right."

"Umph! What other tricks you got up your sleeve, girl?" he joked. Blame didn't laugh; she just kept her magical eyes locked on his. "Yeah alright," he conceded, "I'll see what I can do. But you're gonna pay me back when you find a job."

When he left, because it was getting too cold in the cramped and filthy apartment, Blame moved J'Rick and Karma to her bed—heaving with Karma, who was chubbier than most little girls. While they slept, she dressed them in sweat pants and warm sweaters. She piled all the comforters on top of them, and slid in the bed between them. Instead of sleeping, Blame spent the night rubbing her children's faces, hands and feet, keeping them warm—marveling at J'Rick's firm little muscles, disappointed at Karma's chubby rolls. It took two weeks for Housing to fix the furnace, but Blame had space heaters in two days...no matter that Carl Crown's gray pubic hairs kept getting lodged between her teeth.

It took three straight weeks of fucking and sucking him off, day in and day out, for Carl to find a good deal on a used Toyota Camry. He paid cash for it, and had it titled and registered in his name—for security. He handed her the keys on a Thursday night. In return, she gave him the orgasms of his life, even removing her dental bridgework, for added flair.

Carl stopped spending time with his other "young girls". Four year old Karma liked Carl; little girls tend to gravitate toward father figures. And J'Rick was even beginning to warm up to the old man. Blame began dropping by whatever house he was working on, just to kick it. Maybe J'Rick could learn something useful, she thought. Or if nothing else, at least he could see a man working. She remembered what Toria said about "sucking the right dick", and whenever Carl asked for a payment on the car, she gave him another blow job.

Blame stopped visiting Ricco altogether. Ricco was abusive, beating Blame's ass from sun up to sun down...especially after he got hooked on drugs. With two inches of glass between them, he told her he would kill her if she ever went down on another man. He swore he would be able to tell just by looking at her; and she believed him. Even though he would probably be locked up for the next two decades, Blame was still petrified of Ricco. To be on the safe side, she decided it was better if he never saw her again. Abuse reaches deep into the psyche; and she didn't want her neck broke.

Blame did find a job. She padded her resume with more fluff than a bag of cotton candy; and within no time she was an administrative assistant in the actuarial department of a life insurance company. The job was in Dale City, Virginia. But she told Carl she'd gotten a gig at a bank in Laurel, Maryland. Since she wouldn't have to re-certify for government assistance for another four months, she didn't bother to report her income. She cashed her AFDC checks and payroll checks at the same bank, and saved nearly every dime.

She cleaned up her raggedy apartment and implemented a schedule for herself and her kids to live by; bringing order back to their chaotic lives. On a Saturday afternoon, with nothing better to do, she and the kids even drove across town to take a look at Monique, and to see how Keisha was living.

Monique was the spitting image of her father...looking more like Ricco than Ricco himself. Keisha shared some of Ricco's letters with Blame. They were not like the letters Blame received—they were the sincere reflections of a man pouring his heart out to his one true love. Keisha also apologized to Blame on behalf of Ricco, for all the abuse she'd endured. She assured Blame he had never laid a hand on her during their relationship. Being raised the way she was; Keisha would never have stood for it if he had.

Blame was devastated. She and her children rode home in silence; and she couldn't help feeling like the world's biggest fool. She wanted to march into the prison and throw acid in Ricco's face; but she sat down to write him a letter, instead. She intended to tell him to him to fuck off and rot in hell, even give him a play by play of the blowjobs she was passing out. He truly *had* produced another child outside of their union. And from the looks of things, he was clearly in love with Keisha, whom he'd never punched, socked, kicked or beaten. Even in the beginning of their relationship, he hadn't used the kind of words he penned in his letters to Keisha.

She hated Ricco; hated herself even more for ever loving him. Plus, in her mind, it was his fault she'd been reduced to sucking dick to get by. After all, he's the one who told her to forget about the Buick. He's the one who got on drugs and caused them to lose everything. He was the reason she wore a partial plate with two false teeth—the originals knocked out because he had no money, needed a fix, Karma wouldn't stop crying, and the fish wasn't fried "right".

She picked up the pen and paper, but thought better of it. She said, to herself, "I'm not even going to waste the energy. No more visits, no more letters...he'll get the message. Besides, a nasty-gram from me can't punish him anymore than the courts already have. It was bullshit to begin with. And now it's over. I'm getting the fuck outta this life...as far away from here as possible. And I don't give a damn *what* I have to do to pull it off." Blame used the pen and paper to write to Mrs. Douthit, instead.

The children in the project yard looked toward heaven to identify the source of the loud cawing overhead. Tuppie Rane was plumb tickled, and could not stop laughing at the sheer determination of Blame Rane. "Tole you she was a fighter," she cackled to any passerby listening. "She gone be alright...come hell or high water, she gone be alright." Then Tuppie spread her wings and swept down from the large murder of crows perched on the roof of the project building. She just wanted to pester the fat white pigeon resting on Blame's window ledge. The Tuppie Rane, who had been a slave in life, was dead now...there was nothing more Mistress Gwendolyn Rainier could threaten her with.

She's coming right at me, thought the frightened pigeon. How dare she! The pigeon lifted her wings, still imagining them as flowing silk sleeves, and leapt off the ledge. She batted her wing at the blackbird, screaming, "Shoo! Shoo! You old black crow!"

CHAPTER 8
CROWS

It is her foolish intent to ridicule and humiliate me—"you old black crow". We are so much older than she; and we know what she does not. I don't bother with an attempt to explain; her knowledge cannot encompass the truth. Instead, I laugh, or rather cackle, into the wind and across time, at Gwendolyn's shallow ignorance. And since He commissioned us to gain, above all, understanding...I certainly understand why I move as crow now, through both space and time. *Old black crow indeed...*

A group of crows—be they jackdaw or raven—is called a flock, a murder, or a storytelling of crows. They are believed to be the most intelligent of birds. The "nucleus" of their brains is the same size as that of the human and chimpanzee brain. In fact, crows are so clever; they have been known to manufacture tools, such as knives cut from stiff leaves, for use in finding and obtaining food. And believe it or not, they've been observed dropping tough nuts into heavy traffic, allowing the cars to crush the nuts open, and waiting for the lights to change at the crosswalk with pedestrians, before retrieving the nuts.

The crow has been highly revered throughout time. You've seen us plastered across the hieroglyphics in ancient Egypt; we were the subject of Aesop's fable in ancient Greece; and could be found ever-accompanying the Norse god, Odin. When the first Dalai Lama was born, legend has it that robbers attacked his family's home. There was no time for the fleeing parents to reach the infant Lama. The next morning, the parents returned to find their home untouched, and the Dalai Lama was being cared for by a pair of crows. In Japanese mythology, we symbolize the evidence of divine intervention in human affairs. As far back as Gilgamesh, it was the crow that found the means of survival—land, in that case—when the dove failed at the task. And deeper still into antiquity—a crow scratched the earth for the murderer Cain, teaching him how to bury Abel, along with his shame.

So you see, we were always there, observing, sometimes intervening...always utilizing our cunning and creativity to sustain. It is true that we feed upon carrion, the putrefying flesh of dead things, but we make no apology— surviving, you see, by any means necessary.

I see the cardinal and the pigeon, travelling alone. I fly with the family...loving this notion of family. I am delighted I can have one now, a family—which won't be stolen away or sold to the highest bidder. What's that? Come closer, I cannot hear you. Mind you, I am ancient.

Surely you can come closer than that. I understand my blackness is difficult to look upon, because you've been taught to associate negativity with this hue. And yes, we crows are very black. We are black as the life-giving womb *and* black like death. We are black like every corner of the universe; and black as the innards of the fruit-producing earth, where all Roots live. Black like oil—father of industry, and coal—mother of diamonds...black as the midnight sky. We are black like the period (.) when the story is done. And we are black like the mud—fashioned into shape—when God first made Man.

If you can't come any closer, then please speak louder...again I am ancient as the original tick tock of Time. Why you wonder, are we always to be found at the graveyard, perched atop the tombstones?

I've told you, we are a storytelling of crows. And the dead, quite frankly, have the very best stories. The living can only speculate; but the dead know, for certain, how the story will end.

What is that you ask? Are we good or are we bad? Ah, well now, isn't that the most timeless of questions—and the *only* one that really matters in the balance of this universe. Such a weighty question, such an easy answer: We simply...Are.

CHAPTER 9

DALE CITY, VA

April 2000

　　She could have worked at the Insurance Company until she retired; but it wasn't enough for Ethel's daughter. Blame lived the high life in the fast lane with Ricco; and now that she was out of her project funk and ghetto mentality, she wanted it all. Uneducated on the significance of delayed gratification, Blame wanted the whole world, immediately. The birds were screaming, "Slow Down!" But she couldn't hear them. She had on earplugs as well as blinders. She developed a sort of tunnel vision that would not let her stray off course, pause, assess, weigh or reflect. When the mind is stuck on one track, it can move blindly, like a computerized subway train; and actual *thinking* is never required. But trains sometimes derail.

　　"What about this mommy?" Karma questioned, holding up a baby doll missing its head.

　　"No honey, she has to stay. We can only take what will fit in the car. Just the toys you play with. Mommy's gonna buy you all brand new stuff anyway. J'Rick, how are you doing with your pile over there?"

　　"I'm ready to go! You want me to help you take them boxes and bags downstairs?" J'Rick was anxious to begin the journey his mother had painted as a truly excellent adventure. There was a knock at the door and J'Rick ran to answer it. Blame tackled him in the hallway and put her hand over his mouth.

　　"Hush," she whispered.

　　"Say Blame, its Carl. I know you're in there. The car's parked out front. What's going on, Blame? You haven't returned my calls all week. Open the door, already." The trio sat perfectly quiet and still until they were sure he was gone. Then for good measure, they sat still another twenty minutes longer. Karma looked confused and wondered why her mommy wouldn't open the door for Carl. Blame assured her she was just playing a game, which was true.

Blame finally cracked open the heavy steel door and checked to see if the coast was clear. Then she ran the packed up boxes and bags down to the Camry as fast as her legs would carry her. Her neighbor Lish helped, and the vehicle was jam-packed in under an hour. She hurriedly squeezed her children in where there was room, bid her neighbor farewell, and promised to keep in touch (though she knew she would not). She headed for the highway, taking what had become a very familiar route on her morning commute to Dale City, Virginia.

Once on I-95 South, Blame relaxed enough to stop checking her rearview mirror. But she couldn't resist the urge to check her purse, one more time, for the set of keys to the three-bedroom townhouse she'd leased the week before. The power was already connected; the cable would have to wait. There wasn't any living room furniture yet, or even a kitchen table. But the kids' bunk beds had already been delivered. Blame would suffice with a mattress and box spring for now. J'Rick was out of school for spring break...making it the perfect time to escape D.C. Blame was so tickled with her coup, she laughed out loud. Her children didn't know what was so funny, but they laughed too. She popped her worn-out, bootleg copy of "*The Miseducation of Lauryn Hill*" into the cd player, and they sang along jubilantly, cruising down the highway to their warm and comfortable new home.

Once inside the city limits of Dale City, Blame stopped at KFC for a bucket of chicken and fixings; then pulled into the parking lot of Polo Manor. Blame's co-worker, and self-proclaimed diva, Charlene Tucker, had recommended the spot. She lived there as well with her three girls: Shaniqua, Dyshay, and LaDawn. Blame rang up her girlfriend and invited her over to burn a blunt. She had officially arrived and it was definitely on and poppin'!

The world had not come to an end with the Y2K scare. She had a job, a car, a place and money in the bank. She wasn't about to pay Carl back for the ride either...as far as she was concerned that debt was paid in full with coochie coupons, and plenty of head to cover the interest. Fuck Carl! Ricco was last year's news, the world was still riding the wave of the Clinton boom, and she was only 29 years old. Blame Rane thought life was definitely looking up; and in her estimation, the sky was the limit.

The birds sang sweeter in Dale City. The air was even fresher than the stench and stank of D.C. The pace of life was a bit slower, calmer...but tragically, Ethel's daughter failed to notice.

Blame took a few days off work to register J'Rick in the elementary school, and Karma in the Head Start Program. She bought some household items and did a little decorating, making her townhouse a home. She didn't have any real credit established, and would have to wait another six months to get the rest of her furniture. She had her eye on some pieces that were definitely going to have to be financed—top of the line furnishings that would make even her mother proud.

Her friend Charlene, at age 32, was only 17 years older than her eldest daughter, LaDawn. For fifteen year old LaDawn, babysitting was not an option; it was a requirement. Shaniqua was eight—the same age as J'Rick. And little Dyshay was six...a year older than Karma, who would be turning five that month.

With a permanent babysitter in their camp, Charlene and Blame hit the clubs nearly every night. Charlene was born and raised in Dale City (which the locals called Little DC); so she knew *everybody*. Blame, because of her exceptional good looks, and also just being a new face in the crowd, soon became the hottest ticket in town.

Blame grew heady from the spotlight. Every race, color and creed of man in the progressive, mid-sized city seemed to have her on their radar. Of the variety of eligible bachelors vying for her attention, there was only one courter she felt amicable about. Even though she was approached by a college professor, a small business owner, a successful account executive, a high school math teacher/basketball coach, several hard-working blue-collar brothers, and the vice president of a local bank; she seemed to be drawn, (or rather pushed), toward a man named Nicholas Gentry—known around town as Nick at Nite.

Nick was a mixed kid who dated Black women exclusively. By trade, he was a well-known club promoter, talent scout/agent and entrepreneur extraordinaire. He had his hands in a little bit of everything, including moving tons of prescription drugs, on the low. Charlene's downing and clowning of the other brothers, and her big-upping Nick every chance she got, also helped persuade Blame he was the man for her. Charlene went so far as to make up outright lies about the college professor, when Blame started getting too close—saying she knew for fact he was on the down low...aka, an undercover fag.

Since her high school days; Charlene desperately wanted to be included in Nick's clique. Plus she had a set of pipes like Whitney Houston, and was sure Nick would put her on, if she could get close enough. Blame was her ticket in.

Blame still had not learned most of the people she would encounter in her lifetime, would have some angle, some agenda of their own, some purpose she could serve to their greater need—never having her best interest in mind or at heart.

Nicholas was dubbed Nick at Nite for a very obvious reason. The man was 100% nocturnal. He might as well have been a vampire bat; he was so rarely seen during the day. But when the sun went down, Nick Gentry glowed as bright as the northern star...in Dale City. Anybody with an inkling of talent flocked around him, believing he had the right connections to make them superstars. If he was in the house, that's where the party was. If he was a no show, your event was a flop. Nick always sat VIP, had access to the back rooms and private parties, could draw the biggest names and managed to close the most lucrative deals. He was a very big fish in a very little pond; and he preferred it that way. At 33, Nick was a man who knew what he wanted; and in Dale City, he got it. At present, he wanted, and would have, Blame Rane...the mysterious, cinnamon-colored beauty from D.C., with the pretty eyes.

It was a new millennium and the industry was changing. The 10-man entourage was fast becoming a dated look. The new trademark of a true Boss was rolling solo, with a dime piece trophy on his arm. Blame certainly fit the bill, and thus far, from their romps around town, it seemed she was born to play the part. She knew when to be brassy, sassy, shy, chic, friendly, rude, front row and invisible. She was so good in fact, that Nick began wondering who trained her. He knew from her exquisite taste and knowledge of the finer things in life; whoever she rolled with previously, dealt in big bills too. When she let her guard down enough to powder her nose with a little cocaine, Nick knew he had a winner.

With the nature of Nick's occupation being so nocturnal, and Blame quickly becoming his number one sidekick, she began to see less and less of her children. She held bankers hours at the insurance company—9 to 5, with weekends off. She paid LaDawn to get her kids off the bus and watch them until she got home. LaDawn didn't mind; her mother wasn't her paying her anything to handle the exact same responsibilities for her little sisters. Blame would get home around 5:30, collect her kids and do "family time". This included: homework, dinner, playtime, television, baths and bed. Her children were in bed promptly at 8:30, *every* night. Then, either LaDawn would come over for the remainder of the evening, or Blame would drop the kids off at Charlene's for a sleep over, because she rarely made it in before 4 a.m.

The nights and the weekends were made for partying! At first it was a foursome, Charlene and friend of Nick included, with the jet-set crowd. Soon, the invitations to go here and there were no longer extended to Blame's coworker. Charlene had long ago played out in Dale City, and Nick said she just didn't fit in. He never did get her into the studio, either, as promised. Blame tried to maintain the friendship, but eventually that too faded.

Blame wanted to keep her coke-dabbling a secret from Nick; but she found it more and more necessary to partake, just to keep up with the whirlwind pace of their lives...weekends in Montego Bay and whatnot. Before long, Blame grew curious about Nick being able to move so fluently in all circles. He knew the old heads and the young kids, both male and female. He mingled with the blacks, whites, Hispanics and Asians—rich, poor and middle class, alike. Nick had been around a long time. He knew if a person had *any* association with drug activity, they had the capacity to be *fully* associated with drug activity. Since

Blame snorted powder, he thought it wouldn't be a far stretch to induct her into his prescription drug ring.

He needed someone he could trust. His original partner in crime, and studio soundman, Joey Piscatti, was a smooth operator and a first class hustler; but Nick knew the man was a snake. The more money they made, the more his fangs showed. Nick's uncle, Stanley, had once told him, "you gotta know your players, and put 'em the right positions." Blame was definitely a player, and using her on his team to replace Joey was a better option than getting snake bit.

Besides, he knew people; so he did some checking, and found out about a cat named Ricco up in Lawsonville on fed time. He figured Ricco must have been Blame's trainer, her molder. It wasn't like he was turning her out or anything; his woman had been bitten by the drug bug a long time ago. She was already infected and just didn't know it, yet.

Nick worked it slowly into the mesh of their relationship. Can you pick up a package for me on your way over? I got some people I want you to meet. I need you to drop that off at this address. So and so is going to give you some money for me; bring it to the club. Then it graduated to: we're going to a college rave tonight, mingle with the crowd and see who's looking for Ecstasy, Oxycontin and Xanax. Pass some of this shit around in the back room at the poker game and see who bites. Can I have some mail delivered to your address? Put this in your purse when we go in the strip club, take it backstage when I give you a signal. I got Usher coming to sing *Burn*...you know what to do.

Meanwhile, Blame's apartment got fully furnished and since Nick had three cars, she kept the Lexus jeep. By the time she was sorting and repackaging pills abc for party xyz, serving late night customers and putting stacks on the counting machine; she required a safety deposit box for her cash and jewels, the use of her children's closets for her wardrobe, and a loaded gun for a good night's sleep.

With Blame on his team, replacing Joey, Nick decided it was time to venture outside his little Dale City pond. Trustworthy Blame would hold down the locals while he shopped the markets in Alexandria, Manassas, and Fort Washington. Everybody knew her by then, and he kept a few henchmen on the payroll in case things got out of hand.

The various runners he had stationed in key locations of the city would report directly to Blame, meaning she supplied their daily work and collected their daily take. So, quite naturally, she had to cut back her hours at work, to part time. When the out-of-town action picked up, like they knew it would, it seemed a bit foolish for Blame to work at all. She was bringing down a week's salary before brunch on any given day. She stayed long enough to pass employment screening for the new condo she purchased, needing a bigger place to house all her *things* (enough to make her mother proud). She didn't bother giving the Insurance Company a two-week notice when she blew away in her cream-colored Corvette, sipping lattes and readjusting her diamond-studded watch.

J'Rick was settling in okay. He was used to the ups and downs of life with his mother by then. But he suffered from pangs of angst and tension when he saw his mother with Nick. Karma, sat quietly and patiently, waiting to feel something...like love...overeating in the meantime...sometimes singing *birdsong*. They enjoyed all the *stuff*, but it still wasn't enough.

Blame talked to Keisha from time to time; at first just to check up on Ricco. But over time they developed a sort of "sisterly" or "same-baby-daddy" relationship. Due to the nature of her business, she had to cut Charlene off completely. The chic was working class, and no longer in Blame's league. This did not sit well with Charlene, to say the least. LaDawn was no longer at her beck and call to tend to Karma and J'Rick; so Blame started dropping the kids off for weekends and entire summers in D.C. They needed to know their sister, she told herself, and Keisha truly did not mind—thinking she scored points with Ricco, as the glue holding his family together.

Blame still loved Ricco. But it was a different kind of love than it had been back in the early 90's. She was still angry at him too, for getting himself locked up and destroying her world. First her parents, then Ricco just up and disappeared. Blame was constantly blaming others for disappearing and fucking up her life. But things were different now. This time *she* was in the driver's seat.

Even if something did happen to Nick, as far as Blame was concerned, one monkey didn't stop the show. She knew the connects, most of the players, and some of the ins and outs of the business. She figured she could hold it down on her own, if need be. Really, she didn't know the half.

She cut Ricco some slack though. Even without the drug habit; in her mind, he was destined for prison all along. He was a drug dealer! Which Blame, quite frankly, was *not*. Drake and Ricco sold crack. Prescriptions drugs, on the other hand, were legal...FDA approved. Drake and Ricco were just kids—early twenties—when they were on top. She and Nick were in their 30's. Suav-A, and company, were thugs in the smoking hot city of Washington, D.C. She was a business woman and mother of two, in the quiet suburban town of Dale City, Virginia. It was like apples and oranges—it clearly was not the same, to Blame.

She still checked three times to make sure things were where they were supposed to be. She still dreamt of scabies and snaggleteeth, fire and frost, and occasionally Ricco's passion. She would never feel that way about Nick, even though he was generous, kind, funny, handsome, and a decent fuck. He just didn't do it for Blame. Even though he was good to her kids—forever showering them with gifts, he didn't speak to her heart. Even though they sometimes woke up on beaches in Cancun or St. Croix, hotel rooms in New York, Las Vegas or L.A.; he was her companion, but not her love.

Blame was thirty-three years old, and life thus far had created a light glazing of ice over her once trusting heart. Nick suggested she move in on more than one occasion; but Blame wouldn't hear it. She now had, and intended to forever keep, her own shit...the memory of Carl Crown's old man balls, and her project rat hole home, loomed heavy in her memory. She was determined to never hustle backward again.

CHAPTER 10
EYE FOR AN I

When I was WindRider TwoSquirrels, a flesh and blood woman, I grew and smoked the peyote. It eased the pain of feeling so much suffering; and it helped me see the things to come. Once upon a time, when I smoked the peyote, I was allowed to see the most horrible of visions. I witnessed the birth of the Great Witch! She is not a tale for spooking little children into proper behavior; she is very real. And she is full grown now.

The Great Witch lives between the waters called: Pacific, Atlantic, Great Lakes, Gulf and Rio Grande. She is so very beautiful and bountiful, the whole world wants her. But I know she was born from the rancid womb of Genocide. Her father is the Warlock—oath breaker, covenant betrayer. So Genocide—the murderer, and Warlock—the liar, named their beautiful daughter, America.

America is a Great Witch; but she does not ride a broom. She rides the backs of broken men. She does not use a wand; she prefers a different stick—the steel barrel of the gun. She is not regulated to a pointy black hat—she can wear any hat and assume any likeness.

America was a very greedy child, and is greedy still. Her parents filled up her big belly with shiploads of slaves. It was much more fortifying than the maize I was reared on. This diet of slavery made her grow up to be big and strong. Her big feet can go anywhere; the whole world is her playground. The Great Witch has never been chastised for her many indiscretions—like Columbus' dog devouring Arawaks; or strange fruit hanging from southern trees—so she knows nothing of caution or fear; and she was never taught the value of sharing.

She has many powerful spells and magic tricks, too. Her pot of witches' brew is called the melting pot. Like any other witch, her favorite snack for the pot is little children. I will tell you how the Great Witch, America, ate my only child...how she stole my farm, and ended my life.

Aaron and I rode the night wind many times during our walking to the Gulf Coast. By the time we got to Orange, Texas, I was ripe with child. Aaron built a home for us. We fished and scratched out a farm for our living. My beautiful daughter, Dusty, was born in 1839. She was named by her father for the lovely, earthy color of her skin. She was so happy to be alive, and her strong legs never stopped moving. I completed her naming when she was seven, adding Awiyusti, the Cherokee Nation's word for the antelope. She ran everywhere. One would think with all the night flying Aaron and I did, there would have been brothers and sisters for Dusty Awiyusti; but she was our only child. She was a good girl, so helpful and happy. Dusty was the absolute joy of our too short lives.

Life in Orange was sweet. But I know now we should have kept walking to Mexico, where, in those days, all men were free. But Blacks and "Indians" lived free throughout Texas, and we thought we were safe. We knew nothing of the whiteman's law. We did not know about the Great Witch—America—annexing Texas as a state, in 1845. It was then that Orange became sour, like the lemon.

Rumors started. So we built a fence and sharpened our weapons. We never let Dusty out of our sight. We watched and we waited for the signs, hoping the rumors were not true. But Texas was swallowed up by America, and she is an insatiable Witch. When the devils, white like the fishes belly, stole our closest neighbors, we knew it was true. The whiteman was kidnapping free people of color, selling them into slavery, and claiming their lands as his own! (Circles?)

Aaron said it would not happen to us. We would fight with our lives; because his African Muslim mother had taught him that oppression was worse than slaughter.

Under the cover of dark night, in the winter of 1852, they came for us. We fought tooth and nail and my brave Aaron killed at least two of them. Because we were unyielding and fully prepared to die; they set fire to our happy home. As the smoke grew stronger and the flames grew higher...the innate part of me that is mother, pushed Dusty out the window. She was a runner, and I hoped she could get away. A mother wants life for her child, always. She put her antelope legs into commission and took off like the lightening. But she was no match for the Great Witch and her army of devils.

I am so sorry my Dusty! She should have burned with us—it would have been better than capture. But catch her they did. And the 13-year old apple of her father Aaron's eye, the pearl of my broken heart—our precious Dusty Awiyusti, was pulled into the vicious grip of slavery. America ate my only child!

I became cardinal almost instantly, singeing my tail feather escaping my coffin—the burning house that Aaron built. I wished so badly to be alive again in those days. I would have burned those damned plantations to the ground—incinerating its occupants like they'd done to us. Oh, the horrible things they did to our sweet Dusty. And of course she could not understand it. She was born free. Much to the devil's dismay, she could not be broken. She was so much braver than I, and the others from Uweyv had been—she refused to be like the cattle.

Dusty fought, bit, kicked, screamed and remained the very definition of disobedience. Her father died to be free; she would never forget that. I rooted for her bravado. A man on one of the plantations pointed to me, saying, "Look, how the redbird cheers for Dusty." If I could turn my head round, like the owl, I would like to see my back. I believe there are scars there; because I felt every lash of the whip my Dusty endured...so many flesh-ripping strikes, I lost count.

Rather than kill her for her insolence, because she simply could not be a cow; the devils who owned our Dusty kept selling her from plantation to plantation. By the time she arrived on her fifth plantation, it was 1855. My 16 year old fruit was ripe herself with seed. Anyone could have been the father. She had a tiny little flower of a babe. The devil named her Sue. Dusty took one look at little Sue; and I could see—why anyone with eyes could see—her whole spirit fill up with pride. My poor Dusty did not know slaves could not be proud.

Oh, how Dusty doted on Sue...stealing food for her...telling her tales of a perfect little farm in a perfect little place called Orange. She pointed skyward, spinning the most wondrous yarns, weaving magic into stories about brave Aaron and me, the WindRider. Sue believed we were stars, constellations in the heaven. Dusty dreamed dreams for Sue. She planned escapes for them both, and kissed and hugged my tiny granddaughter very tight. She became tamer, calmer...but she still was not like the cow.

When Sue was seven years old, in the year 1862, her Mistress decided she needed to be taught a lesson for some minor indiscretion. I cannot recall the lynchpin now. The Mistress, white like the fishes belly, beat my dear, little granddaughter with the cat-o-nine tails.

Woe to Dusty Awiyusti—antelope and the earth, precious blood of my blood! She had, what is called today, a psychotic break. My Dusty assaulted that Mistress. In turn, every white devil on that plantation assaulted my Dusty, my living flesh. They brought her to the very door of death, over and over again. You may call me a coward; but I could not watch and had to fly away. Though she was near death, it was not enough for the devil. To finally break Dusty, the Mistress, who had only been slapped to the floor, sold sweet Sue, away.

Now, if a slave will slap you to the ground for beating her child, what do you suppose that same slave (born free, mind you) would do if you sold her precious little piece of heaven—her only daughter—away? Well that is precisely what Dusty did.

My daughter scaled the wall with a fractured arm. I flew back just in time to see her throw herself over the balcony, wincing at the pain of her broken ankle and busted knee. She used every little bit of strength she could muster to pummel that devil of a woman. The beating was like the hailstorm that flattened our crops one year, on Uweyv. When the whitemen finally came to her rescue, the Mistress had been beaten to a bloody pulp. Dusty had meant to kill her.

I was very proud of Dusty's bravery. But I suppose you already know she could not be sold again. Time had run out for the daughter of Aaron and I—the WindRider. They drug my flesh to the hog pen, and threw her in with the sows. They forced other slaves to come and witness. The Mistress was carried to the hog pen on her feather mattress, so she too could see, and thus be vindicated.

Dusty was covered in mud. They brought out a rifle—that is another name for the devil's gun, which I have already told you about. Dusty held up her fist, soaked in the mistress' bad blood. She did not cry or even flinch. The rifle made a sound like thunder. The thunder made a hole in Dusty's head. She collapsed face first into hog slop.

I have no words. I cannot tell you this pain.

I reeled up to the heavens and flew down, like the hawk that used to fish on Uweyv. By the time they saw the redbird spiraling like their thunder arrows, called bullets, there was no time to react. I went in with the precision of what you call a surgeon; and I plucked out the sky blue eye of Mistress...America.

I flew to Orange with that eye (I carry it with me still). I did not stop until I reached the graveside of Aaron. There is no tombstone there, not even a grave. It is the place where he took his last stand against evil—the place where his burning body lay down. I languished there for three long years, refusing to fly. But I danced the galv (honor dance) and chanted the names of Aaron and Dusty—like any other warriors on the battlefield, they died honorable deaths.

Then in the month of June, 1865, I woke one morning to a warming wind. The wind was called Emancipation. It was surely sent by the Great Spirit, and it blew away the last of my bitter grief. The hopeful wind tickled my feathers and courted me, until I found myself wrapped up in its arms. I was flying again! With new air breathed into my little bird lungs, I set out to find a ten year old girl named Sue.

I am TwoSquirrels and I was determined to track my granddaughter. The Great Spirit guided my flight, and I found her walking away from a cotton plantation in the river valleys of East Texas. She was still very small, and she had two eggs, a sack of grits and a cooking pot. She was born brave, because she walked alone; covering the state of Texas with only the dotsua, redbird, for a companion.

I did not know where she walking to; but I did not leave her side. If she was going to the end of the earth, then so was I. When danger came, I warned her, so she could lie down in the bushes. When food was nearby, I uncovered it—hidden rabbits, sleeping squirrels—so she would not starve. I plucked berries and dropped them in her path, sang her to sleep with birdsong.

One day, she came upon an old woman, walking in the opposite direction. Sue asked the woman, "Which way is Orange?" It seems Sue remembered the stories of her loving mother, Dusty, and that home was in a place called Orange. Now aware of our destination, I took the lead and guided her all the way home.

She was such a tiny little girl, so brave. She found work, and slept under porches, in woods and caves. When she was old enough, she made a home for herself in a boarding house— in a room no bigger than a closet. She sewed clothes to pay rent for the closet, and to eat. And she gave herself a last name...Dusty.

Little Sue raised *herself*. When she was still too young to know what was bad; I watched as she, sadly, met and married a man named Filip, who seemed allergic to steady work. Filip had already made his last name bad, so he adopted Sue's. They bore a son named Fil Jr., who, like his father, was no count. I had flown to Africa about this time, and did not get to witness the raising of such an insolent boy. I'm glad not to have known him. I understand from the talking, he was in no way like Aaron. Fil Jr.'s daughter, Philomena, was no better. I returned from my pilgrimage in time to see Philomena become pregnant, with no husband. She was a selfish and foolhardy girl, and she left her baby daughter, still in swaddling clothes, for old Sue to rear. They called the baby, Ethel.

Sue, daughter of Dusty, granddaughter of Aaron and I, the WindRider, lived to be 110 years old. She was born in 1855; she died in 1965. She did the very best she could with Ethel. She did the very best she could in life. She prayed to and thanked the Great Spirit often. She never forgot her mother, Dusty Awiyusti, and looked for her everywhere in Orange, Texas...up until the day the she died. And she always put out fresh seeds for the dotsua, redbird, which was her dearest friend.

My only flesh on the earth now, is Blame, daughter of Ethel and Sherman Rane; the little Aaron, called J'Rick; and sweet Karma, who loves the dotsua that shadowed her early childhood. That is my story in this Great Witch called America. I will ride her wind until the Great Spirit brings me home, where I already know, my Aaron will have prepared a place for me.

Miss America...she really is beautiful though, on her surface. And she has a dimple—a pretty little beauty mark upon her face. It is a place that draws your eyes and arouses your senses...giving you joy in springtime just to behold it. It is in the hills and dales of the North Carolina foothills. Her beautiful dimple was once called Uweyv, the river. I shall leave Texas and fly black to the East now. I am going to find the land of my birth; also, I have a yearning to know what has become of my Blame.

CHAPTER 11

MY PEOPLE PERISH

November 2005

Nick Gentry's soundman, Joey, was a Catholic Italian kid from Philly. He'd been loyal to Nick for years. In his estimation, he was half the reason Nick's dealings had been so profitable. He didn't like the way things were going down, and was determined to do something about it. No one had heard from Nick in weeks, but the "scrips" were flowing like business as usual. The only problem was the new chic, Blame, raking in all the dough...money that should have been his. His woman, Gladys, was okay, as far as girlfriends and pawns go...but Joey had seen lots of good soldiers die on the battlefield. She was replaceable. And so he hatched a little plan.

The oxymorphone supplier got popped. Blame hustled a lot of pills, but the flip on Opana® was unbelievable; making no less than nine times her initial investment on the powerful opiate. Gladys, the live-in girlfriend of Joey, swore she could get oxymorphone from her job, no sweat. Blame regretted promising Gladys a ride to her workplace, an HIV clinic all the way in D.C.; but she *needed* those pills. Blame was sure Gladys could pull it off; and Joey himself said it would be a cakewalk. White people, she was learning via Nick and company, seemed to get away with everything.

While Gladys got dressed, Blame serviced her ever increasing drug habit, snorting several lines of coke, to stay on top of her game. She then wrapped a scarf around her head, placed a baseball cap on top of that, and completed her disguise with a pair of dark sunglasses. She hadn't been in D.C. in years, other than to drop the kids off at Keisha's. And she sure as hell didn't want to be seen, pulling up at an HIV clinic. Plus, what they were about to do was, technically, a crime.

When they arrived at the clinic, Blame was delighted to see the non-descript building, no signs announcing its true identity...nothing to single out the doomed community it served. Instead of dropping Gladys off, she decided to park and go inside...make everything look on the up and up.

Gladys talked to a woman behind the frosty glass at the check-in counter. After a familiar exchange, the woman pressed a button, allowing Gladys entry to the back rooms. Blame took a seat and scanned the crowded lobby, reading the posted signs, inspecting the patients waiting to see the doctors...trying to pick out who was a friend or family member, and who had been stricken with the death sentence. Surprisingly, she couldn't tell who might have tested positive.

A woman checking in at the front counter looked awfully familiar, but with the huge red welts on her face—a dead giveaway of full blown AIDS—Blame couldn't place her. She flipped through an old magazine to pass the time, thinking about all the money she would make that week. When she came upon a Mercedes Benz advertisement, she froze. The last time she'd seen a Benz like that, Toria Black was driving it. She glanced up at the haggard, dying woman at the counter and knew without doubt, she was looking at her former roommate.

Blame convulsed, raced to the bathroom and vomited up her lunch of baked salmon and Waldorf salad. When she returned, Toria was sitting in the chair next to Blame's purse. She had no choice but to return to her seat. Even though Toria made Blame feel like a real piece of shit when she last saw her, in the projects, Blame had no desire to reciprocate. Besides, after the ordeal in the Dominican hair spot, Blame knew she had

104

that one coming. She didn't even want Toria to notice her, so she kept her head down, hat pulled low over her eyes.

When Gladys was finished, stealing 700 capsules of the level IV prescription narcotic from her employer; she returned to the lobby. She couldn't get her driver's attention and had to call her name. "Blame, you ready?" She asked, not breaking her stride to the door.

"BLAME?!" Toria gasped, jerking her head in Blame's direction. "Well, well...looks like we both got caught out there," and she attempted a smirk, but her cracked, ashy lips wouldn't allow it. "I knew your funky ass was gonna get yours sooner or later."

"You know what," Blame responded, slowly removing her cap, shades and wrap. "I wasn't even going to say anything to you, Toria. But since you wanna call me out...as you can see, I am *clearly* not here to see the doctor! I'm just riding with a friend, sweetheart. And just like you found yourself back in the 80's, *your* whorish ass is the only one caught out there, *Toria*. I see that shit finally caught up with you. And what was that you said to me back in the day? Oh yeah. Bye bum bitch!" And she strode out of the clinic with her nose high in the air, feeling a million bucks.

Joey's plan worked. Gladys was a fool for thinking it would be that easy. Blame was a bigger fool for trusting it.

The sting was like something off television. Boy did they set her up good. Less than three days after the heist at the HIV Clinic, Blame was caught red-handed and completely off guard. The bewildered look on her mug shot said it all—wide-eyed and dumbfounded—like the caught fish, when it realizes what it has swallowed. Blame made her one phone call to Keisha, giving her the name and address of a bank (coded in ghetto slang, of course, so Big Brother would be none the wiser). Keisha got the cash and jewels out the safety deposit box; she'd had a key for months now...just in case. The bond and the lawyer depleted the jewels and most of the cash.

All Blame could think about, as she sat in the holding cell, fiending for a cigarette, was: How could she have been so stupid? And where in the hell was Nick?!

Weeks later, she looked a wreck and felt ten times worse, as she sat in the sturdy, leather-upholstered chair in her lawyer's office. This was her third visit with Mr. Brookshire. The DA had an airtight case, but Blame believed they should brainstorm, explore all avenues in preparation for the trial...there just *had* to be a way out of this mess. She was a first time offender, after all, and he was really beginning to annoy her with his defeated spirit and slight air of superiority. With the kind of money she'd forked over, he'd better find the needle in the damned haystack!

"Did you know about the outstanding warrants for your arrest for welfare fraud and grand theft-auto?" Mr. Brookshire asked, rifling through some papers. "The vehicle found in your possession was reported stolen by...ah, a Mr. Crown. You deposited payroll checks and welfare checks in the same bank account, for Christ's sake!" her top-notch lawyer exclaimed, throwing his hands in the air. "Ma'am, those are very serious offenses. They speak to your character. You'll be tried on those charges first, and since you're clearly guilty, and will be found so...you won't *be* a first time offender when we go to trial on the drug charges."

"You don't understand," Blame countered, hanging her head. It's not how it sounds. Dammit, I paid for that car in ways you could *never* imagine! And I'll pay back the money for the welfare benefits; every penny of it, I *swear*. If I'm guilty of anything, it was being poor and desperate. I was just trying to get out of **hell**, Mr. Brookshire. "

"And you have my sympathy; but the court does not see it that way. Poverty is not a legal reason to break the law. The prisons are filled with poor people, Miss Rane. I certainly can't mount a defense with that age old excuse."

She wrung her hands and paced the floor. She'd given the man $30,000.00, cash! Why wasn't he telling her what she needed to hear? There has to be a way out, she thought. Mr. Brookshire came so highly recommended, why couldn't he make this disappear, like it was done in the movies? And why was she in this position all alone, any damn way? Where the hell was Nick? Ricco would have had her back. Fuck Nick!

"The person they really want is Nick Gentry. He runs the operation; him and his partner Joey. I just work for him for God's sake!" she shouted, sounding like Nino Brown in New Jack City. "Why aren't the authorities out there looking for *him*?"

"For the tenth time Miss Rane, Joseph Piscatti has signed a deal to testify against *you*. And please, tell me, where do we find this 'Nick'?"

"I don't know," she cried, clutching the edge of his lavish desk. "I don't know! The last time I talked to him, he said he was in some place called Dumfries. He said the town was wide open, 'a pussy waiting to get fucked'. It must've been a goldmine because I haven't heard a word from him since."

"Then I'm sorry to say, Miss Rane, we don't have a leg to stand on. The state's case against you is very strong. The evidence is clear cut; there's nothing for me to dispute. They have you on film at the clinic. They can fill a stadium with the witnesses mounting against you. You were in possession of the drugs in question when you were arrested, and loads more drugs, too. The media is calling you *"the pharmacist"*, Miss

107

Rane! You have more than $3,000.00 a month in bills, and no apparent source of income. And again, speaking to your character, the father of your children is serving time right now for this very offense! Unless you can produce this 'Nick', possibly work a deal to turn state's evidence, I'm afraid our hands are tied."

She flopped back down into the chair, feeling defeated. "I got two kids Mr. Brookshire. I have NO family. I mean *nobody*. I've NEVER been in any trouble before. I'll take probation, house arrest...I'll do community service. I can get the money together to pay a fine...I don't care how much it is. I'm a first time offender Mr. Brookshire! A woman. A mother. An *orphan*, even. I *cannot* go to jail! My children don't have anyone else. Nobody!" She screamed hysterically. Though she'd spent very little time, in the past few years, considering her children; *now*, she couldn't think of anything else.

Mr. Brookshire dropped his Montblanc pen on the open file atop his handsome desk, and handed Blame a box of tissue. He looked her square in the eye and said in his most calm and rational voice, "Blame, I hear you...my heart goes out for your children. They are truly the innocent ones in all of this. I'm a father myself. So believe me, I sympathize with you completely, and I will try to get a jury to do the same. But I'm afraid you are not hearing me. First offense or not, single parent or not, you, Ms. Rane, are going to prison. The *only* part of the outcome I, or any other attorney can affect, is for how long. And I give you my word, I will utilize every resource available to me, to make that time is as minimal as possible."

Mr. Brookshire was an integral part of the judicial system; he knew filling the prisons was a necessary cog in the ever-turning wheels of justice. The jails, courts, judges and police depended on it. His very profession depended on the system working like the well-oiled machine that it was. Besides, he already had the 30K, the less work he had to do, the better.

His tone of voice, the look in his eyes, made the inevitable hit home for Blame. She, at last, actually heard what he was saying. The finality in his demeanor was as sure as the burned down house on Rose Lane. She was going to prison!

Blame rose from the comfortable leather chair and suffered a meltdown. The earth shifted. Her weak knees buckled, unable to support her weight. The thirty-four year old woman collapsed to the richly carpeted floor, in the middle of Mr. Brookshire's office, and cried like a baby. She cried for J'Rick and Karma; for Sherman, Ethel and Ricco...she cried for poverty, ignorance, vanity, greed, foolishness and shame. And she cried without reservation, for Blame.

One week before the trial was to start, Attorney Brookshire's secretary called to arrange a meeting with Blame. As promised, he utilized all available resources, and had a deal on the table from the District Attorney's Office. At 3:30 in the afternoon, she found herself staring at the long list of so-called witnesses: Carl Crown, Toria Black, Charlene Tucker, Gladys Reynolds, Officer Michael Terrell, Officer Amber Kennedy, Marjorie Winters, David Hammond, Joseph Piscatti, Delia Roberts, RN, etc... There was footage from the HIV clinic and the sting operation, where she was caught red-handed. "I assure you Ms. Rane, it's a very good deal," Mr. Brookshire expressed, hopefully. "Do you have the money, in cash?"

The "money" he referred to was $16,000.00. It would cover restitution for welfare fraud and grand theft auto. It would also pay fines and reimburse the state for funds spent on nailing her. If she had the money, and could keep her nose clean for a parole period of ten years...she would not go to prison for a minimum of eight years—maximum, twenty. She would not have convictions for the fraud or grand theft auto. She would plead guilty to possession with intent to sell and distribute a controlled substance. The charges for maintaining a dwelling and vehicle for such purposes would also be dropped. Blame would only serve 18 months! She would be remanded to the Virginia Correctional Center for Women, in Goochland, Virginia, in five days.

She had exactly $18,619.83 left to her name, so she nodded her head, but her eyes continued to plead with him. It was the best he could do, and he was the best, hands down, at his profession, he assured her. "What happens to my bail money?" she asked.

"Upon your incarceration, it will be returned to the guarantor...whoever proffered the funds and signed for your release." Mr. Brookshire called in his paralegal and an assistant DA in to witness her signature. And Blame, accepting the lesser of two evils, reached for the Montblanc pen he offered, and signed away her freedom.

She couldn't lose her kids to social services. She knew if she did, she would never get them back. She paced the floor, wrung her hands, chain-smoked several packs of cigarettes, and paced the floor some more. Oh, the horror stories she'd heard about foster care! Maybe she should run! But where would she go? No, she'd never be able to register J'Rick and Karma in school, she thought, remembering life on the run with Ricco—24 hour diners, seedy motels. Blame resigned the idea. It was unfair to her children—always looking over their shoulders because of mother's mistakes.

Blame had lived long enough to know eighteen months was not a long time. She could swing it, but she could not lose her kids in the process. Her daddy once mentioned some family down south. It sounded like a good idea until she realized she didn't have a name or address, not even the name of a city they might be in. That kind of information would have burned up in the fire. Damned Fire! Her life would never have turned out this way if it hadn't been for that damned fire, she thought, still assigning blame. "God," she pleaded, "*please, please, please* send me an answer for my children!"

A murder of crow invaded the patio of her 4-bedroom condominium. They began cawing and rubbing their wings together, rhythmically and prophetically. Blame couldn't think straight wound so tight; the annoying sound was driving her crazy. The hysterical cawing sounded like kee kee kee; the rubbing wings sounded like sha-sha-sha. She flung open the windows and screamed at the nerve-wracking avian, hurling nasty words and her shoes at them. They did not budge; but looked into her beautiful eyes, and continued cawing and making the agitating sound with their wings...kee-sha, kee-sha, kee-sha. Then, completely out of nowhere, she thought...

Keisha! Yes, Keisha! She watches the kids all the time. Plus she'll be getting the bond money back! Maybe I can get her to keep it in exchange for keeping my kids out the system. Looks like we're going to be one big happy family after all...I hope. Blame got down on her knees, like her daddy used to do, and prayed for the safety and welfare of her children. She had no more pride to swallow, so she picked up the phone and dialed Keisha, her babies-daddy-other-baby-mama.

Blame finished the call, and let out a long sigh of relief. She called her children—waiting outside the closed door—into her bedroom. "I know y'all love your sister, Monique, and Miss Keisha too. So...it's time you got to know them better. J'Rick, you and Karma gonna go stay up in DC with her for a while.

See…I got some things I need to go take care of…put behind me. It won't be for too long. Okay?" She glanced back and forth at them, waiting for a response.

J'Rick spoke first. "Mamma you act like you talking to a kid. I'm not seven years old anymore, and this is not another amazing adventure; like the lie you told when we moved down here! You not going on no damned business trip; you're going to JAIL! We know all about it! All that shit you talk about daddy, and you ain't no damned better!" Smacking him was just an involuntary reflex for Blame. He rubbed his cheek; but being a big boy now, at 13 years old, he did not cry.

"Mamma why I gotta go?" Karma queried. "Why can't I stay here with Dyshay 'nem, so my grades won't get messed up in school? Miss Charlene don't care, she cool. Plus, you say it won't be that long anyway."

"Girl you ain't staying with no damned Charlene! She's half the reason I'm in this mess to begin with! Fuck Charlene! Have you lost your mind?!"

"No. She ain't lost her mind, mamma. You lost yours," J'Rick continued, bracing for another slap. "If you would've been in your right mind, you would've stopped doing the shit you was doing a long time ago…acting like you didn't have no kids. LaDawn and Keisha practically raised us. You wasn't worried about us then, why you trying to act like you worried about us now?" Instead of slapping him, Blame pulled both her children into her arms and wept.

Silly thing, forgot to thank her Maker. And the murder of crow flew promptly away, with Tuppie wondering, how do you put your own self in chains?

CHAPTER 12
JEZEBEL THE WENCH

My momma, Tuppie, was a house niggah, so I was a house niggah too. Momma say she come to Rainier Estate when she was just a little bitty baby. She say Massa Charles fetched her to be the maid and plaything of his first-born, a girl named Hilde. When Hilde, born sickly, died in childhood, Momma was moved to kitchen detail.

When Charlie III was born, she became his nurse. Momma already had her milk, cause she already had me. Me and Charlie grew up side by side. I reckon we musta fell in love way back when Momma suckled us together...cause I surely can't remember a time when I didn't love him.

Momma say I's a fool...say young Massa could never love me, and I's just his wench. I say she's a liar. You ever take a look round the place where I lived and died, after 'mancipation? Love made it possible. Did you ever set your eyes upon the face of Rone Rane during your travels? Das me and Charlie's boy. Now you tell me a fella so handsome weren't the produck of love. Sides, if'n I was his wench, well I was the only one. And 'cept that gal his daddy made him wed; Charlie never took another into his bed. I don't spect.

Charlie III never loved his wife, Mary, nohow. He only married her to please Massa and Mistress Rainier. She bore him five chirren, tho. And momma say that's proof of love...say I'm a damn fool. I watched him with them chirren, I reckon he loved them some; but not as much as he loved our boy, Rone. Rone was Charlie's firstborn. I didn't have to fret too long though. Smallpox took em *all* during the war—Mary, Ole Massa Rainier, and all five of them heirs. I can't help but smile when we dig they graves. Momma say I's a devil and a fool for being happy bout dead chirren.

Momma'd say anything to get my goat though...she hated me so. I bleeve she despised the very sight of me...go figure that, woman hating her own chile. See all these scars here. Dey didn't come from no overseer; and Charlie never laid a cruel hand on my body. Momma done all dis here. She beat me worse than they beat Claude when he took off for freedom one night...she beat me worse than a runaway slave. To this day I don't know why she hated me so. I bleeve she hated me more'n Ole Mistress Rainier did...and she hated me something fierce cause her boy Charlie love me so.

But Tuppie my momma; so I love her, no matter what. Anyhow, after 'mancipation, she never laid anotha hand on me...seem like she took being a slave out on me. She stayed right chere on this farm with me all the days of her natural life.

Humph...I memba 'mancipation like it was yestudee. All summer long folks stirring around, packing up, traveling 'pon the open road. You ought to seen them niggahs with they chests stuck out, heads held high. Them hussies off our plantation sneering and guffawing at me; calling me a damn fool. Little Rone pulling on my skirts, pleading for us to go with the freed slaves. Got so I had to smack him like momma used to smack me—real hard. I say, "boy we ain't goin nowhere. Our place is right chere with yo pappy!" Charlie didn't make it no secret that my son, Rone, was his boy.

Only place I went was with momma up to the Union soldier military post to be counted, names put down on paper. That was one of the best days me and momma ever had...tickle me now jest thinking bout it. The Union soldiers, they asked momma her name, and course she say Tuppie. Then they ask

114

her what her last name be. Well, she went to scratching her head, looking round confused, with no idea what a last name was. Then they ask for her old Massa name, and she get to stuttering. Most she get out is Rain…so that's what they write down—Rane. Then she present us, Rone and me, and they last-name us Rane, too. Chile, we hightailed it outta that place like we stole something…like they was gone take them last names back if'n we didn't get on down the road real fast.

When we was a good distance away, momma look at us and say (in her high and mighty voice), "I's Miss Tuppie Rane, howdy do?"

That tickled the plumb daylights outta me and Rone. When I stop laughing, I curtsy and says back (in my white folks talking), "just dandy ma'am. I be Miss Jezebel B. Rane." And momma bout cried from laughing so hard.

Then little Rone, only six year old mind you, gets to struttin round with his thumbs poking his shirt where some suspenders might be, if'n he had any. Looking just like a full grown planter, he say, "I Rone Rane! That right granny?"

"Tis indeed," she say. And we laugh and talk that way til we gets home. Our home still Rainier Estates. Momma won't leave me and I won't leave Charlie, so there we stay. I still works the house and gardens like ain't nothing changed. Momma, don't come in the big house no more. She say, "Slavery Over!", and she laugh every time she say it. She take to the fields with the other hands, shaycroppin, and she keep Rone with her, teaching him everything she learn bout tending the good earth.

For long, mean old Missy Gwendolyn Rainier take sick. Charlie say she still grieving her husband and her grandchirren, and the Antebellum South. I didn't recall him having no aunty name of Bellum; so I can't figure out what that last part mean.

But I tends to Ole Missy while she dying, jest the same. I can't see nothing particular ailing her, cept she won't eat nothing; but fore long she up and die, too. Might be wishful thinking, but I clare I bleeve her dying word was "Rone". Charlie say she die from a broken heart. But Ion't bleeve she ever had a heart to break.

Not long after she die, Charlie section off a piece of land, way far away from the big house as possible. Ain't the best land, but it look like **heaven** to me. He give me some papers say it nine acres, and it be all mine! None of us could read them papers; but I guards 'em wit my life. Cause nothings better than owning land. Not nothing! And my Charlie, my love, say it be ALL MINZ!

So, Me, momma and Rone go on down there, build us a house and start working our *own* land. Charlie come to see how we faring from time to time. One day, he bring a letter and a fancy pair of cufflinks for Rone. He don't take me in the bed though; he give me two pieces of silver, and I wonders if there be another white gal somewhere bout. But that evening, Charlie went back up to the big house and hanged hisself from the chan-do-leer! I guess he was grieving that Anty Bellum, too. He never said a word to me bout being in such a bad way...only that all his confed'ret money wasn't no mo good. Some distant kinfolk of Massa Rainier's come from Florida to Carolina and sell off the whole plantation. They can't touch me and Rone nine acres though. Charlie made sure of that. I missed him sorely all the years of my life.

We had us a pretty good life down there on that tough place. We kept to ourself and prayed the nightriders wouldn't come for us. They never did. I couldn'a asked for a better boy than Rone. My Ronie, peach-skinned in the winter, color of roasted almonds in the summertime—lord he was a beautiful chile! He worked real hard every day the good Lord give him.

Late in life, he took a wife, name of EulaLee. She a good girl, loving and hardworking. She give Rone two boys, Doany and Baptise. She treat me and my momma real good, too. I bleeve if she had'a lived longer; there would've been more chirren. But she died young. We had us some sho nuff hard times on that place. But all in all, we had us a pretty good ole life...after 'mancipation. And no matter what momma say, Charlie made it possible, cause Charlie loveded me.

Now Doany, Rone's oldest boy, was sure something to be proud of, the way he bought up the land 'round here. Oh now he was dry as a burlap sack left out in the sun too long, but that was jes his way. Made him a right smart and frugal man, I reckon. He kept his purse strings cinched so tight...only allowed himself one Co-Cola a year, at Christmas time. But whenever folks fell on hard times (black or white), Doany would be right there to bail 'em out. He got two acres here, seven there, and fore long, he added another thirty acres to the nine Charlie give us. Made some right smart improvements to the little shack me, momma and Ronie threw together. It's a far cry from the big house; but it's a fine home for people what was slaves.

Baptise, the baby boy, was a different sort all together. He was born one week to the day after my mamma, Tuppie, died. He had a jolly sense of humor and them fretful, wandering legs from the start. Why he was running in EulaLee belly fore he come in the world. He'd wake up in the middle of the night, little legs just kicking the quilt—always itchin to go somewhere. I knowed we wasn't gone have him long. He couldn'a been no more 'n fourteen year old when he took off from here. Said he was tired of bowing and cow-towing to white folks. Sayin, "Yes'um, suh," got caught in his throat; and if he was talking to a man, he needed to look him in the eye. So he run on up north, like the rest of 'em what jest can't be still or stay in they place.

Baptise stopped running when he got to Ohi-uh. Had him a little old boy name of Sherman. I seed a photograph of my onliest great grandboy; but I never laid my eyes on the child. When I died, Doany didn't have no chirren. I can't see no woman ever taking up with him either...he so plain; like the brown dirt he spend his life toiling in and purchasing up. If he had some children, I don't know nothing about it. I'm just laying here under the ground, ground what belong to me...waiting for Ole Gabe to blow his horn. I lay here remembering and dreaming. I keep having a dream momma's not under the ground, like me. I keep seeing Tuppie as a big black bird, flying high in the sky. It don't make no sense to me, though. We all dead. Can't be no difference in death, can there?

TUPPIE RANE

I had four otha chillun, sides Jezzy B—one died at childbirth, other three sold way from me, fore they's even five in yeahs. Alls I ever had in my whole entire life was my Jezzy. Can you imagine not never owning nothing...not even yoself? Most folks can't imagine sech a thing. Now 'spose you only had a rock and a cup...think on how much those two little things would mean to you. What you'd do to keep 'em close by. Are you starting to see? Well, alls I had was Jezzy B, and bein a slave, even she wasn't mine. But I'd do anything to keep her wit me.

Mean old Missy Gwen'lyn, she hated my Jezzy—on account of her boy Charlie loved her so. I bleeve she despised the very

118

sight of my girl. She'd spy on them chillun playing togetha—
Charlie just tickled pink and Jezzy bowled over wit laughter—
and a wickedness would come over Missy Gwen'lyn like I never
seen. (And I seen a might plenty wicked things.) I feared she
would choke the very life outta Jezzy, if'n she ever got her hands
on my young'un. So I's real quick to beat her to the punch. I
beat Jezzy for all she was worth. And when I seen how pleasing
those beatings be to Missy Gwen'lyn, I beat her some mo. Lawd,
Lawd.

I's standing in the hallway one day and I overheahs Massa
Rainier say, "Well, do you want me to sell Jezebel, dear? I'll do
whatever makes you happy, Gwen'lyn."

I holds my breath, waitin on the answer, for what seem like
a whole plantin season. Finally, Ole Missy Gwen'lyn say, "No.
Nobody tans her hide like Tuppie. She beats her daughter like a
dog, Charles. I wouldn't miss those whippings for anything in
the world!" I think they hear me when I let my breath go...so I
run on down the hall real fast.

I loves Jezzy B more'n my very own life. Life ain't much
worth livin no how when you's a slave. You can't dream, plan,
hope for nothing. You can't even decide. You not even allowed
to try and fail at nothing...you betta not fail yo Massa! You ain't
got no idea who yo mammy or yo pappy be...where your chillun
at in the world. You learn not to want or eckspeck nothing...only
thing you can depend on is death.

But I loved my Jezebel B. I adds the "B" on her name;
couldn't nevuh give her nothing else. I didn't care who hold the
note on her; she was mine. And Ole Missy loved to see me
whoop her. So I beat the mess outta my young'un evertime I
thought Ole Missy was anywhere in earshot. I beat Jezzy so
much, I don't know how she ever loved me. But love me she did.
Onliest fection I ever knowed come from her and Rone. Hurt my

heart something powerful evertime I struck her; but I beat her to keep her near me, just the same.

See, that's how messed up a slave mind be—how distorted the thinking. That's why black folks is all mentally insane now. Can you imagine that? Best way I could think of keeping my dear daughter with me was to beat her sun up and sun down. Now ain't that a pitiful shame?

Oh mercy me, there I go again, slipping back into my native tongue. I beg your pardon, I forget myself sometimes. What I was trying to say is; I was afraid. Because that's all a slave ever really has—Fear.

THE LAST OF RAINIER

We Rainier are no more. We went the way of the dinosaurs, the pharaohs, and the Mohicans. I had five beautiful grandchildren. They were all hazel-eyed, strawberry blonds. They were sweet as the bee's honey and I so loved every single one of those little Rainiers. They were taken away from me and I could not understand why. What had I done to be so rebuked?

I did unto my neighbors as I'd have them do unto me. I was a good wife and mother—a model Christian. What had I done to be cut off at the root? My treatment of the slaves did not matter. They are niggers—descendants of Ham—everyone knows they don't count. With no hope of a future; no understanding as to why I should be dealt such a fate; I stopped eating and lay down to die.

Jezebel, (I certainly named her right), tended me in the weeks before my death. When madness set in before I closed my eyes, I came up with the notion she'd poisoned us all. She had to be capable. The way her own mother beat her, she had to be the worst black devil in the world. She surely put a spell on my Charlie, and she wanted him for herself. So I decided she poisoned my husband, my daughter-in-law, my grandchildren and now me. Nevermind that I'd stopped eating and willed death on my own self. Dementia sank in, and I blamed Jezebel for everything. I hated her even more, especially after Tuppie stopped whooping her.

One night, lying in bed, looking at her ugly black face, I decided I'd better get better, get up, and protect my Charlie. He was still young enough to have another family. All was not lost! But once starvation has charted its course; I found there is no stopping it. I'd gotten too weak to speak and I could not even ask for food. Jezebel had long ago stopped trying to feed me. My body was shutting down and I was powerless to stop it.

On that last morning, when I knew I would not survive my suicide—I thought only of Rone. I forgot he was part nigger and only remembered he was part Charles III—part ME. I longed to see his almond-colored hands, find my own daddy's features in his chiseled face. With my last bit of mind, I even prayed to the God of all things for Rone's future and the future of all his generations. Then I closed my eyes.

When they sprang open again, my beautiful gray-brown and copper eyes were in the head of a rock dove—known to some as a pigeon. I stretched my stiff arms and found them to be wings. I lit out of Baylorton as fast as those wings would carry me—hell bent on knowing the outcome of my prayers for the generations of Rone. I flew a very long time before I found his great granddaughter—all that was left of my blood and bone. I flew clear to the coast of Virginia before I found Blame Rane.

CHAPTER 13
BIRDS OF A FEATHER

"She's going to prison you witch! This is all *your* fault!" the crow shrieked.

"My fault?" Gwendolyn gasped, incredulously. "What on earth are you talking about Tuppie? How can I possibly be to blame?"

"Yes...you and yours are the very reason why. Maybe if Blame had some generational wealth, she wouldn't have been so worried about money. She'd be sitting pretty like that 6th removed great nephew of yours down in Florida. Oh yeah, I know about him. We sure as hell worked hard enough and long enough for her to have something besides a lousy Buick to start life on! Maybe if you all hadn't been so evil and cruel, Baptise wouldna run off to Ohio. Sherman could have known his people and maybe he could have put some sense in that girl's head. Maybe if my Jezzy coulda married proper and not been your boy's *whore*, there would have been a man around, and Rone wouldn't have worked hisself to death so young, trying to be a man when he was just a little boy! It all trickles down, Gwen! And it never adds up!"

"Tuppie, I'm sorry! Truly, truly sorry for everything I ever did to you. I know excuses are for the birds...but since we are birds now, please let me explain..." The crow listened to her testimony. The cardinal, perched on a branch in the same tree, listened as well.

When the pigeon was done with her story—uncovering her "daughter of a slave" shame; the crow somewhat understood. She'd seen her own family undergo the same sad denial. The generations born free pretended the older folk had never been slaves at all. They did not speak of it to each other, and outright hid it from their children. They should have shared the history with their seed—the knowledge would have made them stronger, wiser, Tuppie thought.

I, Tuppie Rane, watched my people shaking the shame off their boots, as if they never walked and lived in dung. I shielded my little raven face with my wing when I came around my freed seeds—such shame they instilled in me for having ever been a slave. Like I had a choice in the matter!

So...Gwendolyn was the child of a slave. It took me a minute or two to adjust to that there morsel of information. It was a new light, a new seeing. I'll never agree with the way she went about things; but I reckon I can somewhat understand. When Baptise asked his grandmother Jezzy about me, she responded simply, "my mamma was a cook." A cook?! She made it sound as ordinary as a prep or pastry chef. "I was a damned slave Jezzy!" I screamed, but she couldn't hear me. "Tell that boy the truth; make him know so deep he never forgets!" If he'd known the truth to pass down to his generations, Blame might've known better than to be such a damned fool.

Blame was never the legal property of no man, but she sure acted like it. Blame could have completed her education. But the silly girl thought there was something better to be doing at the time. Blame wouldna never got herself locked up in a cage if she knew how many generations of us was locked up before her. And she certainly wouldn't have taken up with those white folks...trusting them crackers like they was just regular people. Foolish woman!

But Jezzy didn't tell Baptise. So who was gonna teach Sherman the history, which he should have been reciting to his baby girl as early as the cradle? I wish I would have lived long enough to teach them chirren some sense. Jezzy believed nobody going forward, ever needed to know such a time existed. No one should have to tell their own children, or anybody else for that matter, their parents, and their parents' parents were the downtrodden property of other people. My foolish girl always fancied herself as something other than chattel.

I understand Madam Gwendolyn now. Her crazy mind is just twisted. But I still don't cotton to her way of doing things. Because we were raped, beaten, fingers...my beautiful fingers...worked to the bone. Degraded, humiliated, kept ignorant and suffering, malnourished and pitiful. Whole generations upon generations upon generations of me, and mine, *ruined*. The pigeon might have a good excuse, but she was WRONG! The whole damned institution of slavery was WRONG!

Blame gone learn, though. That prison'll sure teach her what common sense could not. I pray to God she learns some sense. Maybe the spinning world won't scare her no more...it's not so bad when you know why it's spinning. Knowledge brings about wisdom, and wisdom leads to understanding. I'm finally getting some understanding; I hope Blame gets some, too.

I, WindRider TwoSquirrels, listened to the pigeon's testimony. I now know the pigeon is from a place in Tennessee, which her family stole from people like me. I know that in life, she was white, like the fishes belly...like the people who set fire to Aaron and me; like the people who killed Dusty, framed Blame, and turned my proud pappa into cattle.

But...going for the worms in the morning dew, she is no different from me. When it rains, she seeks shelter under the same forest canopy as me. We molt our feathers together—her old feathers fall to the ground white, mine red, but they are feathers, just the same.

Though she is white, like the fishes belly, I have seen the tiny pigeon tears she sheds for Blame. I believe she feels somehow responsible for the ignorance and the shamelessness of Blame. I feel her sorrow...she has much sorrow, now.

I, Mrs. Gwendolyn Rainier, sincerely apologize. I don't know what else to say. I cannot undo the past. I am dead now and cannot right my wrongs. I can now only hope I will somehow get to heaven with the cardinal and the crow. But with the blood on my hands, and all the pain I have caused...I fear the devil—in planning his menu—might soon desire a taste of roasted squab. I am filled with regret that I shoulder some blame for Blame. And I am deeply and *truly* sorry.

CHAPTER 14
VIRGINIA CORRECTIONAL CENTER FOR WOMEN
GOOCHLAND, VA

Virginia certainly was a beautiful state, Blame thought, admiring the scenery through the window of the bus...even in the dead of winter. She tried to commit every tree limb and icicle to memory; knowing it would be a year and a half before she would see such wide open spaces again. She found it hard to believe she could find beauty in an icicle. Blame wished she could be free like the birds keeping stride with the prison bus— the pigeon, cardinal and great flock of beautiful, black crow.

Her affairs were in order, as best they could be, considering the circumstances. J'Rick and Karma were with Keisha and Monique. Keisha would get the $20,000.00 bond refund as soon as the paperwork of her incarceration went through. Blame had already mailed four $500.00 money-orders to the prison in her name, for her commissary. It was every penny she had left in the world.

There were thousands of dollars tied up in drugs in the streets still; not to mention the cache she got busted with, but she charged it to the game. Nick finally showed up...in two suitcases in Quantico Creek. His legs, arms and head were in one suitcase; his torso in the other. Poor Nick, thought Blame. She remembered him saying the town of Dumfries was "a pussy waiting to get fucked"...quoting *Scarface*; looks like he's the one who got fucked, she mused.

She looked around the bus at the women who were going into lockup with her. They were a touch bunch of females; half of them looking like men. She reminded herself again, it was only 18 months. All she had to do was keep her mouth shut, keep to herself, and stay out of trouble. She wasn't a fighter,

126

but she wasn't a chump either. She figured she'd gone enough rounds with Ricco to handle herself with the average female. Still, she wanted to stay off anybody's radar; she did not want to be tested.

When the bus entered the big steel gates, the birds dropped off, circled around and took off toward the nation's capital. The inmates were unshackled, checked in, thoroughly searched and given their supplies for prison life. They entered general population to a raucous of hoots and cat calls, sneers, name calling, evil eyes and mean-mugging. They were assigned their cells and left alone. There was no tour or initiation process; they would have to find out on their on how things went down in the big house.

Blame would share a cell with an old tattooed Mexican woman, named Muerta, a methhead from just outside of Richmond. Muerta was doing nine years for armed robbery. It was her fifth time behind bars. She acknowledged Blame's presence by spitting on the floor. It was going to be a long 18 months.

A light and an alarm went off and the cell doors slid open. It was time for lunch. Blame fell in line (still very adept at fitting in) and marched down the hall with her new peers. She noticed each line going to chow seemed to be led by a real character. At the front of her line was a 6-foot woman with a bald head and gold teeth, who went by Big Sheila. Directly behind her in line was a mousy white girl, named Cassidy, who walked too close to Blame for comfort, and couldn't have been any more than 19 years old. A couple of unmistakable dykes smiled at her, flicking their tongues and licking their lips.

An inmate or two tried to make light conversation with Blame, but she had nothing to say. She wasn't a child anymore. She was 36 years old, with children of her own. Blame didn't want to make friends, join a gang or clique up with any particular set. She wanted to do her 18 months and get the hell out of there. If she had to fight to maintain her space and peace, she was more than willing to do so. Still, she didn't want to be tested.

Big Sheila got word about the new chic who thought she was too fly to speak. In less than a few hours in prison, Blame managed to land on the radar of the baddest bitch in the clink. She was, without a doubt, going to be tested.

The veteran felons determined she needed some tough lessons about prison life. Within the first thirty days or her incarceration, Blame had been in numerous fights—one on one, she kicked ass. But the three times she got jumped, she got creamed. She had her canteen stolen; her hair cut off, and was sporting a long sleeve made of gauze and ace bandages. If she hadn't thrown her arm up when she did; it would have been her face, and not her forearm, receiving the three-inch scar. She was presently being extorted for toiletries, because her $2,000.00 in commissary funds had been recently discovered.

Blame was afraid to leave her cell; Muerta, though mean as hell, was safe. But she had to attend a mandatory counseling session. So off she went, eyes darting around like a frightened kitten, on the lookout for trouble. She passed one of Big Sheila's flunkies en route to the session. The woman was wearing Blame's stolen sneakers, while Blame shuffled down the corridor in a ratty pair of too-big flip flops. Blame was furious! As they waited in line to take their seats, someone popped her in the back of her shaved head. She didn't even turn around to confront her assailant. She sat down quietly and bit her lip, but her blood was boiling. To add insult to injury, it seemed the counselor was picking on her as well.

"So why are you here?" the smug counselor continued, singling Blame out, and studying the new prisoner's peculiar eyes.

By this time, Blame was completely fed up. She snapped and responded, "I'm here because my mamma and daddy died and didn't leave me no insurance money! And Mrs. Douthit didn't let me stay in a room nobody else in the world was using. So I was homeless, cold, and living in a fucking car! I'm here because I roomed with a fucking whore who got me caught up with some bad company—a crazy ass niggah who used my face for a punching bag and dropped two babies on me while he was fucking another broad and banging dope! I'm here cause banks keep bullshit records and old men can't let go of good pussy! I'm here cause a dumb ass wigger got hisself cut up and put in the river, when he was *supposed* to be having my back! And a stupid bitch swore she could get some work, no problem; but it was all just a set up! I'm here cause bum bitches hate! And a sheisty lawyer robbed me! I'm here cause I was poor with kids to feed and couldn't get a job worth a damn cause my greedy ass mamma didn't teach me how to do nothing but sew! Here cause my daddy smoked cigarettes and probably burned the fucking house down! I didn't know my ass from a hole in the ground when they died on me! And 632 Rose Lane ain't on the fucking map! Dammit that's why I'm here!"

"I see," the counselor responded coolly, unmoved by Blame's tirade. "And none of the blame rests on you?"

"Man fuck this!" Blame yelled, wishing she could have stayed in her cell. "I didn't sign up for this psycho-babble bullshit. You don't know nothing about me lady...where I come from...what I've been through! It's not all my fault I'm in here. I'm not the only one to Blame!" She stood up angrily and kicked her chair across the room, where it glanced the leg of the counselor. That display of emotion gained her three weeks in solitary confinement.

The time spent in solitary was a Godsend for Blame. For the first time in her life, and only because it was forced upon her, she finally had the opportunity to sit still, and think. She thought honestly on her present situation, and the years leading up to this outcome. At every pivotal point in her life, she realized, while it was very easy to point the finger, whenever a vital decision had to be made in her life; she made a poor choice. The longer she reflected the more apparent it became that Blame Rane bore the responsibility for her life. Bottom line...she fucked up. She started off making poor decisions and didn't stop until she wound up in a cage.

When she was released back into the general population, Blame was sent to a mock court and convicted of assaulting the counselor, adding another ninety days to her sentence. Blame was outraged! Another three months?! She wanted to choke somebody...anybody; but she took a deep breath and calmed down, instead. She promised herself going forward, she would think, at least twice, before speaking or acting. Moving too fast had cost her too much in life already. And her stupidity had just earned her another whole season away from her children and her freedom.

The funds in her account were astronomical compared to that of other inmates, so Blame was still on quite a few radars. Rather than get herself killed over a couple thousand dollars, Blame thought of clever ways to get confined to solitary...without adding any more time to her sentence. She managed to spend thirteen of the remaining twenty months in solitary. While she was confined, she developed a valuable new habit—reading.

In her lifetime, Blame hadn't cracked the spine of any book that wasn't required reading in high school and college. It just wasn't her cup of tea. But she had to do something to pass the time, lest she go insane. The more and more she read, the angrier and angrier she became. Then the more enlightened she became. And suddenly, out of nowhere seemingly, her mind opened up and she began to think! She couldn't believe she knew so little about the world she lived in. She was beginning to see how everything was related: politics, society, religion, education, medicine, poverty, wealth, economic conditions, global trade, race, etc...

Maxine, a corrections officer on the solitary ward, picked out the reading material for the prisoners. She kicked it regularly with Blame, who enjoyed building with woman, discovering so many new things. Blame liked Maxine's necklace too, called dhikr beads, and all the quiet wisdom she possessed.

She read everything she could get her hands on and finally started to gain some knowledge. Blame's favorite book, the green one, blew her mind with its plain truth. Maxi joked that Blame was becoming one of those opinionated militant sisters, with ideas on how to correct all the social ills of America.

On her last release from solitary, Blame discovered there had been some changes. Big Sheila was transferred to a maximum security facility for maiming the youngster Cassidy. Nearly all of the violent offenders, including her cellmate, Muerta, had been relocated to other facilities, as well; Goochland was being reclassified as minimum security prison. Blame relaxed a little and decided to do the remaining six months in general population. Another day in solitary (good books or not) was one too many.

On her first day in gen pop, she was required to attend another mandatory session, about rehabilitation. When she got to the classroom, a counselor, with a laid back personality, asked her about her interests. Blame shamefully admitted she hadn't any. "None?" The counselor queried, flabbergasted. She dug a little deeper, "don't you enjoy cooking or painting? What about poetry? Do you play an instrument? How about cosmetology?" Blame shook her head "no" too all of these suggestions. "Do you enjoy reading books? Play ping pong or checkers? How about sewing? Can you crochet? "

Blame finally perked up. "Oh yes! I love to read, and I can sew *and* crochet. I knit, needlepoint and cross-stitch too!" It had been so long since she employed the few skills taught to her by Ethel, she'd almost forgotten she possessed the knowledge at all.

"*Really?* Wow, that's a pretty rare set of skills in this day and age, Blame." The counselor tapped her notebook and scratched her head. "I'm supposed to enroll you into some of the classes or programs that interest you. But we aren't actually offering a sewing class...I just threw that out there," she reluctantly admitted. Blame perked down. "But hey, here's an idea. If I can round up some ladies who want to take up sewing, how would you feel about doing some teaching?"

"Me? Oh no, I couldn't. I don't even know if I remember how," Blame responded.

"No problem." Adrienne, the really cool counselor, responded, always a step ahead. "Tell you what, you make a list of whatever supplies you can think of, and I'll get them to you. Practice in your cell until you remember how, and we'll talk about those classes later. You've got nothing but time here Blame. The more ways you can think of passing it; the faster it will go."

Blame made the list, Adrienne secured the supplies, and before long, Blame was knitting slippers and sweaters, crocheting scarves and kufis. She was so engrossed in detailed needlepoint, she missed outdoor rec a time or two. Some of her tier-mates developed a strong interest in what she was doing. The caring counselor approached Blame within three weeks and told her seven ladies had signed up to take the "All Things Sewing" class. There was money in the budget to buy more supplies; but she was lacking a teacher. Blame was honored.

She wrote excited letters to her kids and Keisha; letting them know how and what she was doing. She exercised daily, enjoyed her outdoor rec time and the surprisingly vast array of reading material available in prison. But the highlight of her days was the time she spent teaching her sewing class. Adrienne was right, it really did help the time fly; and before she knew it, Blame was being paroled.

The Blame Rane who was leaving prison was hardly the same woman who'd been incarcerated twenty-one months earlier. In the darkest of places, she blossomed. The new woman was stronger, wiser, more patient and thoughtful. She was (self) educated, considerate, humble and thankful. And all she wanted was to get back to her children, make a home for them and herself, and teach them what she could about this thing called life. She was an avid, diehard reader too, and knew that would never change. She wanted to be a productive member of society—one that might somehow affect change. She'd also been reminded she loved sewing—creating with her hands—and hoped she would find the time to do more of it.

CHAPTER 15
J'RICK & KARMA

I saw him put his hand in her blouse; and it reminded me of
things I saw similar men do to Dusty, when she was just a child,
as well. Karma did not fight back, as Dusty had. Karma, from
where I was watching, seemed to enjoy the negative attention.
I could not believe my eyes and I wished the other birds were
near. I would have appreciated their insight on the horrific
spectacle before me.

The other birds were not with me though, when I finally
found the children in spring. The black one travels with the
flock, some of whom are older than Methuselah; and the white
one is just plain fat. Plus I am a better tracker, so I beat them in
our flight to the D.C. suburbs—to find the children of Blame.
That is how I came to be the only witness to the crime.

My great-great-great-great-great granddaughter, Karma
Rane, had just celebrated her eleventh birthday. She was, like
all the girls in this new generation of children, "big for her age".
She was without a mother or father—wards of the state and
federal penitentiaries, respectively. Her bff (best friend
forever), big brother J'Rick, had just turned fourteen...so quite
naturally, his attention had turned to girls his own age. Her
second closest confidant, little sister Monique, age nine, was
not old enough to understand what was happening to Karma. I
use Monique's age as an excuse, because truly, even I had
trouble comprehending what I saw; and I, the WindRider, have
seen 182 years.

The woman, who cared for her, was very busy—working a
fulltime job, completing her nursing education and trying to
hold a family of misfits together. Besides, Keisha had a
daughter of her own, whom she adored; and J'Rick, the spitting

image of Ricco, had a special place in her heart as well. Karma fell precariously into the "middle-child" syndrome—feeling apart and left out—craving attention and ever searching for love.

I loved her. And I tried to gain her attention by juggling my memento eyeball with my wings—a favorite amusement when she was a smaller child. She never noticed me though. Her mind was on other things, like the image seared into her memory of J'Rick and the neighborhood girl he'd snuck into Keisha's basement. The naked laughing couple seemed to be enjoying themselves; Karma noted, as she spied from her hiding place, behind the busted recliner. She had a painful emptiness inside and she wanted a reason to laugh and giggle too. Mr. Perkins filled that void.

He was the gym teacher at her middle school, in his mid-thirties, chubby, balding, a boyish face which he kept clean shaven. He flew under the radar of law enforcement, always choosing loners like Karma, who would not tell his dirty little secret, and thereby never landing on any list of known pedophiles or sexual predators.

As he fondled Karma's pre-pubescent breast, she giggled, like J'Rick's girlfriend, Tasha, had done. I sized up his beady little green eye and thought seriously about adding another cornea to my collection. I will not go with the devil into the details, because they are too wicked to recite. There was, however, blood, a broken hymen and a very confused 11-year-old mind.

When Mr. Perkins' attention turned elsewhere, Karma withdrew into herself. Food, and lots of it, became her only comfort. She re-enacted the events of her rape with any boy who looked twice at her. She told herself she was fat, and ugly, and not worthy of love. Looking back, I believe she felt this way all the days of her short life—shorter even than mine.

J'Rick was a freshman in high school. His unassuming good looks, athletic ability, and laid back attitude, made him instantly popular with his peers. Since they were all new to the neighborhood (Keisha and Monique, included) people assumed Keisha was his mother. He didn't make any corrections. It was easier that way. He didn't like to stand out; and admitting both your parents were in prison was a sure way to become a sore thumb.

Still, he loved and missed his mother very much. He tolerated his father, only because it was a necessity, living with Keisha—upon whom he was completely dependent. He wrote to Blame every week and delighted in the letters she would send back. He read a lot. And because he had no other teacher; he tried to teach himself how to be a man.

Considering his limited resources, he was doing a pretty good job at this effort. Since men sharpen men like steel sharpens steel; he spent a lot of time at barbershops, gyms, political gatherings, churches, mosques, sporting events and other places where men, of a positive nature, tended to congregate. He didn't talk very much at these gatherings, preferring to watch and listen—waiting patiently for any little nugget of wisdom he could carry with him into the future.

He practiced at home, in the mirror...how men who took care of their families behaved. He learned, amongst other things, in his "man training", accepting responsibility was a key element in his quest for adulthood. He was glad his mother was learning the importance of this, too. And he couldn't wait until his mother was released, so he could show her what he'd learned; show her the man he was trying to become. He hoped she would be proud.

He was certainly proud of Blame. J'Rick could track his mother's growth in their correspondence. Where her earlier letters were full of shifting blame; her later letters were from a woman who'd learned to take responsibility for her actions. He thought that was admirable. The latest letter he'd received, read:

J'Rick Rane,

This is my last letter to you, as I'll be coming home soon, son. I appreciate the letters you've sent me over these months…they've really helped me see this time through. Prison is like hell, J'Rick. I pray you never wind up here. But, it is not completely without its advantages…like plenty of time for reading. I was able to do a lot of thinking—honest reflection on the paths I chose in life. And I've truly learned a lot.

I believe this life is about: right, wrong and responsibility. Remember that, son. The sooner you learn to take responsibility for your actions and deeds, the sooner you will become a man. From your letters, I understand that is your ultimate goal. You're on the right track, son.

It is easy to blame others for your mistakes. But trust me, J'Rick. You can blame rain, the devil, or the deep blue sea…whatever your preference of boogeyman may be. But the truth of the matter is, we are each individually responsible, and will be held accountable for our actions—in this world and the next.

So try to think beyond immediate gratification. Consider the implication and outcome of what you do. Try to use sound judgment and make good decisions. I did not. And that's why I'm writing to you from this prison cell today. Be better than me, J'Rick.

But! This is the last piece of prison correspondence you'll get from me! I will see you soon. Until then, take care of yourself and your sister. And thank you, for always being in my corner, son. You are my rock, and the best <u>man</u> I know. I love you.

Forever your Mother,
Blame

J'Rick was still a teenaged boy, doing the things such boys do. He played his music too loud, had unprotected sex, and missed some homework assignments if there was a good basketball game at the court. But, all in all, I knew J'Rick, the little Aaron, was the one I had to worry least about. He was the kind of son any mother would be proud of. And I, being one in the long line of his mothers, was definitely proud of him. I only wish I could say the same for Karma, the daughter of Blame.

CHAPTER 16
BLESS THE CHILD

June 2007

She was taken to prison by bus. Upon release, she was entitled to one bus ticket to any destination within the state. Blame chose Norfolk. At the bus depot, she caught a cab and gave him the address of her destination—632 Rose Lane. The cabbie plugged it into his GPS, and advised her there was no such address on Rose Lane. She sighed, laughed bitterly, and told him to take her to the street anyway. Blame just wanted to go home.

The ex-con exited the cab and looked slowly to her right. There was no burnt out carcass of a house, no ashes or stench of death...just a bright, open lot, overgrown with wildflowers and honeysuckles. To her left, she noticed a hearse, limousine and long row of cars—unmistakable signs of a funeral underway.

Blame crossed the street to Mrs. Douthit's house; her tears began streaming before she reached the front porch. She was greeted at the door by a woman who introduced herself as Beverly. Beverly inspected Blame's odd funeral attire, then ushered her in, pointing out the guest book and the old Formica table, piled high with hot food. Fresh out of prison, Blame helped herself to a plate of fried chicken, collard greens, potato salad and cherry tomatoes. She sat quietly in a corner, wolfing down the meal, and listening intently as the mourner's eulogized Mrs. Douthit. Beverly made her way to where Blame was sitting and asked, "I'm sorry, I can't place your face. Were you a friend of Aunt Cathy's?"

Blame wiped crumbs from her mouth and answered, "Yes, she was my friend. We were neighbors years ago. My name is Blame, Blame Rane."

"Blame!" Beverly exclaimed. "Little Blame from across the street? Well my how you've grown!" She took Blame into her arms and hugged her tightly. "I always wondered what became of you. You have my condolences by the way, on the passing of your parents."

"Thank you, and likewise," Blame responded. "I didn't know Mrs. Douthit was ill."

"Not ill; just old. She went peacefully. We'll have to catch up after the funeral. Oh! That reminds me, I believe Aunt Cathy has some mail for you." Before she could say anymore, the funeral director had gotten Beverly's attention, and the attendees began making their way to the door. Blame filed out with the group and slid quietly into the family car.

She stood at the coffin for a very long time...studying death. Mrs. Douthit looked peaceful, she thought. And that was good. She walked away with her head bowed and was very thankful to be alive. She was poor, hungry, and homeless again; but she was alive...and so thankful for that. When the funeral was over—scripture recited, flowers and earth lain on the casket, and Mrs. Douthit lowered into the ground—the procession made its way back to her Rose Lane home.

After quietly reflecting on the kindness of Mrs. Douthit during her time of need, Blame made her way to the first bedroom off the hall—where many years earlier, she'd cried enough tears to fill a canyon, and seriously contemplated suicide. Weary from her travel and the long years of a misspent life, she lie down across the guest bed and quickly fell asleep. Blame hadn't slept in a real bed, with a real mattress, in nearly two years; and she slept soundly until late the following afternoon.

She woke to the clatter of dishes in the kitchen. After she regained her senses—remembering where she was; she went to the kitchen to apologize to its inhabitant, feeling quite embarrassed. Blame was greeted by a smiling Beverly. "Well good morning sleepy head!" Beverly announced cheerfully.

"Ma'am, I am *so* sorry. I didn't mean to…" Blame started, but was cut off by Beverly, handing her a plate of warmed up leftovers.

"First of all, wash your hands, and don't Ma'am me. I'm not that much older than you. Don't you remember me, Blame? I used to spend some weeks in the summers here at my Aunt Cathy's. You were such a little girl; I guess you wouldn't remember me. I remember you though; and your pretty mamma. Such a shame, I mean about the fire and all." She handed Blame a fork, napkin and table salt; then continued. "And second of all, no need to apologize. I noticed you didn't have any luggage, and I didn't see a car parked outside. But I know my Aunt Cathy was quite fond of you. And whatever your situation is; well, it's really none of my business. I know Auntie would have welcomed you into her home. And the way you were snoring, I thought it best not to wake you," Beverly laughed.

Blame spent nearly two years locked in a cage with animals; she found herself breathing easy for the first time in years. Perhaps it was the kindness of this strange woman—with no apparent hidden agenda…or maybe it was the culmination of a long, sordid and tiring life…perhaps it was just the simple goodness of perfectly fried chicken and the three birds singing sweetly outside. Whatever the case may have been, Blame dropped her head in her hands and wept like the repentant sinner she was. Beverly, born of a good nature, wrapped her soft arms around the woman and rocked her like a baby. They remained that way for a very long time.

When the tears subsided, Blame poured out her heart to her patient and considerate listener. She ran the gambit of her thirty-eight years: from her childhood at 632 Rose Lane, to her escapades with Toria; from her rocky relationship with Ricco, to the birth of their beautiful children; from her fall from "grace" into the trashiness of the projects, to her life of crime in Dale City. She finished with the hard months she'd spent behind the prison walls in Goochland, and her subsequent bus trip home. Beverly did not judge or admonish or criticize. She did not interrupt or question or even shriek in horror. She listened and comforted. And when Blame was finished, she poured Ethel's daughter a warm cup of tea, and excused herself to Mrs. Douthit's bedroom.

Sitting alone in the familiar kitchen, Blame felt as if the weight of a hundred years had finally been lifted from her spirit. The window was open, and the warm, summer breeze blowing through, felt as cleansing as a hot shower. She wasn't ashamed or fearful of having exposed too much. She was instead, relieved, and overcome by a welcome and peaceful calm.

Beverly returned to the kitchen carrying a large manila envelope; and smiling. She said, "I am leaving today Blame. My Aunt Cathy left this house to me; but my home is in Richmond. I am going to close this house up and catch my flight later this evening...deal with renting or selling it some other time. If you had come home 24 hours later, I would have been gone. And you would have missed the Good News. God brought you here right on time, Blame. And I want you to get on your knees and thank Him before I tell you what's in this letter."

The very tough skin she'd developed in life almost made Blame rebuff her kind hostess; but the singing birds outside the open window and the gentle touch of Beverly's hand upon her shoulder, made Blame slide from the worn kitchen chair and onto her knees. She looked up at Beverly questioningly, and asked, "What do I say?"

Beverly softly replied, "Give thanks, Blame. So little is it that you give thanks. And say whatever is on your heart."

Blame began in silent prayer and ended crying and shuddering in blissful release and relief. Beverly wiped the tears from her own eyes and lifted Blame to her feet. Both women sat down and Beverly exclaimed, "Your prayers have already been answered!" She pushed the manila envelope across the formica table, the same way Mrs. Douthit had done nearly two decades ago with a yellow legal pad.

Blame opened the envelope slowly, like she was handling an ancient document which might turn to dust if she wasn't careful. She read the contents to herself, and then, to be sure she understood correctly, she read it again, out loud. She lay the documents down and got back on her knees, shouting, "Thank you God! Thank you. Thank God!"

The letter was from a law firm, representing the estate of Mr. Doany C. Rane, of Baylorton, North Carolina. Mr. Doany Charles Rane did not have any living children, only one nephew, Sherman Rane—last known residence: 632 Rose Lane, Norfolk, VA. Death records indicated both Sherman Rane and his spouse, Ethel Rane, were deceased. Therefore, their only known living daughter, Ms. Blame J. Rane, was sole heir to a four bedroom home and 39 acres of farmland in Baylorton, NC. She'd also inherited a tractor, a 1983 Chevrolet truck, several items of farming equipment and $4,672.00 certified funds, enclosed.

"Ain't He good girl?" Beverly beamed.

"Lord yes!" Blame yelled, staring at the enclosed check in disbelief. "May I use your phone, Miss Beverly? I need to call my kids! I gotta figure out how I'ma get to D.C. to get them.

Where is Baylorton? Oh who cares?! We have a home!" Her thinking was all over the place. Blame jumped up and down, squealing at the top of her lungs, and hugging the documents close to her delighted heart. But she could hardly be heard over the shrill warbling, whistling, cawing, cooing and tweeting of three ecstatic birds, in the kitchen window.

"Slow down," Beverly cautioned. *You* trying to figure out how *you're* going to do something, is how you got your life all turned upside down to begin with. Let go and let God, girl. Now, as I was saying, I have a plane to catch tonight. That rental car in the driveway needs to go back to the airport, too. But this is what *we're* going to do Blame. You're going to take me to the airport; then you're going to drive that rental to D.C. to get your kids. You all can stay here, spend some quality time getting to know each other again. You owe them that. Don't overwhelm them by moving too fast. When you're all rested and refreshed, you drive on down to North Carolina. Turn the car in to any Hertz location down there, understand? I'll call and put another two weeks rental on my card. Is that enough time to get things in order, Blame?"

Blame threw her hand up to cover her gaping mouth. "Oh No! Miss Beverly I couldn't! You've done so much already. I just...I can't accept that...it's too much! I mean, how will I ever repay you?"

"You won't, Blame. The Good Lord will repay me. Just consider it my way of tithing. I promise you I'll get it back, tenfold! Don't you worry about that. Now go call your kids and that law firm...let them know you're coming to claim your crown. We need to find a bank that will cash that check so we can get you some new clothes to go with your new life. And stop ma'am-ing me! I told you I'm not that old. Oh, and Blame, try to make thanking God a regular habit. You'll be blessed for

144

it." Beverly finished tidying the kitchen; then handed Blame the keys to the rental car and her Aunt Cathy Douthit's front door. She wasn't the least bit hesitant. Blame had been through so much in life, and she truly needed a break. Beverly had been moved by the Spirit, and was delighted to oblige.

"Oh no," Blame sighed, terribly dejected. "I knew this was all too good to be true. I can't go to Carolina, Beverly. I'm still on parole. Damn!"

"You let me worry about that," Beverly smiled. "You haven't asked what I do for a living, but I'll be happy to tell you now. I am a 5th circuit judge, Blame. I know people, and I have *earned* the power to bend the law. Who's your parole officer?"

Blame handed her the packet of documents she'd been released from prison with; Beverly scanned them and tucked them in her purse. You go on to Carolina and start a new life for yourself and your family. This little budsaw is right up my alley. You leave this burden on my back; this is one I can definitely carry…as long as you promise me your life of crime is definitely over!"

"Oh yes ma'am! I promise on my mamma and daddy's graves, that life is behind me forever!"

"Done deal then…and stop calling me ma'am!" They laughed and hugged and knew they'd created a bond, a friendship which would last all the days of their lives. Even though they no longer had any family remaining on Rose Lane, they would forge new bonds, and be each other's family.

CHAPTER 17
FAMILY REUNION

Blame checked her reflection in the rearview mirror. She'd stopped perming her hair in prison, and her lively brown curls, with a few strands of silver, danced in the midday sun. She moistened her lips with a little shea butter and wiped a tiny tear from the corner of her radiant eye. Blame was pleased with the stronger, wiser woman looking back at her. She hoped her children would be too.

She pulled up outside a neat brick house in Fort Washington, Maryland, the suburbs of Washington, D.C. Before she could get out of the car good, J'Rick and Karma came bounding out of the front door, followed by Keisha and Monique. Blame dropped her purse in the yard and they all shared in a warm and uplifting group hug. Everybody was talking at once as they entered the well-kept house, a Welcome Home banner draped across the front room wall. Once inside, Keisha pulled her daughter into the kitchen, allowing Blame some time alone with her children.

Fifteen year old J'Rick loomed a full foot taller than his mother. Twelve year old Karma, though a little on the heavy side, was blossoming into a beautiful young lady. All Blame could do was laugh and cry. Her head moved left to right, as if she was watching Serena at the US Open, back and forth, between her excited teenagers. They had so much to tell her and it appeared they were going to do it all in one breath. They showed her their report cards, their sports awards and other accolades, family photos from a recent visit with their father, their bedrooms, the books they were reading, the cat, Felicity, and their matching cell phones.

When her head stopped spinning, Blame kicked off her shoes and relaxed on the back deck with Keisha; the kids started up a basketball game in the driveway. Keisha brought out two glasses of Pinot, some light refreshments and a Gucci shoe box. Blame noticed for the first time how pretty Keisha was, and she suddenly understood Ricco's attraction. She couldn't see it before because they'd been such staunch enemies all those years ago. Blame grabbed Keisha's hand and said, "Thank you."

Keisha batted her grip away and responded, "No. Thank *you*! I used that $20,000.00 bail refund for the down-payment on this house. But...I've been paying you back a little every month." She placed the shoe box in Blame's lap, and added, "There's $4,300.00 in there. I finished school...got my RN! I promise I'll pay you back every penny, Blame. Things are just a little tight right now, with these student loans hanging over my head. But I promise you'll get every single dime. You have no idea the difference that kind of money made in my life."

"Pay *me* back?! Girl, are you crazy?!" Blame cried, pointing to the house and yard, "Look at the life you gave my kids when I couldn't give them nothing but a sad prison song. If you told me I still owed you a million dollars for keeping them safe, I swear I'd be trying to figure out how to pay *you* back! You better take this money and pay off them student loans," she added, placing the shoe box on the patio table in front of Keisha. Both women looked into each other's eyes and laughed, to keep from crying.

"So," Keisha asked, after a peaceful pause of watching the children at play, "do you have any plans? I got three bedrooms Blame. Me and J'Rick got our own rooms, Karma and Monique share. But I do have a basement. Nothing down there but an old mattress and a beat up recliner; but you're welcome to it...until you can get on your feet."

"Okay now you're going too far, Keisha. Girl we're gonna end up on Jerry Springer if you don't stop," Blame joked. "No seriously, I appreciate the offer. But I'm actually gonna be okay." Blame filled Keisha in on her trip to Norfolk, her weekend with Beverly and her incredible inheritance. They ordered and ate Chinese, watched dvds and played a few rounds of spades.

The next morning, Keisha went to work at the hospital, dropping eleven-year-old Monique off at summer camp on the way. Blame woke up early and cooked a big breakfast for her children. Over pancakes, eggs and hash, she broke the news about their windfall and the home waiting for them in Baylorton, NC, making it all sound very exciting. J'Rick was immediately skeptical.

Karma took her lead from her big brother. She noticed the doubt on J'Rick's face and responded to her mother, "but ma, why we got to leave? I like it here. Miss Keisha said you could stay, too. All my friends are here. And I don't want to leave my sister." She pushed her plate away from her and added defiantly, "I'm staying here!"

Blame bit her lip and looked questioningly at J'Rick. He stared into his mother's eyes for a long time recalling the correspondence they'd shared for nearly two years. He knew his mother was not the same women from D.C. or even Dale City. They'd both grown immensely over the months and he desperately needed to believe her...to trust her again. He put his juice glass down and picked up Karma's hand. He looked her in the eyes and said, "Sis, it's not like last time. Miss Keisha looked out for us when mamma was away; but she's back now. And she's our mamma. We go where she goes. And Monique will always be our sister. She can visit anytime, and you can

148

come back up here and visit when you want. Right, mom?"
J'Rick asked.

"Right," Blame agreed.

J'Rick continued, "I promise you it's going to be okay,
Karma. We'll make it okay, because we're a family. Plus, you'll
have a room of your own now. And come on…39 acres! That's
almost a whole town! We have a responsibility to each other,
Karma. So you cool? " Karma begrudgingly nodded her head.
Blame let out a sigh of relief and leaned across the table to kiss
her son on the forehead.

On a lighter note, she stated, "but first, we're going to take
a trip to Norfolk. I'll show you where I grew up. How does that
sound?"

"Interesting," smiled J'Rick, sarcastically. And Karma
laughed.

The next day, the children rode with Keisha and Monique
to the nearby workcamp to visit with Ricco. They needed to say
goodbye. Blame did not go with them. She was no longer on
the visitation list anyway. She stayed at the house and packed
up her children's things, loaded the rental car with what would
fit, and put labels with her North Carolina address on the
remaining boxes. She would send for them after they got
settled. She would also send for Monique, thinking a visit from
her sister might make Karma's transition a little smoother. Plus,
Keisha could definitely use the break; she'd spent nearly two
years parenting kids who weren't her own. And from the looks
of things, she'd done a marvelous job.

Blame looked at the framed photo on Karma's
nightstand, of: Karma, J'Rick, Keisha, Monique and Ricco. Ricco
and Keisha looked like the perfect couple, flanked by their
loving children. Her heart skipped a beat at the sight of a drug-
free, well-rested Ricco, looking handsome in his kufi and khakis.

149

But after the years of distance between them, her heart had finally broken free of the love, and her mind, free of the vice grip. There was nothing left now, but memories of pain and long suffering.

He looked to her, like a devil in a good disguise. She found it hard to believe a man could be so physically and emotionally abusive to one woman and not the other. Life had taught her something about the nature of people, and Blame would bet money, unfortunately for Keisha, it would only be a matter of time before the *real* Ricco reared his ugly head.

Blame wanted to warn Keisha, but knew how it would be received. She'd learned it was impossible to reason with a woman blinded by love. She envied Keisha's patience and conviction; but she did not envy the outcome. Whatever she had with Ricco was long over; and she truly wished them well. Her "sister-friend" had done well for herself, and Blame loathed the idea of Ricco fucking it all up. She only hoped he had grown into the man Keisha believed him to be.

When the family returned, they had a light lunch together and bid their farewells… finishing off the roll of film in the camera. Monique cried, and Blame offered to send for her as soon as they got to North Carolina. The summer was just starting; the girls would have lots of time to visit before school started, she added.

Without any further ado, Blame, her nearly grown children, and the cat, Felicity, backed out of the driveway in Beverly's rental and headed south to Norfolk, and Rose Lane. They would spend a few days there, as Beverly suggested. Then they would pack up again and head to Carolina—where, all three prayed, a better future lay ahead.

PART II

NORTH CAROLINA

The sun rises and the sun sets. ~ **Eva Fulp Martin**

CHAPTER 18
THE MIDDLE OF A THING
TUPPIE RANE

I already know how this story ends, because I am its very beginning. And I'll be here still, when it's finished. Even if you know the beginning and the ending, the middle of a thing is always the best part. Being the Alpha and the Omega, I can tell you, *now,* how to better maintain the eye-blink of time that lies between...the middle time, called Life. Oh, what I would give to have had some knowledge, wisdom and understanding during my living years. I'm learning some things now, though. I've learned...

It is what it is, in this world. You have to do the best with what you are given. Like a bird building its nest. Country birds will use whatever country things they can find. While city birds, on the other wing, utilize the castoff of great metropolises. You won't see fern nettles or magnolia leaves in the nests of New York City avian; any more than you'd see shoes on a slave's feet. So if you are a coastal bird, and must build your nest from dried seaweed, broken seashells and bits of plastic from busted beach balls—learn to make the most of it.

Try to follow the Good Book, the lessons of your upbringing, and your own good sense. Now if, like me, you can't read and nobody tells you what's in the Word; you will have the harder row to hoe. If, like me, you had no upbringing because you had no parents—your row will be the hardest. But you are living in a different time now, and you should not be like me. You can learn to read; you can know both your sire and seed. Your journey to the straight path should be much smoother than mine.

At least we all have some modicum of good sense...most of us, anyhow. Why even a jackass knows the coyote brings trouble. But if you've no sense, none whatsoever...and haven't learned any sense by the middle of your years...you ought to throw yourself down the well. Really, there's no hope for you. And I know about having no hope—I lived most of my life in the purgatory of bondage. But there was always the chance I could get free. A fool has no excuse. An Ethiopian proverb says: "A fool at forty is a fool indeed!" So I assure you, if you've no sense, no wisdom at all, when you become long in the tooth, and hoary of hair, a leap off the barn roof would probably be in your best interest.

And keep your shoulder to the plow. I thought I slaved as a slave; but I never worked so hard in all my days as I did on Jezzy's farm. We reaped what we sowed; and we sowed like our lives depended on it. Because, no longer dependent upon our master for basic sustenance; our lives did depend solely on our ceaseless labor and sound judgment. As you know, he who loves the bed will see poverty. As poor as we were, imagine if we had not pounded and struggled every waking moment. Why we'd be worse off than the very dust we toiled in.

The sun rises and the sun sets. You can depend on that. And you need to make your word as dependable. The days and nights of the rising and setting sun make up a whole life. Squeeze as much joy out of those days and nights as possible. Do so without being intentionally cruel to your neighbor. Do so by doing what is right, versus what is wrong. Again, make your word as dependable as the rising and setting sun. And you will have a good middle—a fine life.

What of love? Since you are born free, just live the best life you can. True love will come. Your story will not end without it. Mine came in the form of freedom. It manifested itself on a farm where I was surrounded by my family. I could not be sold away from them, nor could they be sold from me; and I did not have to abuse them to keep them near. I did not go to the grave without being able to give and receive love to the fullest. You will know true love before you close your eyes, too. As will Blame. And hopefully, you all will be wise enough to recognize it when it comes knocking at your door. But if you are too foolish to recognize your blessings when they come...go now and seek out the well bottom or the roof top. Your living is in vain.

CHAPTER 19
ONE ACRE SHY & NEEDING REPAIR

Karma turned the map upside down and still couldn't figure out where they were. J'Rick checked the Mapquest print out again. The lawyer, who'd given her the deed, title and other paperwork, also gave her directions to the farm. There was supposed to be a highway off that stretch of road, but they couldn't find it. They drove on, getting nervous about the gas level, and finally came upon a sign that said "Welcome to Baylorton. Population: 2,933." Their mouths dropped open. "We had more people in our high school!" exclaimed J'Rick from the back seat.

Blame was abuzz with the excitement of being a landowner! And a whole thirty-nine acres at that! She had no concept of the value of land, but was determined to make it her business to find out how it could support her family. Finally they came upon what looked like any other place in America: a town with a McDonald's, Walmart, Exxon Gas Station, Movie Theater, High School, Pizza Hut, Food Lion, etc... They stopped at the gas station to fill up. J'Rick pumped, Karma paid, and Blame asked a cheerful-looking black woman for better directions. "Excuse me; do you know how to get to Rane Lane from here?"

"Yes ma'am, you go on down to the third light and make a left onto Rainier Road," she explained, gesturing with her plump arms and hands. You'll be leaving the city limits, going out into the country. That'll take you into what folks round here call Rainier Place. Go on down about two miles and make your first right. You'll see the sign—Rane Lane," she graciously responded. Then she added, because country folk are the nosiest, "What are you going down there for? Nobody lives down that road anymore." Blame left her hanging and got back in the car, smiling at the idea of her name on a street sign — symbol of ownership, she mused.

She almost passed Rane Lane, as weeds were taking over the olive colored street sign marked private. Weeds and small pine were also swallowing a cinder block building at the top of the road, which looked like it might have been a country store, in some earlier century. They turned onto the gravel road, pitted with potholes and heavily guarded by a border of thick oak trees. The road went down a small incline, then back up, into a bright, sun-filled clearing. In the midst of the clearing stood a tall, badly weathered, two-story farmhouse with a wrap-around porch, a hanging front door, peeling paint and several broken windows. Just like the street sign, weeds were quickly claiming the dwelling as well. Since there was no clearly designated driveway, they pulled right up to the front porch.

The three looked back and forth between each other and the house. Each had their separate thoughts, but was afraid to share. They sat in the rental car for a long time; no one brave enough to be first to enter the ghostly abode. Their gloom was interrupted by the sound of tires on the gravel road, approaching fast. A newer model SUV crested the hill and came to a stop beside the rental car. Abraham Ismine emerged with a curious, yet perturbed, expression on his bearded face.

"Good afternoon," he greeted the family, after Blame cautiously rolled down her window.

"Good Afternoon, to you," Blame said, waiting for the stranger to make his next move.

'You folks have business down here?" he asked.

"Do you?" was her snide reply.

"Ma'am I don't mean to be rude, but you're trespassing on private property," he alerted, getting peeved at the obvious intruders.

"No sir, to the contrary," Blame quipped, stepping out of the rental, *"you* are trespassing on *my* property! And I'd appreciate it if you'd leave." She proffered the documents certifying her ownership and fanned them in his face. He snatched the papers from her hand and read over them. "Hey! Give me back my papers!" Blame exclaimed, reaching skyward. Mr. Ismine didn't pay her any mind, holding the documents from her reach until he was done reading. He removed his hat, folded the papers neatly, and returned them to Blame.

"Well, it looks like apologies are in order then, so I must say I am quite sorry….Ms. Rane. I'm Abraham Ismine, your neighbor to the right, just beyond that row of cedar," he pointed the direction. "Mr. Doany Rane was a friend of mine. Well actually his deceased son, your cousin Wilbur, was my friend. Since Doany passed, there's been a lot of vandalism down here. I sorta look after the place."

"Well," she answered, motioning toward the overgrown weeds and hanging door, "you haven't done a very good job of that. And how'd you know we were here? You couldn't see us through the…what'd you call those trees, cedar?"

"You asked for directions to Rane Road at the One Stop. News travels fast in Baylorton. I knew you were here before your tires hit the gravel." Blame thought about that for a moment, then turned away and started removing boxes from the vehicle, signaling for her nervous children to do the same. Abraham introduced himself to the family with handshakes, momentarily loosing himself in Blame's magical eyes. The Rane resemblance was clear, and he was most impressed with J'Rick's fine manners. Abe helped himself to some of the boxes and jumped up on the sturdy porch. The family followed. "Looks like you're planning on staying a while?" he asked.

"That's right; if it's inhabitable."

"Oh, she's fine…just needs a little work is all. Say, where you all from" he asked kicking away the shrubbery inhabiting their path. Blame answered Virginia, while J'Rick responded, D.C., and Karma blurted out Maryland. No corrections were made, and they followed Mr. Ismine inside. "Yeah," he added, batting at cobwebs and fanning away sheets of dust, "she needs some work, but you have a fine home here Ms. Rane. You must be Sherman's daughter?"

"Yes I am," she beamed at the mention of her father's name. "Did you know my daddy?" she asked, hopefully. "No ma'am; never met him. Just heard talk of him is all."

Let down and wanting no further small talk with the stranger, Blame changed the conversation to matters of business. She asked, "Since you're here, could you give me directions to the electric company so I can get the power on? And where's the water bill office?"

Abraham laughed at the last question and informed her she had well water…free water for life. He clicked open his cell phone and called the power company; he seemed to be on friendly terms with whomever he was speaking with. Blame heard him say her name twice, and spell it once. He closed his cell and informed her that her power would be on before 5:00 p.m.; she just needed to go by the office and sign the contract. Then he called Waste Management and ordered a trashcan and pickup service, handing the phone to Blame so she could give them her personal information. Blame and the kids were still busy unloading the car when they heard Mr. Ismine's truck leave.

Their good neighbor returned ten minutes later, now driving a Ford F250 long bed pickup. He got out and lifted several items from the bed, including a gas-powered weed eater and a container of gasoline. Abe ripped the engine on the weed eater and began clearing the porch and grounds of overgrowth. Yelling over the whir of the machine, he told J'Rick to take a look in the barn, nodding the direction, and ordered him to fetch the lawnmower. J'Rick did as he was told. Mr. Ismine showed the boy how to fill the tank, prime the mower and turn it on. J'Rick, who'd never cut grass before in his life, lit into the chore like he'd been born for the job. Blame and Karma looked on in astonishment from the porch.

After the weed eating was complete, Abraham went inside and returned with a broom and dustpan, which he handed to Karma. She rolled her eyes at him and he rolled his back, adding, "well if you're the kind of young lady who likes to live in filth, help yourself. But if you believe cleanliness is next to Godliness...and it is...I'd suggest you get this place cleaned up. Those bags there are for the trash." Karma reluctantly started sweeping the front porch.

Abraham turned to Blame and asked her to follow him. He retrieved a bucket of tools from the truck bed and led her down to the well. He showed her how to remove the heavy cement cap and prime the pump. After several attempts at the outside spigot, water eventually came gushing out. "Pine Sol, bleach and gloves are in the truck. Doany should have a mop and bucket in the kitchen. What you can't find in the house, you'll find in the barn!" he yelled over the lawnmower motor; then went about the business of fixing the hanging front door.

When the power company showed up, the family took a break. They didn't realize how much time had passed. They took a look around at their work and were quite pleased. At least they'd banished the first layer of grit and grime. Abraham Ismine handed Blame a business card. "I'm a contractor by trade, Ms. Rane. I don't work cheap, but my prices are fair. Let me know what you want to do about those windows and I'll see if I can't work out a good deal for you. I think you need to go with storm windows all around. I may have a few for starters in my storage." He looked over the sweaty children and asked, "how about some lunch, my treat?" Everybody was down with that. The family went inside to wash up, and rode with Mr. Ismine to town.

They enjoyed burgers and fries while Abraham told them all about Baylorton. He was smart and funny, so the family enjoyed his company. Their group was met with stares and whispers, nods and smiles. Newcomers were always noticed in the small town. The children received the most attention...boys going gaga over Karma; girls giggling and shoving each other, trying to catch J'Rick's eye. Blame took it all in. A few men looked in her direction, but they looked at Abraham and turned their attention elsewhere. Everybody in Baylorton knew Abraham could hold his own. No one wanted to get in a pissing competition with him, or any other Ismine man, for that matter.

After lunch, they went to Walmart for new linens, towels, kitchen wares, toiletries, rolls of heavy plastic for the windows, (until she could do better), and a few other creature comforts for their new home. The house had been left as is, following Doany's death, so it was completely furnished. Aside from the litter of teenage parties: broken beer bottles, used condoms and empty cigarette packs...it was in pretty fair shape. Blame knew she had to get rid of the sofa and antiquated television, wash down and Febreeze the mattresses, and pull up the worn carpet. But it had four huge bedrooms, a dining room, an oversized kitchen, a living room, a big bonus room, pantry, parlor and a small sewing room...the possibilities were endless. She couldn't wait to get back and have a better look at that truck in the barn.

The truck, it turns out, was in pristine condition with a good strong engine. Blame had it registered, titled and tagged in her name. Then she returned Beverly's rental to the Hertz office two towns over. She sent the Rose Lane house keys back to Beverly, with a letter telling her how wonderful life in North Carolina was shaping up to be, thanking her friend again for her incredible support. Once her phone service was connected, she called her other friend, Keisha, and told her which train to put Monique on. Besides cleaning, clearing and more cleaning, J'Rick and Karma spent their days discovering treasure in the attic and barn, and taking long nature hikes all over their land. There was even a thin creek and a small lake on the property. The Ranes were in country heaven!

Blame was especially pleased with all the hardware in the sewing room, including: an antique sewing machine, as well as a modern-day Singer, bobbins, a box filled with old patterns, pins, measuring tape, bolts of materials, scissors, baskets full of every notion imaginable, thimbles, rolls of yarn, spools of thread, and needles of every kind—from sewing to knitting to crocheting. Since renewing her passion for the art of textile design and manufacture in prison, the sewing room quickly became Blame's favorite spot in the house. In the evenings, she sat in the tiny alcove designing and creating one-of-a-kind hats, dresses, sweaters, wraps, blouses and lingerie. With a bottle of wine, a pack of cigarettes, and copies of the latest fashion magazines, she could easily spend hours on her newfound hobby, sometimes not coming up for air until daybreak.

The next few weeks were spent applying for jobs and getting the house spic and span—polishing wood, washing down walls, windows and baseboards, waxing floors and throwing out the things they simply would not need. They painted the interior of the house, scrubbed the bathrooms clean and repaired the legs of a few chairs and tables. The Rane home was finally coming together; but the job hunt wasn't going so well...Blame being a convicted felon. She still had the majority of her small inheritance, but it certainly wasn't going to last forever. And she had begun to worry about their future.

CHAPTER 20
BIRD'S EYE VIEW

Crow:

Blame's come home! I almost didn't recognize the place when we flew up. Doany must have added the other rooms, second floor, *and* indoor bathrooms, too!

I was plumb tickled to see them kids tromping in the fields what we used to work in; and you could have knocked me over with a feather when Karma found that picture album in the attic. She opened the cover and there I was, a living woman! Only time my likeness was captured. Rone had it done, back when they used to lay me out on the porch...when I was old and dying. I remember Rone saying, "it can't steal your spirit, Granny Tuppie, gone and smile at the box." Seems Doany had our photos put together in a book, with me—matriarch of the Rane clan—on the very first page.

Blame sewed pretty curtains for the kitchen. We didn't have no sewing room when I was alive. Maybe that was Jezzy's idea? Naw, she wasn't much good with needle and thread. EulaLee died fore I did, so it musta been put in for Doany's wife, Cin.

That was back when I first got my wings. First place I come to was home, to see bout my people. Wasn't nobody on the place but Doany, an old man by then, and his wife, Cin. Cin was the dancehall type, and couldn't have loved Doany if he paid her. But she was getting along in years, yearning for a home of her own. Well beyond her season, she did manage to give Doany a son—Wilbur. I suppose that's what he was after all along. Birthing a child so late in life killed ole Cin.

Doany and Wilbur got along right fine, farming and talking, fishing, playing checkers, going to ballgames. Wilbur had such plans for this place, even planted apples trees. But he died in the 1st Gulf War. I seen it with my own eyes, over in that Arabian Desert. He only joined the Reserves to help pay taxes on the farm; but got sent to kill other brown boys, like himself. Wilbur was by hit by what they call "friendly fire". The words some folk come up with! Wasn't nothing friendly about it. In the end, it doesn't matter how your country fared. If you don't make it off the battlefield, you personally lose the war. I stayed with him in the hot sand 'til his spirit rose up from his body. He was a good boy...kind, hardworking, gentle spirit, like his grandpappy, Rone—the joy of my old heart.

Oh, but enough with the past. It's a new day! Blame Rane done come home! I danced all over the place, strutting the way little birds do. I'm so happy I don't even care that ole Missy Gwen'lyn followed me here. Her and that quiet cardinal. I'm going to have words with that redbird someday, figure out why she's tailing me. I'd sure like to know the story behind that eyeball she's always toting around, too. There's got to be a rich tale behind that sort of thing. I picked out a place in the barn, high in the rafters, for my nest; reckon I'll be here a spell. I ain't seen the pigeon for a few days now. Last I saw, she was flying in the direction of the big house. Wonder if it's still up on the hill?

Cardinal:

I did not know where we were going; only that Blame had a home in Carolina. When we arrived, I noticed right off it was beautiful country, and it reminded me of a place I dream about. I circled the farm, familiarizing myself with the lay of the land.

Then I heard it! Just beyond the distant hills behind Blame's property was the sound of rushing water. The sound, the scenery, even the aroma called out to me. I flew beyond the hills and there in the valley, what did I behold?! UWEYV! THE RIVER! My dream river, and land of my birth! Our proud Cherokee home!

I landed in a clearing, where, nearly two centuries ago, my mother warmed fresh vegetables over an open flame. I could almost see the faces of my brothers and father, dancing around the fire. And I laughed, chirping heartily, the way little birds do.

I thought to myself, look how this life/death keeps moving. We think we are going in straight lines; but time is really a circle. Everything comes back around to its starting point, eventually. I have circumnavigated the entire globe— studying Africans, Asians, Australian Aborigines, Brazilians, Inuit and the tribes of Eastern Europe—only to return home.

I dipped my beak in the sweet water of Uweyv, and made a comfy nest high in the limbs of a stoic Virginia pine. I was close enough to keep a bird's eye view on Blame. She would be fine in Baylorton; my intuition told me so. It was good earth, so bountiful that a little girl, not properly trained to hunt, could easily nab two squirrels from its giving forests. This was a good place. It was Home, *sweet* home.

Pigeon:

Rainier Estate! Could it be? Why yes, it's my glorious queendom, my beautiful home! I flew on ahead of the others while they inspected an old farm house at the edge of our plantation (which I do not recall in my living years). I raced the wind to my former throne. Was the big house still on the hill?

I passed the overgrown graves of my family and myself, and pushed through the sweet magnolia. The shanty of slave quarters had been torn down, but there was still some tobacco growing in the fields. When I crested the hill where my mansion should have been, I was met by the unsightly metal heap of a trailer park. I winced, cawing the way little birds do, and floated woefully to the ground.

A school bus and other junked vehicles lay abandoned where our stables—housing the counties finest thoroughbreds—once stood. A scraggly band of Mexican children played soccer in the dust; their mother's hung clothes where my flower garden used to be. Men played checkers at a picnic table and clamored on in a foreign tongue. I do not have to understand Spanish to know they were not talking about me. No one remembered me, my dear husband, our long dead daughter, or my five precious grandchildren. No one eulogized my poor boy, Charlie. No one thought to trim back the blackberry bushes covering the crooked crosses that marked our graves. *Nothing* of my former prowess remained.

I hung my pigeon head and cried. Was my living in vain? What did it matter now if I came from a humble past? Who cared now if my grandparents were indentured servants? It made no difference at all that my parasols were ordered from Paris, France, or that I owned four little nigger girls, whose sole purpose in life was to fan and keep me cool. There was no monument erected proclaiming me "Toughest Mistress in the County". No memory of my forged pedigree. Nary a soul even remembered my name.

I was erased from existence, in the same way I'd erased my own family. I wondered if there was anyone in the whole wide world who might still know my name. So I took to the sky and flew towards the setting sun. Perhaps they still spoke of Gwendolyn O'Grady in the land called Tennessee.

CHAPTER 21
BUSINESS BEGETS BUSINESS

Blame familiarized herself with the town of Baylorton and its limited resources. She discovered their particular section of the county was known to all as Rainier Place (though no such signs were posted), because of a pre-Civil War plantation in that area. She was pleasant to the ladies in town, but made it quite clear she did not care to make any new friends—most women, she'd learned, were more trouble than they were worth. Even though they lived rent free, the rising cost of healthcare, home and auto insurance, utilities, cable, groceries and gas was quickly eating away at the money left by Doany. And Blame still had not found a job.

Mr. Ismine, rarely visited, but when he did, it was always with welcome relief. The family liked his easy company. He taught them how to fish in their lake and operate their farm equipment. They'd arrived too late in summer to plant, he explained, but promised to show J'Rick how to turn the ground over for next year's harvest. He even showed the boy how to hunt, giving him a rifle from his very own collection. When it became apparent financial constraints were becoming a real burden for Blame; Abraham hired J'Rick as an apprentice in his construction business. Blame really appreciated that. J'Rick would be able to make his own money, because she certainly didn't have any extra cash. Karma was getting restless, but the arrival of Monique nipped that in the bud.

Blame didn't have an extensive wardrobe, so she started sewing clothes for herself and the girls—letting them design and help create their own fashions. They began wearing their creations when they went into town for groceries or other necessities; and they were always met with pleasant stares.

One evening, when Abraham and J'Rick were riding home from a long and rewarding day's work, J'Rick asked if he could get more hours. School would starting soon he explained, and he wouldn't be able to work as much then. He admitted he was worried about not being able to help his mother out as much as he had been. Abraham, usually very talkative, drove on in silence, scratching his beard and looking off in the distance.

When they reached the Rane house, J'Rick bolted from the truck's cabin with his toolbox, always anxious to fiddle around in the old house—fixing whatever he could find in disrepair. His little bit of tools, donated by Mr. Ismine, were precious to him; somehow they made him feel more like a man. And being a man was what he strived for most, bless his heart.

Instead of dropping J'Rick off and circling out of the driveway as he normally did, Abraham exited the work truck, piled high with materials, and joined Blame on the porch. She was busy scouring the local paper for possible job opportunities...her brow furrowed like her daddy's, her teeth clenching a pencil. "Good evening Blame."

"Mr. Ismine," she responded, ducking her cigarette, but not looking up from her depressing task.

He brushed sawdust and sheetrock off his jeans and shirt and began measuring the windows. "That's a pretty blouse you have on, Blame. J'Rick says you do a lot of your own sewing. Did you make it yourself?"

"Yes," she responded, blushing at the compliment.

"I thought so; it's not the kind of thing you see around here. And I'm not the only person who's noticed," he added, jotting down the window measurements in a notebook.

He'd gotten Blame's attention. She was at first offended, wondering if people were clowning her outfits. "What's that supposed to mean? Anyway to hell with what these country bitches think…they wouldn't know fashion if it slapped them in the face." She snapped, defensively.

"Whoa, slow down, Blame. And watch your mouth. I meant that as a compliment. Several ladies in our church, and some others in the community, even schoolgirls, are talking about the stylish clothes they see you and Karma and Monique sporting around town. I'll bet they're wondering where they can find some of those fine city hats and dresses. Have you ever thought about selling your wares? Might not be much in it, this being such a small town full of fashion-deprived 'country bitches'…as you put it," he winked. "But I reckon if you could sell a couple of pieces, it might help on the groceries, pay a light bill or two…it might be worth a shot. Plus, it'd be an easy way to make some new friends. Some of these 'country bitches' are okay. Besides, if you stay cooped up in this house all the time, you're subject to get a bad case of cabin fever," he laughed…then waited quietly to see if she'd taken the bait.

Blame laid the paper and pencil down on the tiny wrought-iron table beside her butt-cluttered ashtray, and took a sip of Karma's homemade tea. She didn't respond right away, but you could almost hear the gears turning in her head. She asked Abraham if he'd like a glass of tea, and returned with both tea, and a large 3-ring binder she'd been working on. She absentmindedly handed Abraham his glass, then started flipping through the pages of the over-stuffed binder. It was filled with drawings of clothes she'd designed, swatches of material in different colors and textures, clippings from high-fashion magazines, pictures of the girls in their getups, and her own journal entries.

Mr. Ismine finished his tea, and in his usual way, excused himself from the porch without saying a word. Blame looked up to apologize about her characterization of the Baylorton women, and to ask if people were really saying all those nice things about their clothes; but Abraham was nowhere in sight. She started daydreaming about a little boutique somewhere in town; but the details of pulling off such an operation grew overwhelming, and the frustration that accompanies poverty, rapidly set in. She closed her binder and lit a fresh cigarette; then went back to the daunting job search in the want ads.

Blame was startled by loud knocking and banging in her barn. She looked up and saw Abraham lugging out all kinds of equipment. He yelled up to the house, "Blame, tell J'Rick to come give me a hand with this, would you?" Blame called for her son and wondered what her neighbor was up to. Once outside, J'Rick and Abraham loaded up his truck and took off up the gravel road. After a while, quite a bit of racket could be heard at the top of Rane Lane. It seemed to be coming from the old cinder block store on the corner. Blame tore Karma and Monique away from the videos on BET, loaded them in the truck, and drove up her long driveway to find the source of all the clamor and commotion.

CHAPTER 22
ABRAHAM

Abraham was not on the Grid and lived in a most natural way. His was the house powered by the elements—wind, solar, water(hydro-electric), and the fourth element, too, earth—growing the food he ate...rotting compost used as methane fuel...pine and oak for heat. Of course there were generators, it being the 21st century; but they were seldom used. The result of this natural way of living; was that Abraham Ismine had no electric bill. Never.

He saved his money...all of it. If there was something he needed, like a car, suit or bulldozer; he bought it, paying cash. Trucks, motorcycles, construction equipment, computers and furniture were never financed. And thus there were no car payments or credit card debt for Abraham. Not ever.

When there were trials (random tests of faith), and in his lifetime, they came periodically—he was prepared. For the occasions when a man must be tested, financially; he went to the bank, or dug into the earth, uncovering tens of thousands of dollars, if necessary, in cash. And thus there were no unsustainable emergencies or insurmountable crises, in his life. Not any.

Abraham owned a construction company, and of course, built the house he lived in. And quite naturally, as with the other large ticket items in his possession, there was no mortgage on his home. He'd paid cash for every board of lumber, every window, shingle, brick and screw. He'd done the work himself, paying his crew a fair wage, occasionally using the scraps from other jobs. So there was no note...just a recent appraisal, valuing the home at more than three hundred thousand dollars.

And because he had zero debt, a few rent houses and a thriving construction company, Mr. Ismine's wealth was always abundant. Not to mention the acreage he had planted in 2nd generation loblolly pine—maturing nicely up on the plateau. Maybe someday he would harvest it to the tune of $100,000.00. But there was no hurry. The local scrap yard was paying $12.00 a pound for metal. He had tons of old equipment, with vines growing through it, just rusting in the fields. Because there were trailers at his disposal—the ones he bought and paid cash for—he could easily haul his unused metal to scale in less than a day's time. But the $24,000.00 it would garner was not immediately necessary. He might scrap his rusting metal someday, perhaps, if the rate doubled.

If the car he was driving, his mode of transportation, the thing he depended on to get from point a to point b, should break down—no worry, he had four more vehicles—titled, registered, tagged and insured. They were all insured as "farm use", of course, so the annual fee was minimal. The herd of Boer goats he bred was a no-brainer. His Honduran neighbors up the road were his only customers. They were grateful such fine eating was a stone's throw away.

None of the Ismines had ever sought "regular" employment. They were a lot who created their own jobs, started their own businesses. Abraham, with his construction company, was just following in the footsteps of his ancestors. He didn't know any other way.

And though his financial genius would have been quite remarkable to any Wall Street advisor, it was just second nature to Abraham. He'd learned the magic from his father, who was taught by his father's father...and so on. The skills of farming, carpentry, animal husbandry, welding, irrigation, business, and engine repair had been passed down in this fashion as well…along with shrewd cunning, ancient wisdom and a passion for life's simple pleasures, including the unchanging Word of God.

Abraham had never heard of Blame Rane, but her eyes…Wilbur's eyes, were unmistakable. Wilbur, Doany Rane's only son, had been Abraham's one true lifelong friend. Wilbur died during the First Gulf War, losing the battle to "friendly fire". Abe and Wilbur grew up in the countryside of Baylorton, both with much older fathers, and were more like brothers than neighbors. Abraham loved Wilbur, and felt it his duty to look after the place when Doany finally passed on, of very old age and a broken heart.

He wondered about the kind of woman—who would show up in a rented car, packed tightly with her belongings and two teenaged children—who'd never so much as visited the place in previous years. He was immediately skeptical about Blame, with her upstate accent and citified attitude. He had seen her type before. City slickers who came to the country thinking it would be easy living—running back up north, with their tails tucked between their legs, at the first sign of trouble…like a moccasin under the porch, a racist sheriff's department, power outages from ice-downed lines in winter, or the army of pests that invaded every summer—mosquitos, possums, army ants, sweat bugs and coyote. Plus the lack of high-paying jobs and big-city entertainment kept most outsiders at bay. There were no nightclubs, pool halls or semi-professional sports teams in Baylorton. No bowling alley, skating rink or water park. There was, however, plenty of fresh air, sunshine and wide open fields, as well as a multitude of fishing holes, dirt bike trails, card parties and fish fries; if you were into that sort of thing.

Blame seemed, to him, like the type who was running from something. Her secretive ways made him think she was hiding something terrible in her past. That, and the pinched way she walked—like an animal kept caged too long. Oh she was pretty enough, but Abraham knew pretty women were a dime a dozen. And the majority of them thought their beauty entitled them to behave badly. His mother used to always say, "pretty is as pretty does", so he'd defer his opinion of her true beauty until they became better acquainted.

He wasn't interested in any kind of a romantic relationship with Blame. Abe had his hands full with an assorted array of Baylorton's eligible bachelorettes. Being the catch he was, women from all over the county regularly invited themselves to his home and his bed—cooking his meals, doing his laundry, scrubbing his toilets, massaging his neck and organizing his sock drawer—until they realized he wasn't the commitment type. He heard tell of a cat fight, down at the drugstore, between two such suitors; he just shrugged and laughed it off, wondering what exactly the victor was supposed to win? Blame, on the other hand, was more like family— cousin to the best friend he could ever hope to have. It was obvious she needed some help getting anchored; it was clear she had no place else to go. So, being the godly man he was, he extended his help. Besides, Blame didn't seem the least bit interested in him, anyway.

Now J'Rick was a different story. Coming from such a family-oriented clan as the Ismine's he grew especially fond of the awkward teenager. The time he spent training and instructing J'Rick made him long for a son of his own. The boy was calm and patient and eager to learn. He wasn't a hothead, like Abraham had been at that age; and Abe liked that, too. He knew his place, and loved and honored his mother—endearing

qualities in any kid. Karma, on the contrary, was a slick one.
She smiled on cue and always knew just what to say; but
Abraham was especially leery of her. He knew with the
certainty that autumn always follows summer—Karma would
surely break her mother's heart.

All in all, Abraham Ismine was a good man. Blame came
from good stock, and she wasn't very talkative—which he
admired. Plus, J'Rick and Karma both needed a man they could
look up to. There were things he could help with, teach them,
about country living, and life in general. He did enjoy their
company too, and Blame's cooking. They were his neighbors
after all, and the long lost family of Wilbur, his dear friend. He
felt obliged to do all he could to welcome them to Baylorton
and to help them settle in as easily as the hard country
permitted.

CHAPTER 23
B.R.O. BOUTIQUE

We spent most of our time revitalizing my great granddaddy Rone's old cinder block, general store...turning it into a boutique for my line of "Blame Rane Originals". It might be a shot in the dark—this boutique idea—but at least it's an opportunity. Even if I fail, at least it's an opportunity to try.

Besides, I have to create my own opportunities in Baylorton. This town is *way* different from any of the places I'd lived in before. Talk about racist! It doesn't really matter too much to me, though; as I imagine racism didn't concern my ancestors. On this farm, the next man's ideology doesn't faze me one bit. Hate can't touch me on my homeplace. I'm queen here, period.

I'll admit I'm a bit nervous about starting a business that caters to the women of Baylorton—a gossipy, meddling bunch, in my opinion. There just aren't enough men in this two-horse town to keep the hens settled down. But they know from the way I carry myself when I take my girls to town, we ain't about a bunch of country mess. We smile, exchange pleasantries and keep it moving. Anyway, my trips to town are few and far between. I prefer my farm to any other place on God's green earth. Like I said, I'm queen here.

We were busy installing the dressing room one day when a car pulled up in the small parking lot outside. Monica David, one of Abraham's many suitors, breezed through the open door. "Well hello, Abraham, I thought I'd find you up here," she walked right past me, without even a nod of acknowledgement, and leaned against the new dressing room door. As an afterthought, she rolled her eyes at me, forgetting to speak.

Now normally, I don't pay Abraham's harem any attention, but this particular chic really got under my skin. Old girl drove a raggedy, ancient Jaguar, sported a few low-grade jewels and kept her nose in the air. Back when I had it going on—with Ricco, and again with Nick—I could have bought a chic like Monica David with my lunch money. She thought she was a real big shot in the small town of Baylorton; and she couldn't stand me. And quite frankly, she got on my damn nerves.

I focused on polishing the wood of my refurbished counter, while Abraham, looking perturbed, led the skank outside to talk. I overheard him tell her to stop popping up on his jobsites. Then the chic got loud, and accused him of having something going on with me...throwing in something about a criminal record. Well that was it. The woman didn't even know me, and she really needed to keep my name out her mouth.

Since they *were* on *my* property, I handled my business. I may or may not have been interested in Abe; but I damn sure didn't care for Miss Monica. Besides, I can't be disrespected in my own store. So I made my way outside, did the white girl hair flip with my natural, and told her, "We're not open for business yet. So you're actually trespassing on private property and you really do need to leave." Then I thumped my cigarette butt in her direction, which landed beside the balding tire on her throwback Jag. Hell, the bitch didn't like me anyway; might as well give her a real reason to hate.

Her mouth dropped open and she looked to Abraham to defend her. He was clearly caught in the middle, so I helped him out with which side he needed to get on. "Mr. Ismine, we have a lot of work to do. Do you mind?" I smirked, and pranced back into the store. Like Tupac said, "I put a little twist in my hips cause they was watching." I didn't have to turn back, I knew he would follow. Abraham is all business and I was actually paying him by the hour for that day's work. Plus, don't get it twisted, I am Blame Rane, Ethel's daughter, and ex-con or not, I still got it going on. Abe was hot on my heels as a deflated Monica David peeled out of my parking lot. I couldn't help but laugh.

"I owe you one," he chuckled once we were inside, "that woman just will not leave me alone."

"Whatever...but she can't be stalking you up here...not on my dime. Anyway, y'all's relationship is y'all's business; but she and nobody else ain't about to come up in my store and disrespect me."

"Umph, I didn't know you were so feisty, Blame. And me and Monica are *not* in a relationship. As a matter of fact, I'm not in a relationship with anyone. But I am a man, with needs like any other man."

"Uhm hum. Don't front Abe, you telling them ladies something, and doing something too, to keep them coming around...hunting you down. Like I said, what you do is your business. Come on, let's finish up so I can get back to the house and get dinner started," I responded, handing him the knob he needed to install in the dressing room door.

He took the door knob, holding on to my hand a minute too long. "And what about you Blame? Don't you have needs like other women?" he asked, looking me dead in my eyes. I don't know why I blushed, but I did. I rolled my eyes and pulled away, and went back to polishing the counter. He got back to work on the dressing room. When I looked back a few minutes later to see how he was coming along, his knowing eyes were glued to my backside, and he was smiling.

Done with a day's work, we packed up the tools and equipment and drove down the lane to my house. We were a tight squeeze on the truck seat, and Abraham's leg, rubbing against mine, stirred up something rather carnal in me. Abe pointed to the tractor sitting in the field and asked, "How much do you think that's worth?" I answered with a reasonable figure and he nodded and smiled. He then asked, "And if you had to sell your farm Blame, which we know you would never do...but if you did, how much would you ask for it...house and all?" I couldn't figure out the point of the exercise, but I played along. I had no ready answer for that question...not a numerical one anyway. After much reflection, I answered, "there is no price, Abraham; because you're right...it's not for sale and never will be." The beautiful, full-toothed grin he offered told me I had given the right answer.

We unloaded equipment, transferring it my barn. Abe grabbed me from behind, by my hips and turned me around to face him. "And what about you, Blame? How much are you worth?" he asked, with passion in his eyes. My heart skipped a beat. I worried, for a second thinking he knew about my past—the times I sold myself for pennies on the dollar to the likes of Carl Crown—and wondered if was propositioning me? But, Abraham Ismine was not that kind of man; so I put the thought out of my mind. I thought about an answer, instead. Damn near 40-year old single mother, convict on parole, former drug dealer, landowner, struggling entrepreneur...no sum seemed adequate.

I remembered a line from *Their Eyes Were Watching God*, referring to Janie Crawford (before Teacake). Zora Neale Hurston wrote, "She didn't read books so she didn't know that she was the world and the heavens, boiled down to a drop." Well, I read books, hundreds of them, so I answered, "I am as priceless as the universe, Mr. Ismine...the whole world and the heavens, boiled down to a drop."

179

"Go head girl," he responded, laughing robustly. "What you know about Zora and "Watching God"?" I laughed too, as something in his eyes grabbed a hold of me. Something so deep and powerful, I couldn't name it and had nowhere to put it...so I turned away and finished putting away the equipment, blushing and trying to catch my breath.

Besides working on the boutique, Abraham also taught J'Rick how to use the tractor and farm equipment. They turned over a little piece of land out back and planted late season vegetables—squash and salad. J'Rick took to planting like he took to every other kind of work he was introduced to...he loved it. He couldn't' wait until next summer, going on and on about what all we would plant. Karma was in her own world, as usual, and Monique, missing her mamma, was ready to go home.

Abraham and I passed the evenings on his porch, or mine, reading books to each other and discussing everything under the sun. The man is deep, possessing such a wealth of information; and I enjoy our conversations, even the heated debates. Little moments continued to pass between us; but I can't afford to be another notch on his belt. I got too much on my plate...finances being front and center.

He has some fantastic reads, though, like hidden treasure. Reading all Abe's literature gave me a brand new appreciation for my fore parents. I admired their struggle and enterprise. I was slowly beginning to understand the true value of owning 39 acres of land. To hold on to the land, especially in the Jim Crow south was something short of a miracle! Abe's wealth of reading material was instilling in me, for the first time, a great sense of Black pride, and a solemn reverence for my persevering people who endured all manner of trials and tribulations

If we didn't have lights or heat (and you *know* how I feel about some heat!), I would make damn sure the property taxes got paid every year. Five generations of Ranes struggled to keep this place, and I'll be damned if I was gonna be the one to lose it. The knowledge I was gaining just gave me strength for the fight. Come hell or high water, I would not be moved. All I needed was a solid source of income to hold us down.

I hoped and prayed the boutique would do well. Lord knows I needed the cash. I sewed my butt off; and in a month's time, my line of Blame Rane Originals was ready for the showroom floor. Monique was especially helpful. Karma, however, had taken to wandering off daily, coming home just in time for dinner, because that child don't miss no meals. J'Rick kept showing up with things he swore he found on a jobsite, like used clothes racks, a cash register and boxes full of hangers. Before long my great-granddaddy's old general store was transformed into a posh little boutique...even if it was out in the middle of nowhere.

Nobody in Baylorton would give me a job; so I gave up on the search completely. I figured, hell, if my folks could make a go at it back in the day, then I could be an entrepreneur, too. Abraham said it was the Rane blood; I wasn't born to be a hireling; and it was my destiny to run the show! His entrepreneurial spirit has been such an inspiration to me. I said a long prayer the morning of the B.R.O. Boutique's Grand Opening. Then I waited.

My very first customer was Erma Wynn, the same lady who gave me directions when I first came to town. She lives on the other side of Rainier Place, just pass the trailer court. She brought her sister, Aggie, and her niece Rita with her. I was so fucking nervous! But Karma and Monique were cool as cucumbers and terrific at breaking the ice.

Erma's minivan was parked out front, and country folk being what they are, a few other ladies just *had* to stop in, too. They weren't about to let Erma be one up on them. Some of the Honduran ladies up the road came by, along with a group of giggling teenage girls, who kept asking if J'Rick was around. When the last customer left, I'd taken in a whopping $91.00!

OMG! I thought, and I thanked the God for answering my prayers. It might not sound like much to you, but it might as well have a million dollars, to me. I could sit at home and make money doing something I totally enjoyed! Life just doesn't get any better than that.

Abe was right when he said news in Baylorton travelled fast. The next day, I had a regular little flow of customers. Teenage girls brought their mothers, and pointed out the things they absolutely had to have for the upcoming school year. Monica David even dropped by; she knew if she wanted to be "dressed to impress" in Baylorton, she better get with these cutting edge Blame Rane Originals! Every day after was the same, and in no time, my boutique on the corner of Rane Lane was a sure fire hit!

At weeks end, I treated the family, Abraham included, to a celebratory dinner/going away party for the girls (they were headed to Maryland for the second half of the summer). Over dinner, Abraham, with his funny self, made us laugh until we cried. J'Rick, my good boy, was all smiles, even adding, with a big bear hug, that he was so proud of me. Hell, I was right proud of my damn self!

CHAPTER 24
THE SWEETEST THING

Tuppie

Sweetest thing I ever did see was the itty bitty toenail of a thing. The tiny crusty end piece that nobody wants—making it that much sweeter—was a brief whisper in *long* time, called: **segregation.** LORD IT WAS A BEAUTIFUL THING!

Imagine, if you can, all black communities, with general stores, tailors and schools, hospitals and restaurants, hotels and banks. I have seen it...tiny little crescents...just the toenail of a thing being born. Imagine, if you can, no assimilation, no crossover, no integration. Black folks was something powerful then...with an *economic plan*. Landowners, shopkeepers and schoolteachers...we took care of, and patronized our own. My heart warmed at the progress and the peace.

If you had seen the Black communities in east Winston-Salem, Goodwill (Madison) or Rainier Place (Baylorton), North Carolina; Eatonville, Fort Mose and Rosewood, Florida; Brownsville, Texas and Tulsa, Oklahoma; you would understand how segregation was a God send. *Sweet* segregation.

I have traveled the entire globe with the storytelling of crow, diving and reeling through space and time. What our eyes have seen, your mind cannot comprehend. I bear witness that when we were busy, incorporating our own towns, governing, policing, entertaining and educating ourselves; we lived like kings and queens. Left alone, we created enterprise. With only one another to do business with, we flourished. From music to literature to business and engineering endeavors, we *were* the beacon of light.

My own family was a part of that perfect Negro time—during and after the Reconstruction. We had our own land; we harvested and sold our own crops. We canned our own goods for winter. We even built a little store to serve the community, and our closest neighbors, the Ismine's, built the old colored schoolhouse on their property. In no time, our communities were ripe and overflowing with carpenters, blacksmiths, tinners, seamstresses, bakers, chefs, farmers, mechanics, preachers, nurses, dentists, politicians, singers, boxers, newspaper publishers, musicians, actors, business owners, traders, fishermen, shoemakers and jewelers.

Now granted, "Jim Crow" made it an uphill battle. But if we could come through the horn of slavery and survive; we could damn sure climb up a hill. If I've learned anything, it is this: When we got free, we should have stayed free. Niggers on the plantation now worse than we ever was—cause now its *voluntary*. It's much worse now than legs in chains. Today my people have shackled brains.

Regretfully, I watched the little toenail of freedom and economic independence, commit suicide. It slithered backward into the putrid belly of the beast. I saw all the people fleeing in droves...running away from what was good. It was confusing and chaotic and most backward. Like the children of Israel running out of the Promised Land, re-crossing at great peril, the Red Sea, backtracking to beat down Pharaoh's door, demanding readmission into Egyptland. That is what they looked like to me. I watched them leave the schools, hotels, restaurants, stores and hospitals they created...and claw, kick and beg their way back to their master; demanding he allow them to spend their pennies in his establishments—making him richer, themselves poorer. I saw them pleading with their former masters for a place in the back of the line; when, had we continued down the road of segregation, we would surely have taken the pole position.

Instead of marching forward, we marched on
Washington. Instead of making a run on land, we insisted upon
living next door to our open enemies. Instead of demanding a
job from our former masters, we should have continued to
create our own...we always do a thing better, anyway. You'll
never again see the kind of baseball that was played in the
Negro Leagues, or hear the kind of music that was dubbed the
Original Blues. Instead of protesting for humane treatment in
their shops and eating establishments, we should have
continued to patronize and invest in our own.

And *ohh*, the poor children. That fine fellow, Malcolm
X, once said, "Only a Fool would let his enemy teach his
children!" I've witnessed an era when the children were not
second-class citizens in the school system, but the cream of the
crop. Now our seeds, our precious little black boys in particular,
represent more than half of the nation's high school drop outs.
It's such a pity.

I fly back and forth, up and down, to every corner of
these United States, and I don't see any sign left of our
greatness. The way things were before we decided we should,
collectively, concentrate our efforts and energies into making
them love and accept us. Back when we had dignity, honor and
respect—for and from one another—and to hell with getting it
elsewhere!

Like Blame says, "Fuck them!" What did they have that
we didn't have? Better stuff, hunh? Better equipment, better
jobs, better wages... well we'd only just begun. We could have
surpassed them in no time—no matter the industry. Just like
the children of Israel, we spent our time worrying and
complaining and wishing we had a piece of Pharaoh's pie
instead of just baking our own...hell, we had all the ingredients.
All we had to do was believe in the power of ourselves.

Then, when the people really became confused and defeated, I watched them rush hard and fast to the wooden, brick, steel and vinyl sided buildings they called their churches. Running blindly, like this building here can save us. Nine times out of ten, the only thing happening in those buildings was a horse and pony show—more robbing and raping of the people. How foolish to believe salvation could be found in brick and mortar. Praying in open fields would have served them better, 'cause God don't live in no church...just pimpin preachers putting righteous money in their own slick silk pockets. The people had the power, always, to save themselves. Such a shame they didn't know it.

Yes, segregation was the sweetest thing I've ever seen! Oh, the growth it allowed my race. Instead of trying to fit in, we should have worked on passing laws to stay out. Rather than fight for inclusiveness, we should have demanded to be left alone. Imagine where we would have been today if we had continued the mantra "Separate but Equal." If left completely alone to grow into our perfection and into our season...hell, the toenail of it was beautiful, imagine an entire uplifted community! ...A nation, even! WOW!

But alas, the toenail got clipped away. It's lodged in a carpet somewhere in some rich man's abode. But you know how toenails are...they tend to linger around. I hope somebody can find it someday; resurrect it, nurture it and help it grow. I hope the people can be taught and then believe that we need to go for self, do for self.

Do you remember how we loved each other in those days, when we were all we had? How dignified, decent and clean we were. How we did not promote, nor allow, violence in our beautifully intertwined communities. Do you think we could do it again? This time let it grow up at least to the knee before we go trying to cut it off? I believe it is possible.

　　　　We, as a people, just need an economic plan, fuck a social plan. We don't need to be socially accepted, we accept and love ourselves. There are hundreds of acres of land for sale all over this country. Some of us should get together and buy some of it…start making self-sufficient black towns again. Some of us should pool our resources and create industry, banks, hotels and hospitals again. Use our tax money in our small black municipalities to benefit our own communities, our own schools, our own social programs.   And we should never beg for acceptance, inclusion or parity, again! We should concentrate solely on making ours the very best that it can be. And trust me, in time it would be the best thing in the world. We are so miraculous at making miracles!

　　　　But to achieve any of it…we'd have the one great task of first coming together. Now that's a mother. Willie Lynch knew what he was doing when he implemented a program of separation which would last for hundreds of years in the minds of its intended victims. If we could get beyond hating on one another, and learn to work together, I promise you we could get back to the Promised Land. I've seen it work for all the other races, and once upon a time, I saw it flourish for Us.

　　　　We can't depend on the politicians to do it. We have to depend on ourselves. Hell, politicians have their own agendas— defined by lobbyists and corporate interests. Even when we finally got a black president, he wasn't really Ours. His father was African, his mother Caucasian. He is not the same kind of Black that we are. He had not one single solitary ancestor come up through slavery. He cannot identify with our struggle, injustice or pain.

Stop waiting for someone else to make it right. YOU make it right, starting with yourself. Stop spending your pennies on foolishness. Get together with your people and turn your pennies into productive dollars...all the other races do it, right here in America. Why can't We?

We gotta go for self. Get together at the grassroots level. Sit down with your family, friends, and neighbors, have meetings and put together an *economic* plan to get you and yours at last out of slavery. Start amassing your resources. There is power in numbers, you know. Get your money together, and your workers and engineers and mechanics together, and open up the closed down plants and factories— jobs gone to China and Mexico. Make textiles, clothes, furniture, batteries and toys again. Trade with one another. Start you own stock market. You know we used to have a Black Wall Street. Invest in yourselves. Put those pennies back into your own community. Enough pennies can create a bank; that will lend to borrowers in your communities to start new projects for growth and development. Create your own retirement plans. Get your begging hand out of your master's face! He has nothing good for you!

If we can amass the kind of industry we have in the illegal trades of vice, just think what could be done if we didn't have to look over our shoulders, or figure out how to launder money. The hair alone these silly black girls are buying, making whites and Koreans and east Indians rich, is enough money on any given Saturday to launch any tech company worth its salt...open any manufacturing plant that can produce goods the whole world needs, and if not on a global scale...then a business serving the needs of our communities at home.

Now is the time to strike—while the iron's hot. There are no jobs? Create your own! We did it. EulaLee was an excellent seamstress, and that is how she brought money into the home. Jezzy and Rone, then Baptise and Doany were farmers and the crops they harvested and sold at market took us through the winters. I ran a store for Rone...in my old age! Mr. Ismine is going to turn that same old building into a boutique for Blame! Those men were carpenters, mechanics, you name it. And we didn't need but a little bit of cash money anyway. We lived in paid for houses. None of us were ever hoodwinked by a car payment or credit card debt. Not until Sherman, anyway, led so far astray by that woman of his. It's just foolishness what goes on these days! Folks putting their own selves back on the plantation!

In my day, after freedom came, we grew our own food, sewed our own clothes, built our own houses and made our own furniture. We vacationed at beachside resorts and inner city hotels owned by other black entrepreneurs. We bought music, books, and art created and published by our own artists. All we paid were taxes, period! The rest was gravy...icing on the cake...for things like Sylvester's piano in Rosewood...the tools and equipment a young son needs to branch off into a business of his own—adding to the whole...computers and scholastic materials necessary to start our own learning centers. We are a nation within a nation. We need to start behaving as such. All the other races do so. Why don't We?

Develop a plan for economic growth and independence. Two or three of you; 10 or twenty; 200 to 400 of you...just imagine what you could do TOGETHER. It doesn't take that much; less than you presently spend on vice. I guarantee it!

Buy the land. Bring your engineers home to design the cities your builders will build. Create the infrastructure, incorporate the towns, and tell Miss America, witch bitch, to kiss your collective asses. Go green and get off the grid. Create your own libraries, swimming pools and road-resurfacing crews...paid for with your own money.

Oh! The families we could boast; generations upon generations of black men and women knowing their fathers and mothers. Whole, intact families...and we all know what kind of strength and leadership that produces. Just imagine it, if you will.

But know too that the devil plans. So be steadfast and aware. He will be steadily working on a design of his own...a plan for your failure and demise. So shrewd they are...always thinking ahead, like Bob Marley's Sheriff... "he say kill it before it grow...he say kill them before they grow". And what a fine job they did...taking the shackles off our ankles and wrists and filtering them into our minds—locking our thinking brains down in bondage.

If only you knew what I've learned in death...those are the easiest shackles to break. You merely have to change your thinking. Gain some understanding as to why you think the way you do. Is there something wrong with it? Can it stand some improvement? Then seek out information that can guide you aright, and change your thinking. Voila! No chains.

Just look at Blame! Nobody was going to give her a job. She *had* to create her own. It may be a longshot, but I'll put my money on that horse every time. When you're up against it and you have zero room for error; things tend to work in your favor...as long as you believe in yourself. God blesses the child that's got his own, they say.

So go find that sweet little crescent of a thing and make it whole again. Get together and get it done—house by house, block by block, community by community. Don't keep talking about it children; be about it. Start today!

And for God's sake, **Love** each other!

CHAPTER 25
RANE BLOOD

J'Rick poured over the maps and deeds of the property. His Uncle Doany had bought up a lot of little plots and parcels from people over the years; and J'Rick's favorite pastime was walking the land, trying to figure out which section once belonged to Mr. Craft, Mr. David or Miss Brown. He was getting so he could walk the entire thirty-nine acres with his eyes closed—becoming familiar with every hill, holler and tree.

The only thing that puzzled him was the eight acres in the far northwest corner of the farm—knee-high in tobacco. The adjoining property—sixty-two acres belonging to Richard Noggin, called Dick—was completely planted in tobacco. J'Rick thought he was mistaken about the layout of the land, figuring that eight acres must have belonged to Noggin, because they certainly hadn't planted any cash crops. To be sure, he asked Mr. Ismine if he wouldn't mind taking a look at it.

Abraham hadn't been on that part of the Rane farm for a number of years. It was cut off from the rest of the property by a grove of tight pines and overgrown brush, and couldn't be reached by vehicle. He remembered it fondly as the secluded place where he and his friend, Wilbur, laid in the tall grass hunting deer...dreaming about their futures. Abe got some light gear together, and set off on foot through the pine with his young neighbor. When they finally came upon the clearing, Abe was shocked, to say the least.

"Well I'll be damned! You called it right J'Rick. When you told me tobacco was growing down here, I didn't know what to make of it. I figured, you being a city kid and all, you wouldn't know tobacco from tall grass. But you're right on the money, son. Looks like you've got a bad case of squatters!"

The men went to Abe's house and collected "No Trespassing" signs, stakes, wire, tools and a camera. Abe sent J'Rick back to the clearing to section off the Rane property, post the signs and document the crime. Meanwhile, he informed Blame what was going on, contacted the Sheriff's Department, and went to pay a visit to Dick Noggin.

Dick laughed in Abe's face and the Sheriff's Department dishonestly told them it was a civil matter, for the courts to decide. Blame filed the appropriate papers. When it became clear that the biased legal network would delay the proceedings until Noggin reaped his harvest, Blame decided to take matters into her own hands. She sent a certified letter to Mr. Noggin advising, since he'd already planted the crops, she would lease the land to him, and demanded immediate payment. (Abraham told her what the fair price for leasing eight acres would be.) She found the letter a week later, in the parking lot of her boutique, a wad of chew spat upon it. With no recourse left, Blame and J'Rick got in the truck (Karma and Monique were in Maryland), and paid a visit to Abraham's old Uncle Mack, to ask him, "Sir, how do you harvest tobacco?"

When the crops matured, they battened down the hatches and circled the wagons. Blame, Abe, Mack and J'Rick, along with their neighbors, the Wynns and Gutierrez', harvested the entire eight acres in one day. They worked as a team, pulling up the plants, loading Abe's trailer, and standing guard with loaded guns. They made a party of it, playing Bob Marley loudly on a boom box, eating boiled peanuts, passing around a jug of Uncle Mack's finest, telling jokes, and daring the Noggins to cross the barbed wire boundary. The Sheriffs were called out; but knew better than to trespass on private property. Someone even had the foresight to bring a video camera.

192

While Sam Cooke sang "A Change Is Gonna Come", Mr. Noggin screamed to the sheriff, "Them nigg...they got guns!" Each gun handler politely handed his registration over the barbed wire fence for the officers' inspection. Those carrying rifles were within their legal limits without any paperwork. The authorities retreated. Dick Noggin was not a violent man; he'd just underestimated his opponent. He bowed his head in defeat and even laughed at the irony.

As the sun set, the group sewed and hung the harvest in Uncle Mack's old tobacco crib to cure. In time, Abe and Blame took the crop to market. Blame divided the proceeds among the neighbors who stood by her. Uncle Mack got a little more for the use of his barn. And J'Rick, discoverer of the faux pas, and the man who owned the land, deservingly received the lion's share.

A chain-link fence was put across that parcel, officially and forever separating it from Richard Noggin's place. J'Rick and Abraham made regular rounds to ensure there were no other violators. Since it was good earth, Marco Gutierrez asked Blame if he and a few friends could lease it for the next year's tobacco season. Blame conferred with her children and gladly obliged—charging a little less than the rate they'd offered Dick Noggin.

Their stand was talked about in every house in Baylorton. Some people repeated the tale with scorn, others with pride...depending on the teller and the audience. It was widely understood that Blame Rane and her kids were definitely the blood relation of the legendary Rone Rane, and his shrewd boy, Doany. A land-owning Rane was a serious person, not to be trifled with or tested. Nobody was quite sure what part of the North they came from; but everyone agreed they were now home...and home to stay.

CHAPTER 26
A DOG WILL RETURN TO ITS VOMIT

Keisha Lorraine Murdoch made her final rounds, checking on the welfare of her patients, lingering too long in Miss Isley's room—a patient who received no visitors—just so the old woman could see a friendly face and engage in polite conversation. She called Monique to be sure she'd gotten in from school and completed her homework. And then, in a roundabout manner, she asked Monique about her father's mood. Monique peeked down the hallway to see if her dad was still napping, then told her mother everything was everything.

Keisha and Ricco were married behind bars, when he was on short time at the work camp. They'd excitedly gone downtown to have Monique's last name changed to Murdoch. Monique could have cared less. Her father was always moody and temperamental. Nothing her mother did was good enough; and he paid Monique little to no attention.

In the three months he'd been home; Ricco had been unable to find a job. He blamed everybody in the world for his shortcomings, but himself. Keisha kept assuring him there was no hurry. She was an RN and could easily hold things down, financially, with or without his help. But the more she stroked his fragile ego, the worse his behavior got.

So, being the patient and long-suffering woman that she was, she started thinking up things for Ricco to do—things that might make him feel useful. The deck needed to be pressure washed and the kitchen sink leaked. Could he take care of that, please? She pretended not to know what a pipe wrench was, even though she had one in her well established toolbox. She was suddenly inept at grilling steaks...could he show her how it was done? And oh the money she could save on lube jobs, if only she knew how... "Ricco, do you know how to change the oil and check the transmission fluid? Oh, such a blessing." Then finally, the bumper-to-bumper traffic on her commute to John Hopkins was frightful...could he drop her off and pick her up, too? He didn't know what a help that would be. She thanked him endlessly.

Ricco had to retrieve the spices from the top shelf so Keisha could prepare dinner. (Keisha was too little to reach them, and Ricco, being such a big, tall, strong man, was just right for the job.) After dinner, the awkward family sat around the table and tried to make small talk. Keisha talked about Miss Isley, her patient in room 210. Monique reminded her mother she needed her dance boots by Friday...repeating again the name of specialty store in downtown D.C. that had the boots in stock. Ricco talked about "the man" being on his back, and how somebody needed to blow up the whole damn congress...bunch of rich ass faggots, he said, who couldn't cut it in the real ass streets he came from. Mother and daughter went to bed, while husband/father sat brooding on the supple leather sofa, babysitting a bottle of Bombay gin, and catching up on the latest with Sports Center. He paced the floor for the better part of the night, bothered by a little itch...which needed scratching.

The next day, as Keisha was getting out of her Volvo, she handed Ricco a hundred dollar bill and reminded him of the address to the specialty store holding Monique's dance boots. She told him the boots were being held under the name "Murdoch", and she beamed when she said it. Keisha turned to go into the hospital, but turned back, thinking of something else to say. Ricco had already peeled out of the parking lot, radio blaring and wheels screeching. She took a deep breath, pressed down the front of her smart scrubs and went inside the sliding glass doors to do her job.

"Ahhhh, now this is what I'm talking about." Ricco mused, as he neared the fast-moving, ghetto sprawl of downtown D.C. The streets were packed! He reclined the Volvo's driver's seat a little more, tilted his ball cap just so, and turned up the radio a little louder—mentally bashing Keisha for not having a "real" system. He double-parked on his old familiar block, just outside the Chinese Restaurant, and took a long look around. The more things changed, he noted, the more they remained the same. It took three months of searching since his release from prison for Ricco finally find what he was looking for.

Monique sat in the bay window, cursing and peering out into the rainy street, waiting for her mother to come home. Finally, she heard the brakes of the city bus and noticed her mother's familiar scrubs just up the sidewalk, underneath a polka dot umbrella which she didn't recognize. Monique cursed again, wondering , "what the fuck was her mother doing taking a city bus home when she had a damn brand new Volvo with ridiculous payments?" Whether Keisha wanted to hear it or not, Monique was definitely going to give her a piece of her young mind.

Keisha walked through the opened front door and shook rain off the umbrella she'd had to borrow from a co-worker. "Any news?" she asked her daughter as she dropped her purse on the foyer chair.

"No mamma. He hasn't been here and he hasn't called. Why did you let him keep your car? Why is he even staying here? I'm tired of this mess! And I hate him! You need to tell him to leave!"

Keisha reached out to console her daughter, but Monique thwarted her advances by retreating to the kitchen. "Monique, honey, you have to understand; coming out of prison is a hard transition. We have to be patient, your daddy will come around, baby. It's just gonna take a little time for him to get acclimated to society."

"Mamma *please*. He's a bum! He's mad at the world and he's not even trying. We don't need him. We do fine without him. Miss Blame had sense enough to leave him alone. Why don't you?!"

"Just hush, Monique! And watch your mouth little girl. I need to think! When was the last time you heard from him?" she asked, going to the kitchen to start dinner.

"Last night at dinner, just like you, mamma. I told you he hasn't called or been home all day. He probably stole your car! You need to dead his broke down butt!" Keisha tried to ignore her daughter's good sense. She looked over Monique's homework and kept finding a reason to go in the front room and peek out the window. She was still looking into the empty street at four a.m. when she fell asleep on the sofa.

The following morning, Keisha put her daughter on the school bus; then boarded the city bus to her job. She went through the day in a haze, was even tacit and short with Miss Isley. She kept telling herself it would be okay. When she got home, her car would be in the driveway and Ricco would be there to explain. Monique would just have to get over it. They were a family, and everything would be just fine. Still, she kept calling the cell phone she'd bought for Ricco, but got no answer.

Three days later, Friday evening, Ricco finally showed up. Monique was crying. The middle school football game was starting in less than an hour, and without her boots she wouldn't be performing at halftime. Monique raced to the door when she heard the car pull up, still hopeful there was enough time to get her uniform, boots included, and get to the field. The pitiful, raggedy man stumbling out of the Volvo made her want to vomit. Keisha moved in front of her daughter and ordered her to her room.

"But I have to get to the game, mamma. Come on; let's just get my boots and go!"

"Monique," Keisha yelled, "Go to your room!"

A woman's intuition works independent of the woman. So for some odd reason, Keisha moved her purse, with her cashed payroll in it, from its normal spot on the foyer chair. She scrambled around and quickly stuffed it up in the fireplace chimney. Then stood in the front door and waited for Ricco to enter.

He smelled like he hadn't bathed in three days, because he hadn't. His eyes were wild and filled with a deep-seeded need, which Keisha instantly knew she did not have the power to sate. She stopped him at the door and asked for her keys, her hundred dollars and her cell phone. He pushed past her and made a beeline for the pots on the stove. He ate directly from the pots with the serving spoon, washing his meal down with the corner of hot gin he'd left in the cupboard. Keisha sat quietly, waiting until he was done. Little Monique stood in the hallway, waiting as well.

Ricco," she finally started, "where were you? Why didn't you call, or at least answer your phone. We were worried about you. And where are Monique's dance boots?"

"Woman, would you shut the fuck up?! A man can't even eat in peace around here!" He scratched his neck and polished off the corner of liquor.

Keisha tried again, "Ricco, you can't just leave for days at a time and then show up with no explanation. What's going on? You owe me an answer, Ricco. And give me my keys, please."

He scratched his neck some more, then his face and arms. She'd seen it before—it was called a dope itch, and there was only one known cure. She dropped her face in her hands and began to cry.

"Ahhh, Keish, come on, man. It ain't even like that. I been taking care of some business. Making some moves so we can get back on top. I seen my niggah Drake and we gone put a plan together, but I'ma need a coupla dollars to get it popping. You know how it is. It take money to make money, baby. So I needed to borrow that l'il change you gave me. But don't sweat it. When I get on my feet, Monique gone have twenty pairs of boots in whatever color she want! I promise I'ma make this up to you baby. But I do need about another $200.00 to get this ball rolling. Where yo bank card, baby?"

"*Ricco,* you promised," Keisha cried. "No more drugs. You promised. I waited on you for more than 10 years and this is how you repay me? How could you, Ricco? Why?!"

Monique bolted from the hallway and launched at her father, "you sorry son of a bitch! You spent my boot money getting high?! Give my mamma her damn keys and get the fuck out this house!" Her rage had led her to the chair he was sitting in. She was suddenly beating him in his back and head and she couldn't stop—her body jerking from sobs. Perhaps it was self-defense, more likely, just plain meanness, but Ricco backhanded her off of him. His daughter slid across the kitchen floor and into the dishwasher. Keisha sprang to her feet, like any other mother tiger, but she was too late. Ricco caught her in mid-air with a punch to her jaw that sent her sprawling into the warm stove. He stormed through the house looking for her purse. Keisha, covered in their supper, reached to comfort Monique. Monique pushed her away, and pulled her cell phone from her jean pocket. Keisha snatched the phone from her daughter and, not knowing who else to call, she dialed Blame.

"Blame!" she screamed, when her friend came on the line. "Blame help me! He's gone crazy!"

Ricco rounded the kitchen corner in a furious rage and asked "Blame?! What the fuck that bitch gone do for you? She know good and goddamn well I'll whip that ass if she even think about coming over here. I thought you said she was in North Carolina anyway. Give me that damn phone!" He snatched the phone from Keisha's grip and dashed it to the floor, crushing it under his boot. Monique meanwhile, crawled past him and ran out the door for help. Because Keisha was on the ground, Ricco kicked her, over and over, demanding to know where her purse was. She kept crying and screaming, yelling and pleading for him to stop. When he heard the sirens, he threw the keys at her, hitting her in the lip, and bolted out the back door into the woods.

Monique and their neighbor, Mr. Shaw, returned to find Keisha sprawled out unconscious on the kitchen floor. Mr. Shaw put his baseball bat down and picked her up out of the floor. Monique ran through the house with Mr. Shaw's butcher knife, looking for her father. He was nowhere to be found. The ambulance came from John Hopkins and took Keisha and Monique to Keisha's job, for emergency medical attention. Mr. Shaw locked up her house, held onto her keys, and stayed vigilant on the lookout for her sorry ass man.

CHAPTER 27
ME AND YOU US NEVER PART

They were sitting at the dining room table playing a game of bid whist. Blame wasn't expecting a phone call, but was pleasantly surprised when the caller id read: K L Murdoch. Immediately into the conversation, she clutched the table and winced in agony. J'Rick leapt to his feet and was about to swat the phone away, thinking it was somehow causing his mother pain. Karma cried, "What is it mamma?!" feeling her mother's distress.

Blame pounded her fist into the table over and over and kept screaming, NO! NO! NO! Keisha? Keisha? Please say something, Keisha?!" Abraham looked on in bewildered astonishment, ready to spring into action, but not knowing exactly what to do.

Her feet wouldn't move fast enough. "Dammit where are those keys?" she screamed. Blame ran to J'Rick's room and took his rifle down from the gun rack. She snatched her purse off the table on her way out the door, and ran barefoot to the barn where they kept the truck parked.

J'Rick was hot on her heels. "Mamma what's wrong?"

"Your damn sorry ass daddy is what's wrong!" she threw over her shoulder, her brown curls blowing in the wind behind her. "I don't know J'Rick. That was Keisha! She's in trouble. You keep trying to get her on the phone. Tell her I'm on my way!" She threw her purse through the open passenger window and ran around to the driver's side, oblivious to the damage she was doing to her bare feet. Abraham and Karma raced to the barn door, placing themselves between the truck and the entryway. Blame revved the engine, blew the horn and told them to move it! She inched forward and they, along with a trio of nervous birds, retreated.

But J'Rick did not. He jumped on the running board and tossed himself into the truck as it raced up Rane Lane. Abraham and Karma got in his car and followed; they could hear Blame and J'Rick screaming at each other inside the Chevy. J'Rick wrestled with his mother, and being stronger, managed to snatch the keys from the ignition and throw the truck in park. As it came to a screeching halt, Blame jerked forward hitting her head on the steering wheel.

"Mamma, you a convict on parole!" he screamed. "Where the hell do you think you're going with a loaded rifle?! Mamma I'm sorry," he added embracing her face and kissing her head where it'd met the steering wheel, "but please, it's got to be a better way. I can't lose you again, please mamma! You ain't making no sense!"

Abraham and Karma were at the truck by this time; Abe's eyebrows raised at this "convict" statement. But he didn't have time to really consider the newsflash. This was a family in crisis and all he wanted was to somehow help. He just didn't know how.

Blame fought and screamed and pushed Ricco away from her, "You don't understand boy. He's gonna kill her, if he hasn't already. Let me go! I gotta help her. I damn near owe that girl my life. If I had lost y'all when I went away, I wouldn't have a life worth living. Let me go J'Rick! You just don't know what I know! The man is capable of murder!"

J'Rick, crying as well, yelled, "Why don't I know, mamma? What, you think I was too little to remember? I remember mamma! Who you think was trying to keep Karma quiet when she was a baby, cause he hated to hear her crying. Who mamma?! Who you think had to lay with they baby sister

202

under the bed and listen to him beating on you...knowing I was too little to take him. Who mamma? What you mean I just don't know? Why the hell you think I'm sitting in this truck? Why the hell you think I'm in North Carolina? I'm with *you* mamma. I'm not a little boy no more. And I ain't never gone let nobody hurt you again. Not as long as I'm breathing. And I ain't gone let you hurt your damn self either. So get out this truck! We'll call the police. We can drive up there right now if you want to. But you ain't going nowhere by yourself, and you damn sure ain't getting sent back to prison for riding through three states with a loaded rifle! If my daddy need his fucking wig split, I'll be the one splitting it!" J'Rick snatched up the rifle and beat his chest, sobbing and crying like a baby, but feeling like a full grown man.

Abraham wrapped his big bear arms around the young man until he calmed down. With his shirt front soaked through with J'Rick's snot, slobber and tears, he slowly took his own rifle from the boy's shaking hands. Karma had run around the truck to try and comfort her mother when her cell phone rang. It was her baby sister Monique, calling from the hospital. They were okay. Blame dropped down from the cabin of her truck and ran around the hood to embrace her son. Her feet ached from the pine cones and sharp pieces of gravel in the road. Mr. Ismine took a step back as Blame squeezed her good boy, holding him tight to her heart.

They cried and cried, and Blame kept repeating through her tears, "Thank you son. You're a good boy. Thank you for loving me. I love you J'Rick. You're a good son. Thank you." They remained frozen that way, in the darkness, in the middle of Rane Lane for a very long time...with three birds humming a solemn refrain.

203

CHAPTER 28

RANE PRODUCE

May 2009

J'Rick loved working the ground, even more than the trade he was learning from Mr. Ismine. He had a stellar sophomore year at Baylorton High, and his junior year was turning out to be even better. At 6' 5", he was a standout on the basketball team, and his coach said he was shoo-in for a college scholarship. Even though he was popular with all the kids, he couldn't wait for school to get out. J'Rick was extremely ready, almost aching, to farm.

When he wasn't in school, playing basketball or working with Mr. Ismine, he spent his time on the land. J'Rick knew every inch of his farm—which soil would produce and which soil wouldn't. He remained vigilant, on the lookout for squatters; but the town of Baylorton knew, just like the Ranes of old, this new generations of Ranes weren't playing, either. Besides being educated on legal matters, they were gun-toting and fearless, and very serious about maintaining what was theirs.

J'Rick planted a half acre garden for his mother the previous summer. He loved turning over the soil, sowing the seeds, tending it every day—watering, weeding, and pruning. He especially loved to reap what he'd sown. This year, he had bigger plans. Inspired by his mother's thriving boutique, he decided to open a produce stand. He'd do the ground work, and Karma, who'd just turned fourteen, could sell the goods. She needed something to do to get her mind off boys anyway. People were starting to talk about his sister, saying nasty things; and she wasn't even in high school yet.

J'Rick jumped off the school bus at the top of his road, with his steady girlfriend, Rita Wynn, and went into his mother's shop. There weren't any customers at that time of day, so Rita dropped her books and went right to work, hanging clothes and rearranging the shelf of Mrs. Gutierrez' whatnots. Blame hired Rita to work part time, and she allowed Isabel Gutierrez, a neighbor down the street, to sell handmade pottery out of the boutique.

J'Rick sauntered thru the swinging doors (which he'd hung himself) to the back of the store, to check in on his mom. Blame was sitting in one of the chairs he'd salvaged from the dumpster of a jobsite. She looked tired. "You okay momma?" he asked, bending down to peck her on the cheek.

Blame spit phlegm into a napkin pressed against her lips, and smiled up at her son, "I'm fine, son. How was your day at school?"

"It was cool. Three more weeks to go! Where's Karma?"

"Your guess is as good as mine. She didn't stop by when she got off the bus. I guess she's at the house. You working today?"

"No. Mr. Ismine doesn't have anything for me this week. I think I'll start building my produce stand. Where should I put it?"

"You and that produce stand," Blame laughed, and ducked her cigarette. "That's all you talk about. You got thirty-nine acres, boy, put it wherever you think is best."

"Bet. Well I'ma go see if Karma wants to help. Rita already clocked in out front. You need anything from the house?" he asked, scooping up the truck keys from the little desk he'd built.

"As a matter of fact, bring me my address book. I need to write a letter to my friend, Beverly."

J'Rick gave Rita a little smooch on his way out the door. He drove down Rane Lane, past the house and barn, and went to check on his vegetable garden. In the last month, he and Mr. Ismine had sown nearly three acres, with everything from squash to cucumbers, peppers to green beans, corn to cantaloupe, tomatoes to okra. It was too soon for anything to be coming up, but they'd had a lot of rain and heavy wind lately and he was worried about the ground being so moist. He picked up a post knocked down by the heavy winds, repositioned it in the earth and inspected his crops.

J'Rick expected the ground to be soggy; but the dry earth crunched underneath his feet. He recalled Mr. Ismine saying, "Wind dries the ground faster than anything, because it pushes the water... you should watch the wind push the water, J'Rick. Hell, by itself, the wind's called a tornado. When it pushes the water, it's a hurricane." And sure enough, he was right. The soil dried nicely; seeds and slips were doing just fine.

J'Rick went back to the house to find Karma. She was nowhere to be found. He made himself and Rita a sandwich, got his mother's address book, and went to the barn to load the truck with the materials he needed to build his produce stand. There were a few things he'd purchased or salvaged from jobsites; but the lumber was donated my Mr. Ismine. He checked around the house and barn one more time for Karma; then went back up the road to start on his project. Mr. Ismine offered to help with the produce stand, but J'Rick declined. He wanted to do this by himself, assuring his neighbor he would let him know if he ran into a problem he couldn't handle alone.

Abraham's 82-year-old Uncle Mack came to watch, and supervise. He rambled up in his '57 Chevy and unloaded his supplies: a lawn chair, crossword book, a can of sardines with crackers, and a flask of his county-renowned moonshine—made from his own daddy's historic still. He looked over the tools J'Rick had assembled for the job, and, being pleased with what he saw, told the boy to carry on.

J'Rick struck the ground with his posthole digger, churning up rich earth, and Uncle Mack said, "You know that's your dirt boy...thirty nine acres wide and all the way to China deep?"

"Yes sir, Uncle Mack. I know."

"Good. Proceed."

While J'Rick mixed cement, Uncle Mack looked up from his crossword puzzle and said, "Boy you know if your vegetables ain't top quality you'll be the shame of six generations of Rane?"

"Yes Sir, Uncle Mack. They gone be right."

"Oh yeah, well, I'll see. You know I got my eye on you, boy."

"Yes Sir, Uncle Mack."

"Ahn hahn...put some more cement in them holes, Rane. Damn sto gone fall down 'fore your squash come in, boy."

"Yes Sir, Uncle Mack."

J'Rick started drilling screws into what would be the frame, and the old man took another hearty sip from his flask and asked, "What color you gone paint?"

"Don't know yet, sir. I haven't thought about it."

Well you better think about it. Your great-great grandpappy Rone didn't 'llow no mess up here on this corner. You gone do it, you better do it right. You hear me boy?"

"Yes Sir, Uncle Mack, I know. What color *you* think I should paint it?"

Abraham stopped by at dusk, on his way home, to see how things were progressing, and to look in on Blame. His Uncle Mack, flask empty, was asleep in the lawn chair. A cardinal, crow and pigeon were dozing as well, on a limb overhead. J'Rick and Abraham helped load each other's trucks. They put the tools on J'Rick's truck, and Uncle Mack into Abe's truck.

"You need some help with him, Mr. Ismine?" J'Rick asked.

"No, I'm good. I'll put him in the downstairs bedroom at my house...he swears it's his room anyway. Here, give his keys to your mamma. Ask her to drive over after supper, will you? And bring me a plate of whatever she's cooking."

"Yes Sir, Mr. Ismine. See you tomorrow."

By the time 12 year-old Monique came down for her summer visit, Rane Produce was up and running. She was impressed with the construction and joked saying, "Wow, it will be a whole strip mall up here when I come back next summer." J'Rick paid his little sister a small allowance to work the stand, though she would have done it for free. There wasn't much else to do in that part of the country; especially with Karma always running off somewhere, without her. Monique didn't mind though, she loved her "Mama Blame's" farm, with wild turkey and deer gathering in the backyard, and the lake she could fish in whenever she wanted. She played chess with Mr. Ismine, fed his Boer goats, and teased him endlessly about being Mama Blame's boyfriend, since they spent their evenings together talking the nights away on each other's porches.

When she wasn't in the produce stand, next door pestering Mr. Ismine, or frolicking in the countryside; Monique spent her time in the boutique with Blame, learning about business and helping when she could. She received a new video camera for Christmas and was doing a documentary on Uncle Mack...which was right down his alley.

Monique exercised a lot, not wanting to become fat like her big sister, Karma. She thought that was the reason Karma was so distant...so secretive and sad. She missed spending time with her sister, who only came home for supper. Mr. Ismine said Karma was having growing pains. J'Rick and his girlfriend, Rita, were inseparable, always sneaking off to the barn. Monique made the most of her annual visits to North Carolina; it was better than the concrete camps she used to attend in summer. She talked to the cat, Felicity, in Karma's absence— even when Karma was there—and waited for her sister to finish her growing pains, and come back to normal...so things could be the way they used to be.

CHAPTER 29
BLAME RANE

I woke up this morning praising and thanking the Divine for my abundant life. My home is safe and comfortable, paid for and clean. My children are healthy, seemingly happy. I can support myself...what more could a woman ask for? Well, I guess it would be nice to have a man in my life; but Abe's just next door. He's good company.

I talked to my girlfriend, Keisha, last week. I hate to see her hurting, because she's been such a blessing to me. She's worried about tracking Ricco down for child support...like that's gonna happen. I understand her being bitter and angry though, especially about the beatdown she and Monique took. I offer the little bit of wisdom I've learned in life—urging her to move on. Point blank, we chose poorly when we chose that guy; that's all there is to it. Still, I feel for Keisha because I *was* her, a hundred times over.

I was there when he was a junkie on the run...got the false teeth to prove it...sitting in the emergency room with two crying babies and my mouth busted open, wondering what *I* was doing wrong? I was there when we lost everything; and I couldn't do *anything* right, standing by my man. I was Ricco's sounding board, punching bag and pleasure palace. Can't believe I had *two* babies for that niggah. What the hell was I thinking? Silly me, guess I *wasn't* thinking. But it's all good; J'Rick and Karma are the light of my life. Today I can honestly say I'm not mad at Ricco. He's just a bad guy; *I* was the fool— young and dumb. I just didn't know any damn better.

Hell I didn't learn any sense until I was forty years old. And Lord knows I'm still learning every day. I was blinded by the bullshit Ricco was feeding me—cars, clothes, jewelry, trips, a comfortable, *warm* place to stay. I had everything my mother yearned for, and then some. Lost it all and got it back again, in Dale City. But the price I paid for shit I didn't even need was too great; up to and including two years in state prison. When I walked out of that place with nothing but the clothes on my back, I felt so free!

I don't know why I thought I needed all that shit. Thinking like my mamma, I guess. I'm so thankful to Most High I don't think like that anymore...fake ass, self-created stress will give you a heart attack. And what does it really matter anyway. All my mamma's "stuff" burned up in a fire...damn near making her life meaningless. I now know the greatest treasures I have are the love and support of my family and friends.

I read an article the other day that said: American women of color spend $180million *every* weekend just on hair care, movies and church! Imagine the total when you throw in clothes, shoes and makeup, too! It's right pitiful. I wish sisters could get together and use that money to change our lives and the lives of our children forever. I know. I know...wishful thinking. I doubt we'll ever truly come together on anything. I spent two years in a prison full of women—all in the same damn boat—who couldn't think of anything better to do than hate each other...such a pity and a waste.

I believed in *myself* though, and B.R.O. Boutique paid off. I make enough money to care of what I need to care of, here at home...enough to keep my ass out of prison anyway. And I don't just mean the kind with steel bars. I'm fighting now to stay out of the prisons of domestic violence, consumerism, self-doubt and poverty.

I can't change or save the world, but I can be an example to my children. I don't gossip, and I reach out to people with love; or I just leave them alone. I refuse to let anybody or anything break my peace. I've been through too much to get here. And not just me, generations of Ranes have lived and died so we can live free, in this little piece of heaven.

Now don't get me wrong, we have our trials and tribulations; but the stress level is at a minimum. At least we're together. When I got caught up in that mess in Dale City; I didn't know if I was ever going to see my children again. That taught me something about the power of prayer. When I was at my lowest point, getting ready to go prison, thinking I would lose my children to the system, I prayed. Looking back on it now, I know God directed me to Keisha. If I had lost my kids, I sincerely believe I might have died or gotten killed in prison. The shit those bitches did to me in there...if I didn't have my kids to come home to, I swear I probably would have just murdered somebody...maybe even myself.

But, praise the Beneficent, we came through it alright, and I have my beautiful family right here with me. I couldn't have a better son than J'Rick, period. When Uncle Mack tells us the stories his grandparents told him about him about little Rone Rane, I think about J'Rick. There Rone was, six years old and newly freed, being the little man his mamma and grandma needed him to be. He never complained and never faltered. That's my J'Rick, hands down.

And Karma...well...Karma's Karma. She reminds me of myself so much when I was her age...so quiet. My mamma *wouldn't* talk to me. I'm here for Karma; she just won't let me in. I tell her all the time how pretty she is, and how much better she would feel about herself if she just lost some weight. And Lord you should hear my baby sing! Anyway...I reckon she'll come around one of these days.

Listen to me...talking about "I reckon"...this country life will sure rub off on you. To see me now, you would never guess

I lived in the projects in DC or in a steel and concrete cage. Yeah, life is good now a' days. I'm in a new place in my life and I loving every minute of it!

Like I said, I have a beautiful (**paid for**) home, a thriving business, and a strong family. I really enjoy spending time with Abraham, too; we have an intense connection. He's so easy to talk to, I find myself sharing things with him, feelings and thoughts, I've never discussed with another soul. Every once in a while he'll make some little comment about taking things further; but I shut that conversation down before it even gets started. Our relationship is good just the way it is; I don't want anything to complicate or ruin it. It's just nice to have someone to talk to; especially when that someone makes you laugh and think and dream. ...But, we'll see.

All in all, I can't cry or complain. Like Bill Wither's said about tears, "wasted water's all it is, and it don't make no flowers grow." Honestly though, I haven't been feeling well. I still have a chill I've been unable to shake since I lived in my daddy's Buick (which I'm thankful he had for me). But there's something else ailing me too; I can't quite put my finger on. Oh well, no fret. I am getting a little older. Plus I've had some pretty tough years...I guess it's finally taking a toll on my body. I know better than to sweat the small shit, so I don't dwell on it. My life is too damn good...too *easy* now to worry about the apparent onset of middle age.

I pray and thank the Creator daily, for health, happiness and my innumerable and wondrous blessings. I'm grateful to all the people who helped me get here, starting with my ancestors...people who I never knew, but who have shaped my life, guiding and helping me in crazy incredible ways. My mamma, regardless of her faults, did teach me how to sew; and that's how I earn my living these days. GranSue had to teach

213

her. My daddy said GranSue was the most God-fearing and best woman he's ever known. GranSue had to get that from somewhere; so I am grateful to the generations that preceded her as well, even if I don't know their names.

According to my daddy, his daddy, Baptise, and his uncle Doany were larger than life; and his grandpa Rone, who was like a lion, was never a boy. Let daddy tell it, Rone Rane was born a man. Uncle Mack says, of the women who raised Rone, my Grandma Jezzy would do *anything* for her family...and her mother, granny Tuppie, was queen supreme, the salt of the earth. He says I have her hands and her figure, too. I didn't know them; but they are my family, and I'm grateful to them. Without their existence and struggle, I wouldn't be sitting here on this porch today.

I am thankful too for my friends: Beverly, Keisha, Abe and Mack, and my cool neighbors, the Wynn's and Gutierrez'. I appreciate Maxine, the prison guard, who helped open and expand my mind, and Adrienne, the prison counselor who reignited my passion for sewing. Shit I'm even thankful for Toria, Ricco, Nick, Charlene, Joey *and* Carl. If nothing else, at least I learned some hard lessons from them. Oh! and I can't forget Mrs. Douthit. She wasn't the warmest woman in the world; but she gave me food when I was hungry and shelter from the storm. And one day, back in '89, she made the earth stand still for me. God bless her.

I appreciate the cat, Felicity, too. She's good company. Her, and those birds of mine...a crow, a pigeon and a cardinal that, believe it or not, follow me around this farm. But mostly, I am thankful to my Maker for finally bringing me _home_.

CHAPTER 30
STAKING CLAIM

Blame's head nearly spun around on her shoulders as the taxicab whizzed by the boutique, taking a sharp right onto Rane Lane. She wasn't expecting any company. She rushed Mrs. Jacob into the fitting room and called the house. Karma answered, and when her mother told her a cab was coming down their road, Karma hung up the phone and nearly tripped over the ottoman trying to get to the front door. She was expecting him earlier that morning...when she told her mother, at breakfast, she had a surprise for her when she got home.

The cab driver laid on the horn, not allowing his passenger to exit until someone came outside to pay the fare. Marco Gutierrez knew Blame Rane was an upstanding woman and a good neighbor. She even let him lease some of her land for farming and she let his wife, Isabel, sell handmade pottery out of her boutique. Everybody in the trailer park knew she was a woman of fine character; but he didn't know this passenger he'd picked up at the bus station, and he wasn't about to get suckered out of another fare.

Karma opened the door, all smiles. The passenger yelled from the backseat of the cab, "Get some money to pay this man, baby girl!" Karma raided her mother's pickle jar of $5's and $10's, paid Marcos—asked about his son, Armando—then showed her guest, with his one worn duffel bag, into the house. By the time Marco reached the top of Rane Lane, Blame was standing underneath the shady awning at the produce stand, flagging him down.

"Good afternoon Marco, did you or Isabel need to see me about something?"

"No ma'am, Miss Rane. I just took a fare to your house. Some guy I picked up at the bus station. It's okay though, Karma knows the guy. Have a good day, Miss Rane," Marco replied, before turning back out onto Rainier Road. Blame stepped back inside B.R.O. Boutique and finished up with Mrs. Jacob. Then she put her "out to lunch" signs on the boutique door and produce stand, and walked down Rane Lane to see what was going on at her house.

"Blame it on the Rain! Hey baby!" Ricco called from the porch swing, as Blame neared the house. "Long time no see. You looking mighty damn good, girl! I like your hair curly like that. Come on up here and give me sugar, mama."

Blame rolled her eyes and rolled up her shirt sleeves. "What the hell are you doing here, Ricco?! Get the hell off my damn porch! How did you even know where to find me?!" She screamed, as she picked up the pace.

Karma jumped into the conversation, grinning coyly at her mother, "Mamma, this is the *surprise* I was telling you about! You know I keep in touch with my daddy. Daddy's on his way to Atlanta, Georgia; he needs a place to crash for a couple of days. I told him you wouldn't mind."

"Girl, have you lost your damn mind!" Blame screamed, now on the porch, face to face with Karma. "This bastard damn near killed your sister and Miss Keisha! What the hell is wrong with you Karma? And as for you, *Suav-A,*" she continued, turning to face her first love, "you got about 10 seconds to get the hell off my damn property!"

"Whoa, hold on now baby. It wasn't even like that in Maryland. It was all a big misunderstanding," Ricco explained. "Keisha was just jealous 'cause she know I still got feelings for you; and she kicked me out. That's all that happened," he lied.

"Niggah please! Who the fuck do you think you're talking to? A damned fool?! You put them in the fucking hospital, Ricco. Now, I mean it. I'm getting ready to call the police if you don't get the fuck off my damn property. Matter of fact, you better get your black ass the hell outta this town!"

"Mamma!" Karma interjected, and Blame wheeled around to see her daughter crying miserably. "You let them Mexicans stay here a whole week when the tree fell on their trailer; and my own *daddy* can't even visit for two days?! Please mamma! I don't know when I'm gone see him again. This ain't about you or Miss Keisha or nobody else. My daddy came all this way to see ME! Please let me have just two days with my daddy. Please?!" she cried, blubbering like a two year old child. "My daddy been gone my *whole* life. And you was too, for part of it. *You* changed. Why you think my daddy can't change? Please mommy, I just want a couple of days with my daddy. What's so wrong with that?!"

Sixteen year-old Karma was Blame's problem child. The one she couldn't seem to break through to. The one she didn't know how to talk to. The secretive, sullen, distant child whom Blame would gladly give both her kidneys to, if she thought it would make her genuinely happy.

Two days...so little to ask, Blame thought. Maybe this will be a way for us to begin a real friendship, a sincere mother/daughter dialogue. Just two days. And I'll straight up murder Ricco if he gets out of hand, she concluded. Against her better judgment, Blame folded like a lawn chair. She wiped away Karma's tears and thought about what two more days with her own daddy, Sherman, would mean to her. She ceded, and said to Ricco, "you can sleep on the couch in the den." She called J'Rick at the college in Greensboro—an hour's drive away—to fill him in.

When J'Rick got home, he was sick. Blame explained they were doing it for Karma...just two days. She told him they'd do a picnic down by the lake tomorrow. Maybe cook something on the grill the following day. They could all catch up, and he would be gone. Just two days...for Karma. J'Rick felt he'd somehow lost his little sister, when they lived in Fort Washington with Keisha. He never knew why she seemed to change so—distant and sad. But if two days might give her a little joy; then so be it. He agreed, as long as his dad would be gone Sunday, before he left for the University. He hoped it would do his gloomy sister some good, and prayed they wouldn't have any trouble. Still, he moved his rifle from the gun rack to his bedside.

It was a bright, sunny day. The family enjoyed a good old fashioned picnic down by the lake. It was one of Blame's favorite spots on her thirty nine acres. Just last week, she and Abraham, and his Uncle Mack fished along that same bank. They caught crappie, while Blame listened to the stories of Baylorton and the history of her people, sipping on a mason jar of Uncle Mack's finest. Blame fried the fish lakeside—Abe having all the modern-day equipment to make the job easy. She'd already made cornbread and coleslaw.

After they'd eaten their catch, Blame and Abe took a walk around the lake, while Uncle Mack took a nap. Abraham casually picked flowers along the way, while they talked and laughed about a myriad of things. They paused at the northeast corner of the lake, where the Indian Cigar trees grew. Because of Uncle Mack's Mason jar, the way the sunlight filtered through the trees—firing up the copper in Blame's magnificent eyes and soft brown hair; because of the sweet perfume rising off the flowers in his hand, and the way she smiled—with her full lips and dreamy eyes—Abe wanted to kiss Blame. Instead, still unsure of how she felt about him, he gave her the bouquet of flowers, and they walked on. It was a good day.

But that was last week. This day, Karma and Ricco engaged in conversation, with daughter doing most of the talking, and daddy feigning interest. Abraham and J'Rick had a sidebar discussion about a problem Abe had run into on a current construction project; he wanted J'Rick's input. Blame made busy fixing plates, going over the books from the boutique...taking a long look around. She enjoyed gazing over her land, but her eyes kept finding their way back to Abraham's strong jawline, muscular arms, and skillful hands. She was surprised at this and hoped no one else noticed. But Abraham had, and was quite flattered. And though it was cool underneath the shady elm trees, Abe was getting warm, having to wipe sweat from his brow, and occasionally adjust his trousers.

Later, as J'Rick regaled the group with episodes of college life, Blame stood up to stretch her legs and scatter bread crumbs for the three little birds, she swore, were following her. Abraham noticed the slight curvature where her back dipped a little then rounded to the high upper part of her buttock. He wanted to place his hand there...and his lips. When he realized Ricco was watching him, he quickly looked away.

Abe suddenly felt uneasy—like the odd man out—at this family gathering, and thought of a reason to excuse himself. He blurted out something strange, like having to trim the goats' hooves, and reached for his hat. Nineteen year old J'Rick jumped to his feet, always eager to help Mr. Ismine. "Well can't it wait?" Blame asked, with a deflated look on her face, and something urgent...almost desperate, in her mystical eyes. "You haven't finished your plate."

219

"Let the man go," urged Ricco, "he said he got some business to take care of. J'Rick, sit down, son. Finish telling me about your college's basketball program." J'Rick looked to Mr. Ismine for direction. His neighbor gave a quick nod of consent (which anyone watching would have missed), and turned to leave, walking quickly through the forest.

Abraham passed the evening on his porch, enjoying the breeze and a plate of Blame's leftover lasagna. He tried to get through a chapter of his latest read, *Villa and Zapata*, highlighting the passages he would discuss with Blame; but his mind was elsewhere. He had a nagging memory of the night Blame cut her feet, racing to get to Keisha and Monique. He remembered the intensity most of all, and couldn't help feeling worried for his neighbors. Maybe he should drive over, he thought, make sure everything's okay. Then he thought he might be intruding, and decided against it. He helped himself to a shot of his Uncle Mack's homebrew and went off to bed.

Abraham woke in the middle of the night, wound up in his blankets and covered in a cool sweat. He tried, but couldn't remember what he'd been, only seconds before, dreaming about. He fought his way out of the tangle of sheets and quilt, and rushed to the kitchen, fumbling for the light switch. He dashed around the island and snagged a photo from the magnet holding it to the refrigerator. If J'Rick, Karma and Monique had been dinosaurs or robots in the photo, Abe wouldn't have noticed. His eyes were completely trained on the gray-brown, copper-flecked eyes of Blame Rane...along with her alluring, open-mouthed smile.

Taken four years ago, Abe still remembered snapping the picture like it was yesterday—Blame's head thrown back, her clear, unbridled laughter causing birds to sing. It was the grand opening of B.R.O. Boutique. She had been so happy! It made him overjoyed to think he had something to do with that. And when he looked at her now—just her still image in a fading photograph—he knew very well, that he loved Blame! And more than that, he knew he needed her.

Abraham was suddenly moved by a passion that no reasonable amount of thinking could quench. He realized it had been there all along; brewing just under the surface. Maybe it took him seeing her with another man for the passion to finally bubble up to the top. He dressed quickly and put on his hat, giddy and almost laughing because he'd just now realized he loved Blame so. He got his flashlight, and headed toward the thin row of cedar marking the boundary line between their properties.

As he got closer to the house, Abraham noticed a figure, what appeared to be someone standing in the front yard, just below the porch. He couldn't make out who; or really even, *what* it was, from that distance; and he saw something shiny, glinting in the moonlight, just inside the front door. He moved a little faster, but much quieter.

The part of him that was hunter took over his senses. Abe hadn't bothered to turn on the flashlight because he'd know the way if he was blind. Now he held it like a club, since it was the closest thing he had to a weapon. His heart raced uncontrollably and he wondered if Blame was in danger; his grip tightening on the flashlight. He kicked himself for leaving them with such a questionable character. J'Rick's father or not, Abe knew when a man was rotten, and no damned good. He started jogging.

The shiny thing in the doorway turned out to be the barrel of J'Rick's rifle. The shadowy figure below the porch was J'Rick's father. Blame tossed a ratty duffel bag out into the yard, and yelled, "Get the fuck outta here. And don't you ever come back this way again!" Karma was just behind J'Rick, crying hysterically. Ricco turned to the sound of Abraham, approaching quickly from behind.

"Is everything okay here, J'Rick?" their neighbor called out. "Blame...you alright?"

"We're fine, Mr. Ismine. Just taking out the trash," J'Rick scowled, looking into his father's eyes.

Ricco turned to Abraham, and said, "This ain't got nothing to do with you man. We just having a small misunderstanding. It's a family affair, so mind your business."

"Well if it's a family affair," Abraham responded resolutely, "then it *is* my business. Because this is my family! Blame, bring me the keys to the truck. J'Rick, you stand down. Don't point a gun at a man unless you intend on using it. This is your father, son. You can't shoot your own father. It's not even an option. Did you hear me J'Rick? Lower that weapon, son!"

Blame and J'Rick, used to looking out for themselves, let down their guards and quickly did as they were told. Abraham threw Ricco's duffel on the back of the truck and ordered him to get in. Blame handed Abraham the keys, and a surge of electricity passed between their fingers. He was a powerful man. He instructed her to get inside and lock up the house. He told her to wait up for him, and promised he would not be long. He told Ricco to get in; and the junkie from D.C., relieved he was no longer at gunpoint, quickly obliged.

Abraham took Ricco to the bus station, asked the man where he wanted to go, and bought him a one-way ticket. Then he handed him $300.00 cash, out the ATM machine. He told Ricco, "Look, you sorry son-of-a-bitch, if you ever step a *foot* back in Baylorton, you have my word, I'll kill you so fast, you'll be dead before God gets the news!" Ricco had spent a lot of years on the streets and even more in prison. He'd met a lot of

222

certified killers in his lifetime. He looked Abraham square in the eyes and knew with absolute certainty the man was not a liar. He stuffed the $300.00 in his pocket and tipped his hat to the victor. Abraham was wound up in protection mode, and thinking of all parties concerned, he added, "And stay the hell away from Monique and her mother, too!" Juan Ricardo Murdoch was never heard from again.

Meanwhile, Blame locked up her house and checked to make sure nothing else was missing. J'Rick had caught his father trying to steal the money bag, which held the cash and receipts from B.R.O. Boutique, out of the desk drawer in the hallway. Blame tried to console Karma, but the girl was incorrigible. J'Rick stayed in Karma's room that night. She could still hear them talking. Good, Blame thought, maybe he can talk some sense into her...that asshole tried to rob us! When Blame was sure her home was secure, checking thrice to make sure everything was where it should be—an old habit—she sat in the front room and waited for Abraham.

She rubbed her fingertips, still feeling the electricity he sent through them. And she smiled. Blame hadn't been with a man since Nick, in Dale City. She'd been approached by a few in Baylorton, but really she'd always had a bit of a secret crush on Abraham Ismine. She just never acted on it—feeling slightly beneath him...considering her shady past. Plus he was almost fifty, and Blame often felt like a child in his presence. Granted she was no spring chicken, at forty-one; but his wisdom and impeccable character made him seem much older.

Still, he'd stood right in her yard, and said "they were *his* family". Her heart melted. The look in his eyes said he meant those words. Their eyes had been conversing for years now, speaking the language of love. She remembered a brief exchange they had while rehabbing the store; over a quote from a Hurston book…there was something extraordinary in his eyes that day as well. Something so passionate she had to ignore it; and had been trying to ignore it every day since. Blame blushed now just thinking about it.

However, as she'd grown accustomed to doing, she thought twice about the matter (a new habit). She was probably getting ahead of herself, she thought. Mr. Ismine had more women calling on him than he knew what to with. And he probably didn't mean anything romantic about them being his "family". He felt that way because of his love for her cousin, Wilbur. She convinced herself she was being foolish and schoolgirl silly. Blame pushed the idea of anything more than friendship out of her mind, lit a cigarette, and put on a pot of coffee.

Abraham waited until Ricco was on the bus, and the bus was on the highway. Then he raced through town, running stop signs and breezing through stop lights…headed straight for the arms of the woman he loved. He didn't even think about what he was going to say; throwing caution to the wind and speeding along, like a miner in the California gold rush—going to stake his claim.

Blame heard the truck tires hit the gravel at the top of Rane Lane. She gripped the handle of her coffee mug a little tighter, checked her reflection in the mirror, and took a deep breath, trying to calm her racing heart. She peered through the curtains and saw Abraham bounding from the truck, taking the porch steps two at a time. Blame sat the coffee mug down and flung the door open before he could even knock.

Abraham blew in like the wind and took Blame up in his strong arms. He hugged her passionately, the fervent way soldiers returning from war embrace their women. Blame was on fire. He looked into her beautiful gray-brown and copper-flecked eyes and told her he loved her. She stuttered and choked on reciprocal words, surprised to hear them coming from her own mouth—but feeling them powerfully in her heart.

Then, because she was a wiser woman, Blame froze and struggled out of his arms. She took a step back and held her head high. "Wait," she said, "before this goes any further, Abraham, there are some things you should know about me."

"I know all I need to know," he responded, trying to pull her back into his arms. But Blame resisted.

"No...you don't. So sit down, have a cup of coffee while I tell you all about it." Just as she'd done with her friend, Beverly, at Mrs. Douthit's house, Blame related the story of her life. She began with an invisible childhood in a house where love and affection were sparse. She continued through, including the most shocking highlights; leaving no stone of her vivid past unturned. Abraham Ismine sat quietly, his face a montage of sympathy and humor, shock and awe, understanding and love. When she was done, and the coffee kettle empty, she showed Abraham to the door.

"You done?" he asked, half afraid there might be more.

"Yes."

"Good, now where were we?" He beamed and pulled her back into his wanton arms, supplanting her lips with kisses more passionate than anything she'd ever known or felt. Their embrace led them up the stairs, and to her bedroom, where they consummated their full grown love. When they were finally able to tear themselves away from each other, they laughed and talked until the sun came up. As their hearts were now adjoined, they talked endlessly about joining their families and their farms. Abraham and Blame made a million plans.

CHAPTER 31
CELEBRATIONS

Before they could combine their resources, families and farms, they would first have to combine themselves—clinging together as one flesh. So there was a righteous gathering at Abraham's church, with the Ismines and Ranes in attendance. The Wynn and Gutierrez families were there, along with Keisha and Monique Murdoch, Beverly Douthit, Abe's and Blame's employees and clients, and a host of other well-wishers.

J'Rick, the best man, was more elated than the couple of honor. To Uncle Mack's regret, Blame walked down the aisle alone. She wanted it that way...preferring to believe her daddy was by her side, witnessing. Keisha stood in as maid of honor at the last minute, when Karma dropped out. The teenager was putting on weight more rapidly than usual, and on the morning of the ceremony, she couldn't get into her dress. Her mother, mean with a needle and thread, offered to make some quick adjustments. But Karma begged off. She'd been sick lately, too, vomiting every morning. Blame didn't push it; she refused to undergo any undue stress that day. Abraham was the proudest man in all of Baylorton when they took their vows. But the crow, pigeon and cardinal, doing a two-step in the church's bell tower, were prouder.

There was a gala reception at Abraham's home, with the entire community of Rainier Place present, along with half of Baylorton, at large. It was a catered affair and everyone, catering staff included, had a glorious time. Abraham and Blame Ismine danced until their feet hurt, laughed until their cheeks ached, and cried tears of joy until their ducts ran dry.

J'Rick was the life of the party—showing off his smooth moves. With all the festivities, and love in the air, he convinced

Rita to cut through the cypress trees, and accompany him home. He figured they could spend at least one uninterrupted hour alone, while Beverly, Keisha and Monique—their house guests—were still kicking up their heels.

They reached the front porch giggling and out of breath. J'Rick stopped laughing abruptly and shushed Rita. He thought he heard someone moving about in his house, and that shouldn't be, since everyone was at the reception. He noticed a light on in one of the bathrooms, and he told his girlfriend to stay put on the porch as he snuck upstairs. J'Rick slipped quietly into his bedroom to retrieve his trusty rifle, tiptoed to the bathroom door, positioned his weapon and kicked the door in! His sister was squatting over the commode, peeing on what looked like a pink stick. Karma screamed and jumped and dropped the stick into the toilet.

Embarrassed at intruding on his sister, J'Rick spun around and fired off a round of apologies. But Rita, who'd heard the scream, was already up the steps and standing in the open bathroom door. Being female, and knowing what J'Rick did not, she rushed into the cramped space and pushed Karma aside before she could flush the toilet. Rita peered down into the water, at the pink stick floating on top, and saw the unmistakable "plus=positive" sign its center. Karma covered her face and cried. J'Rick, still confused, kept apologizing to his sister. "Stop being so sensitive, girl. You act like I ain't never seen you before. Who you think changed your diapers? It's not that serious sis. Damn Karma, I said I was sorry."

"J'Rick," Rita turned to him to explain, "She's crying because she's pregnant."

J'Rick snatched up his rifle again and demanded to know, "By who?! Who the fuck is it Karma?!" His sister ran to her room crying and slammed the door. Rita calmed J'Rick

227

down and went to talk to Karma. J'Rick stomped out to the porch, where he paced back and forth, wondering who the culprit could be. When Rita finally joined him, he was slumped in the swing with his head in his hands.

Rita sat down beside him and rubbed his knee. "She won't say who the daddy is; but she hasn't had a period in over three months. I don't why she pissing on a stick, that girl been knowing she pregnant."

"Three months? And mamma don't know? How?" J'Rick questioned, dumbfounded.

"You know how your sister is Rick; she don't tell nobody nothing. And Karma's a big girl, too. Hell if we hadn't found out tonight, she probably could have hid the pregnancy for the whole nine months. Come on," Rita said, rising to her feet, "I guess we need to go talk to Miss Blame."

"Nah, not tonight. Let mamma have her fun. I'll tell her tomorrow. I'ma kill that l'il niggah when I find out who he is!"

The birds didn't care who, what, where, when, how or why. They loved babies and celebrated the continuity of family...the re-creation of themselves. Karma could hear them warbling joyously through her open window. The melody was so pretty, so full of life, she stopped crying and started singing along—her voice a symphony within itself. Karma was actually glad half the secret was out. She was sixteen, grown as far as she was concerned, and she didn't care what Blame had to say. It was J'Rick she had been worried about telling. And the other half of the secret would remain hidden; she absolutely refused to tell anybody the father's name... because honestly, Karma didn't have a clue.

CHAPTER 32
DUST COVERED DREAMS

The slightest breeze blew through the open window. The house was eerily quiet, empty, save me and the cat, Felicity. The store was closed, because it was Sunday. I'd long ago tired of fooling with the heathens and hypocrites at Abe's church. So I sat alone in my backyard, smoked a cigarette or two, and watched a familiar trio of birds frolicking in the birdbath. The cardinal pranced around on the gray stone, and seemed to be vying for my attention. Perhaps it was just my imagination, but I felt like the redbird was trying to tell me something.

The crepe myrtle hung heavy, sweetly perfuming the air, and the only clouds in the sky were big, fluffy and white. The sun shone brightly, but it wasn't too hot...just right, you might say. I strolled lazily across the warm grass in my bare feet and lay in the hammock, to think. I was troubled about a name for my first grandchild. It would be helpful to know the daddy's name, but Karma, as usual, wasn't talking.

I sipped on a tall glass of fresh-squeezed lemonade and enjoyed a book—I was reading *Queen*, the sequel *to Roots*, that afternoon. Felicity curled up next to me and we drank in the natural intoxicant of a gloriously perfect day. I eventually grew tired, as seemed to be the case most often, and lay my book down, resting my weary eyes on the redbird until I drifted off to sleep. Then I had the most fascinating dream!

I was somewhere along the coast of Texas. Don't ask me how I knew it was Texas. It was a dream, and dreams are that way. You know things you wouldn't ordinarily know. Well, in this dream, I was a flower, worn in a beautiful girl's hair—a tight chestnut bun. She was a tiny, frail, little lady; but I could tell she had a big spirit. The dream started with this petite teen standing in a line, seeking employment, I believe. Seated before the long row of colored girls accompanying her, was a gruff-looking white man... asking important questions.

The little lady listened to the girls ahead of her, as they rattled off their first and last names, their particular skills, and then moved to another line. The slight, copper-skinned girl didn't have a last name and considered how she should answer, when asked. She wondered if they would make her leave, tell her she couldn't have the job because she had no last name. She thought about saying Cohen, her master's name before Emancipation, but it didn't feel right. When it was her turn, she moved in front of the long low table, training her eyes on the white man's knuckles as he rapped his pen against a ledger.

What's your name, girl?"

"Sue. Suh."

"Sue what?" he whined, impatiently.

"Suh?"

"Sue what? Who's your people?" Well she didn't have to think about a response. The answer to that question was on the tip of her tongue; and remained forever in the breadth of her heart.

"Dusty." She beamed. "Dusty my people!" She repeated proudly.

"Sue Dusty, eh?" he scratched his head questioningly, and wrote her name down in the ledger. She looked at the words and smiled. She couldn't read them; but knowing her name was right there alongside her mother's name, made her happy enough in that moment to cry. It was recorded in a book somewhere, that they belonged together; they were a part of each other...Sue and Dusty.

A moment later, she heard a woman calling from the end of the hallway, "Sue Dusty." She was startled to hear it again, and realized she had just last-named herself. She was from that day forward, and forever would be, known to all as Sue Dusty. She giggled sweetly, adjusted the flower in her hair and moved on down the hall. When she completed the interview, she walked out into the bright Texas day where she was greeted by her waiting friend, a little red bird, with a stone its talon.

Abraham kissed my cheek and stroked my forehead; waking me from my dream. Startled, I touched my cheeks to see if they felt like wilting petals, because I had just been a flower in a girl's hair. I glanced at my arms, surprised they were not tender green stems. I looked to the birdbath, and the crow and pigeon had flown away...only the cardinal remained.

"Honey, are you okay?" Abraham asked, helping me up from the hammock.

"I'm fine, Abe," I insisted, wheezing and coughing (which I blamed on seasonal allergies), "I was just thinking about...my grandmother, Sue."

"Well that's pleasant," he smiled, setting his Bible down beside my ashtray. "You know, this is kind of awkward. I know your people on your father's side, but there's so much I don't know about you Blame." He blushed, stroked the prison scar on my forearm, and added, "for instance, I don't even know your mother's name. I mean her maiden name...or anything else about that side of your family."

I took a swig of lemonade, still studying the cardinal, and answered nonchalantly, "Ethel. My mother was named Ethel Diana Dusty." The second my mother's last name left my lips, I was struck with the most enlightening epiphany. I gagged and sprayed lemonade, and a little sputum, all over Abe's fine Sunday suit, as the meaning of my dream became clear as our vinegar washed windows. Abraham gave me a swift pat on the back; I caught my breath and looked quickly to the birdbath. The cardinal, with the stone in its talon, was standing very still, and surprisingly, it was still eyeballing me. In that mid-day haze, I felt like that little redbird and I were, somehow, connected.

I had to be in the twilight zone. I looked at my husband, specifically the mole on his cheek, to make sure he was really there, and I wasn't still dreaming. I squeezed his strong hand for added measure, and he squeezed back. (I love that Abraham Ismine.)

I don't know how to explain this, but I knew, without a shadow of doubt, the Sue in my dream was my mother's GranSue. She was my great-great grandmother…had to be. My family from Orange, Texas was last-named Dusty. Thanks to my dream, I now knew why. Sue gave herself the last name that had been her mother's first name. Sue's mother was named Dusty. My mother never told me that. I wondered if she even knew. Well, it didn't matter because I knew; and the redbird guided my knowing. The same bird was even in the dream. In some fantastic way, that cardinal showed me who my people were…like it knew Sue, and maybe even Dusty, too.

Abraham looked worried, assuming I'd taken ill, again. I slowly released his supportive hand and tipped to the birdbath; half afraid I would frighten the little creature away. But the bird stood very still, watching me. When I got within a breath of the thing, I looked it dead in its beady little eyes and asked, "Dusty?" I swear on my mamma and daddy's grave, that little bird clapped its red wings. Abe was there; he saw it! Then it shook its singed tail feather and flew away, whistling.

I took one of Abe's pain pills, prescribed for his aching back, and went to lie down. I had to be tripping…but something in my knowing told me it was true—I had been a flower in my GranSue's chestnut hair! And I was certain GranSue's mother had been named Dusty. I needed to find Dusty.

The next morning, a Monday, I asked Karma to cover the store and produce stand. She was having such a rough pregnancy, and I felt bad about asking; but Rita had classes at the community college part of the day. It was either Karma fill in, or close up shop. Financially speaking, the latter was not an option. I had business at the library; and it would not wait.

I went to six libraries in four cities pouring through their computer databases for information. Karma's never been too dependable. Due to the impact my absence was having on my shop and farm, I bought a laptop and researched at home, scouring the internet and genealogical websites for any little kernel of information I could find.

One day, after weeding tomatoes and peppers, I sat down to continue my research, with a familiar rainbow of birds looking over my shoulder. Even though the things I found broke my heart and made me cry, I couldn't stop looking for Dusty. After mining through hundreds of pages of microfiche, articles, census data, ship manifests, photographs, property logs, tax statements, and other documents, like these:

New Orleans *Delta*, Aug. 31, 1851   Charleston Courier, Sept 11, 1848

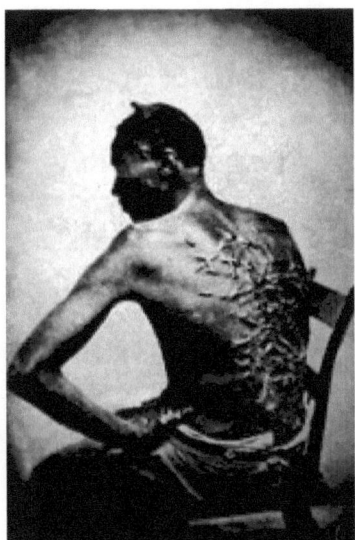

Slavery in Colonial America

ForeverFreeProject.Org

At the Sale by Mr. James L. Gantt, the following prices were realized:

A Woman—cook and washer, 22 years old, with a child 4 years old, $5000.
Girl, 17 years old a house servant, $6000.
Girl, 16 years old a house servant, $5200.
Girl, 15 years old a house servant, $5000.
Woman, 26 years old, and two children, 7 and 8 years old, $8000.
Man, 19 years old, field hand, $6000.
Man, 19 years old, field hand, $5150.
Man, 18 years old, field hand, $5150.
Man, 40 years old, field hand, $3600.
Woman, 27 years old, field hand, $4000.
One Share Charleston Importing Company, $7075
$1000 Non-taxable Six Per Cent. Bonds, C. S. A, at 102
$1000 Eight Per cent Bond, C. S. A., 1568, at par.
$1000 Four Per Cent. Certificate, C. S. A., at 60 cents.
$7600 Four Per Cent. Certificate, C. S. A., at 56 cents.

Charleston Courier, Oct. 27, 1864

AltoArizona.com

Without Sanctuary

The Barbardos free Press File

235

Charleston *Courier*, Feb. 28, 1854   Knoxville (Tenn) *Whig*, Sept. 1, 1849

...

   ...I came across a document from the Cohen Cotton
Plantation in Eastern Texas, cataloging the deed of ownership
and description of purchase for a Negro girl named Sue...7 year
old female, bought from the Morgan Estate in Houston, Texas.
Looking into the records of the Morgan Estate, (where I
discovered the matron had only one eye!), I located a copy of a
property ledger. There was mention of this same child: 7-year
old Sue, and the $400.00 yield she brought at sale. In the
margin beside her name was this obscure little notation:
mother, Dusty, put down. Other related information led me to
believe this girl was the Sue of my dreams. For example, seven
years earlier, in the Morgan ledgers, was the name Sue again,
with a date of birth and the words: born of the Negress, Dusty.
This little Sue was the GrandSue who raised my mother, Ethel.

And Sue's mother, without a doubt in my mind now, was named Dusty!

In the dream, or astral projection, I could feel the love my GranSue had for her mother Dusty. I don't think Sue ever knew what I found out on my journey to find Dusty—that her mother had been "put down". I said a long prayer, and mediated deeply, honoring the memory and lives and love of Dusty and Sue...and the lost generations that preceded them.

I don't know what drove me to search so hard and long for this information; but I was glad I did. My parents died when I was only nineteen years old, leaving me without any sense of family, until J'Rick and Karma came along. But the journey I went on to find Dusty, helped me understand that, because I live and breathe today, I have always had and will forever have Family. I was never alone; my people have always been with me. And it's cyclical, this living. My children and their children will always have me with them, as well.

I logged off my computer, feeling like I'd eaten a six-course meal, and raced to tell Karma the good news. I found my daughter in the boutique, crouched in the floor between the dress racks, over a small puddle of pinkish water. "Mamma, its time!" she screamed.

I panicked, didn't know what to do, so I called Abraham. He and J'Rick were at the boutique in no time. They even had Karma's overnight bag, ready to go. My family loaded up in my husband's jeep, called the doctor's office, and took off for the hospital, two towns away. I looked back at the three birds tailing us, and at the sign which read: Rane Lane – private road. Without thinking twice, I blurted out, "Dusty! Karma, you *have* to name this baby Dusty!"

Gwendolyn Rainier

We couldn't get into that hospital, so the cardinal, crow and I, waited it out at the farm. It took them three long days to come home, with the most beautiful little boy you ever did see! He looked like Charlie and Rone to me—in a breathtakingly beautiful brown sure to melt any grandmother's heart.

There is nothing left for me in Tennessee. The cardinal has a beautiful place on the river, but she's come back this way too. Tuppie has given up her perch in the barn, as well. We worked together and built one big nest in the tree outside Karma's bedroom window...so we could keep an eye on little Dusty.

They're the best birds I know—the cardinal and crow. We share our stories, sing some songs, and try to reconcile our vast differences. I'm certainly learning a great deal. Mainly, what a fool I have been.

Life...or rather, death, is not too bad these days—especially since I've discovered we three are sisters, in humanity. The other birds, that call this farm home, will fly south in autumn. But we will happily endure winter's chill. We three will be right here until the Lord calls us home, with our perfect little grand boy, Dustin Abraham Rane..."TwoSquirrels-Rainier"!

CHAPTER 33
LISTEN KARMA

2012

The fruit don't fall from the tree, and my daughter, Karma, was living proof. She'd gotten it into her head that Baylorton was just too small...said she was leaving. She met some boy on the internet, and was going up north to make a name for herself...have some fun in the process. I wanted her to know that what she was looking for in life was right here. So I sat her down and told her...

"What you don't know, because I never told you...and who else could tell you but me; is that I have been cold; and I have been hungry. Karma, when my parents died, I lived in a college dorm room for as long as I could. But dorm rooms are filled by paying customers in the endless purchasing and selling of education. At semester's end—with no tuition or room and board fees—I was summarily removed. More than a month after I was kicked off campus, my co-worker, Toria, and I rented a raggedy, rundown two-bedroom walkup in the ghettos of Chocolate City aka Washington D.C. So I was homeless Karma, for *thirty-eight* days!

Thirty-eight days, I learned, is a *very* long time when you are cold and hungry and homeless; plus it's the dead of winter. Between the dorm room and the walkup, I lived in a Buick, with a broken heater. I drove around from place to place so I wouldn't get robbed or raped or worse. A comforter, piles of clothing and a coat and hat was *all* I had to keep me warm. The hat was a gift from my neighbor, Mrs. Douthit, God bless her. If I ate at all, I got one meal a day off the value menu at fast food joints. I bathed in the rust-stained sinks of pissy gas station restrooms. I was almost raped one night. And I lost the feeling in one of my toes...to this day, Karma. As pitiful as it was, I couldn't even cry; child, my tears were too damned cold.

I didn't get a dime from my father's insurance policy and there was no insurance at all on my mother. I had nothing, Karma. I couldn't even fix the heater on the Buick. I needed every penny I earned for rent and utility deposits, and first month's rent. Besides, I was nineteen; I didn't know anything about getting a car fixed. When I recalled my daddy getting such repairs, the mechanic usually kept the car a few days. I couldn't hand over my home to some auto mechanic. Working in a textile mill for minimum wage, it took more than a month to get even half of the money together.

It has always stayed with me, Karma, those 38 days. That feeling of having no place to go...not having enough money to eat. No shelter, no way in the world to get warm. A loneliness so cold and absolute it would make an iceberg feel like the burning flames that killed my mamma and daddy...despair so deep, I thought I would drown. And every single night I spent in that car, I swear to you I wished I would die. *Death* was more appealing to me than freezing and suffering!

I knew my roommate, Toria Black, was the kind of girl my daddy warned me about; but she'd gotten kicked out of her Aunt Linda's apartment and desperately needed a roommate. She did not know the true meaning of desperation...not in the way I knew it. What she merely wanted...I absolutely *needed*. So I made a bad decision in choosing a roommate; but anything...anything in the *world*, beat the kind of cold I endured.

Then I found myself in a hotel room in Baltimore, ordering room service—from omelets to underwear—with a man I barely knew. During those 38 days of homeless hell, there was a time when I didn't even have clean underwear to wear to work. You cannot understand the difference between these two realities unless you've lived them both, child. Then this same man, yes, your father, is dangling the keys to a paid for place, in my face. And yeah, I know it's all paid for with drug money. But when you've been **cold**, and hungry and homeless, you don't necessarily make the best decisions. When the man starts to abuse drugs and abuse you; and you can still feel the numbness on your skin from a frightfully frigid, homeless winter...and you have no family other than the one you and he are making; your mind plays tricks on you. You rationalize that it could always be worse...when *really* it could have been much, much better.

Your father beat me Karma. And I don't mean an occasional push here or a shake there. I mean knockdown, drag out, ass whippings, day in and day out. You see these two teeth here. He knocked out the ones God gave me. My right eye stayed closed more than it stayed open...had fractures that had to heal on their own, child. And if I could open myself up to show you the *real* scars...the ones in my mind and my heart and in my psyche, they'd be more horrible than anything you could ever imagine.

And it got worse. Do you remember the projects we lived in, in D.C.? They were beyond shitty. Do you remember a man named Mr. Crown? You might have been too little to remember. But anyway, as bad as the projects were, the heat went out, and shit got worse. I knew I had to get you and J'Rick out of that place. I couldn't let y'all be *cold*, Karma. And I degraded myself to such an all-time low; I pray you never feel like you have to do the things I did, just to survive.

Then, even when you have a job and a place of your own, which was my case in Dale City; there is still the problem of living paycheck to paycheck. When you have two children who are solely dependent upon you; and you are *always* one paycheck away from homelessness—your judgment is easily clouded. Hunger stays with you, Karma. When you are so cold your bones ache, you *never* forget it. How long does it take for an insatiable need to become greed? I don't remember when I crossed that line. But by the time was I was robbing an HIV clinic for oxymorphone...my greed was complete. I grew up thinking I had to get a bunch of shit to make me happy, and I was hell bent on getting it...never really knowing what "it" was.

What I'm trying to say is; you don't have to learn from your own mistakes. I am telling you these things so you can learn from *my* mistakes. I was a fool! Maybe the world's biggest! J'Rick told me as much when he was only thirteen years old. Remember, right before I went to prison? I have not done the best I could have—but I kept you in out of the *cold*, and I staved off hunger from your belly. If I wouldn't have been stuck on stupid, I guess I could have found a better way to do it. But the bottom line is; I *was* stupid. Young and dumb and way past foolish.

When I was nineteen I had *no home*. Because this blessing on Rane Lane fell into our laps—and we come from people who refused to give up; you will *always* have a home, Karma Rane. You do not have to make the poor decisions I felt forced to make. You do not have to accept sharing your bathroom with a whore, or having your face used as a punching bag, or sleeping with a dirty old married man, or laying your freedom on the line for a damned lousy place to stay. Please realize the peace you have here at home, Karma. Please understand it will always be here for you—even if I am not. Be patient and humble daughter, and use this place to blossom into the kind of woman your son can be proud to call his mother. Honey work on making yourself a person *you* can be proud of!

We're doing okay here. The farm, the boutique...they're all
making a little money...enough for us to get by. And I could sure
use your help around here. You could finish school on line,
Karma. They have that now a days. I can give you a percentage
of whatever the clothes and crops bring in. This is your home
Karma. Don't let some boy who has nothing to offer you pull
you out in the streets. And don't you *dare* take my grandson
away from here. You hear me?

We all make mistakes baby. So you had a baby early. So
you dropped out of high school. You haven't even begun to
make the mistakes, poor choices and bad decisions I made. And
you haven't even begun to live. I promise you that you can
change your life and go aright any second of the day. As long as
you still have breath in your body, you can turn your life around.
I'll do anything I can to help you. I'll support your every
endeavor; but I can't get behind no bullshit, you hear?

It's cold out there Karma...*damned cold*. There exists a frost
in this world you can't even begin to imagine. You don't have to
rush your decisions, baby. You don't have to hurry your life
along. I know, through the years, I've let you down. And I'll live
with that. To tell you the truth, I ain't learn no damn sense until
I was near forty years old. But this is not about me letting you
down, or you letting me down. I'm begging you, with tears in
my eyes, for you not to let *yourself* down. Do all you can to
make the regrets in your life minimal...your heartaches few. I
hope you can hear me. I pray that you will heed.

Life really is what you make it, Karma. You will only have
yourself to blame for the outcome. When your mistakes begin
to pile up, you'll find it easy to blame rain...but it's not the rain's
fault. You can blame your father, a teacher, a crappy employer,
or even me; but you won't move forward in life. That's how you
think when you believe you are not responsible for the events

243

transpiring in your adult life—that someone else is to blame. But you only get back whatever you put out there, sweetheart. You bring it all on yourself—the good as well as the bad. Once you've completed your thirteenth year and reached the age of discretion; it's all on you, daughter.

I put *myself* in prison Karma. It wasn't Nick's fault or Charlene's fault, your daddy's or nobody else's. The Blame is mine. I promise you, you will only reap what you sow. And you alone *will* be held accountable for your actions and deeds…even your intentions. So seek knowledge, strive for wisdom daughter; and above all, gain some understanding.

There aren't any champagne parties out there child; just champagne tricks…just strife and struggle. You have to work hard and earn your joy. At least here, at home, you don't have to worry about your most basic necessities—like shelter and food and warmth. Life is real, child. Trust me; you do not want to put yourself in a position where you have to figure out how you're going to eat, and where you're going to lay your head. You're not ready for that reality Karma. Thank God, that's covered here.

Please listen to me Karma. I'm telling you what nobody ever bothered to tell me. I had to find out what I'm telling you on my own. You don't. All you got to do is try to hear and understand. *This is your home.* And we are not a perfect family. But we are a family. I love you. J'Rick and Dustin love you. And as long as we have each other; we're gonna be okay. Go slow daughter. I promise you Karma Rane, you already have what you're looking for."

Karma never uttered a word. She just sat there, eyes glued to the pattern of intertwined roses in the wallpaper, fingering a lace doily I'd made. I hoped some part of what I said got through to her. Well...at least I tried. *sigh* And I don't recall even that much effort from my own mother.

I thought I was dying—hemorrhaging internally—when I got my first period. My mamma hadn't told me a thing about it. Mamma didn't allow me to have company in the house, which made it hard for an already shy girl like me to make friends. So I didn't have a soul to ask what was happening to me.

Once, when I asked my mother for the words, just the *words*, to the gospel song she always hummed; she looked right through me and said, "I got to keep something for myself, Blame. Everything ain't for you. You ought to be glad you even got a mother." Poor Mamma! What hurt her so—that, even if she did not know the way—she failed to warn me which way **not** to go. Surely in her living there had to be some learning. As I am now learning that Time is a magnificent teacher.

It's so easy to sit here and find fault, but all in all, I am my mother's child. Whatever limitations and shortcomings she may have had, are ever present here in me. And heaven help me, I'm afraid I passed on the same sad traits to my own daughter.

My 16 year old daughter, Karma Dominique Rane, left sometime in the night. I woke the following morning to find her room nearly empty. She took her clothes, her pictures, her television set and cd's. She took the diamond bracelet I bought her when we lived in Dale City—purchased more to assuage my guilt than to acknowledge her birthday—along with the hair dryer, her books, an afghan and her BRO originals. She took our family portrait off the mantelpiece and my pickle jar of $5's and $10's.

But she left her cat, Felicity. And, with her breasts still full and leaking life's milk, she also left her baby boy.

CHAPTER 34
KHARMA

She look right through me; like she don't even see me. If she notice anything, it's something ugly, like my weight. Always hustling me up on the scale and trying to put me on a diet. I know I'm fat! I don't need no constant reminders. She wouldn't like it if I was constantly reminding her she's a drug-dealing jailbird. My momma don't care if I live or die; if I'm happy or sad; if I'm home or away. So I stay away.

Too busy to notice me...busy with daddy, Mr. Crown, Nick, drugs, prison, J'Rick, Abraham, the farm and now that damned boutique. She'll buy me a exercise bike, but won't take me to church to join me up with the choir. She probably don't even know I can sing. Don't matter. I *can* sing, and that's *just* what I'm going to do!

My mama don't have to love me. Other people love me. J'Rick and Monique love me. My teacher did one time, boys in Maryland...boys round here, too. I think my baby, Dustin, love me too...I think.

She act like she gone sit me down and love me, but all she did was talk...about her *damn* self. I been singing round the house since I was little girl. She couldn't hear me though...worried more about some sorry man plan or some hair-brained scheme to get rich quick. Whatever...

I even named my baby what she picked out, thinking that might make her look at me, *see* me. But she poured the love I never got all over my little baby boy. He gone be alright here. I can't have no baby holding me down anyway. Dusty gone be alright...

His daddy might be Armando, Isabel's boy. Or it might be Dewey Noggin, or any one of the boys who used to play on

J'Rick's basketball team. I don't know and I don't care. Don't really give a damn neither, just like nobody ever gave a damn about me…big ole fat Karma Rane.

I only did it with all them boys cause it feels good sometime to be touched, talked to…looked at. Mr. Perkins was the first person to love me and make me feel good. I musta did something wrong though, he stopped loving me just like my mamma did.

She used to read to me and play with me…talk to me, when we lived in the projects. I was a little girl, but I remember. The only time she was busy doing nothing was when we lived in the projects; I guess that's the only time she had a minute for me. Two cheers for me—I beat doing nothing. That changed when we got to Dale, though. I mighta saw my momma a total of ten hours a week down there, if that. I miss my sister friends, in Dale City, the girls I grew up with, the ones who raised me. I miss my daddy sometimes too, even though I didn't really get to know him. J'Rick, he gone to college…Monique, she just a kid.

I can't stay here with just me and Blame; old convict always trying to tell *me* something. What she gone tell me? How to get played by everybody you know and wind up in the penitentiary? Cause that's bout all I ever seen her do.

My mamma bought me stuff when she had money, and looked the other way. Down here now sewing and fronting like she had something to do with this place. She didn't even know none of them people in the photo album. Tryna act like she Miss high and mighty now. Beneficent Blame Rane…gone give Rita Wynn a job and lease some farm land to poor families. Yeah right! Ain't a righteous bone in that woman's body. She ain't never even looked at her own daughter, not for real.

I mean, I heard some of the stuff she was saying…but it's too late for all that. I been right here every day, and the first time she want to talk to me is when I'm on my way out the door. Girl bye. Plus, what kind of conversation you call yourself having when you don't never ask the other person what they think, how they feel...or who they even are! She don't know shit about me.

I wish my grandma Ethel wouldn't have died before I was born...she probably would have loved me. And then I might not have got so fat. It just feel good to eat food, and I can't help myself. I get tired of feeling bad all the time. I'll try *anything* if it feels good.

I don't care, though. I'm gone sing! And I'm a show all these motherfuckers who I am. I'm a be somebody, for real...and not no damn farming shopkeeper, neither. I can't stand it down here...people talk too much. That's why I stopped going to school. All the boys who used to like me don't like me no more. All the girls act like they better than me.

I met a boy who like me though. Matter of fact, he love me! And we ain't even did nothing yet. I ain't gave him no pussy *and* he know I'm fat; so he love me for real. He love me for me; and it feels good. He gone make me a star. And all these raggedy fuckers round here can just kiss my fat black ass!

Especially my mamma...Fuck Blame! She ain't never gave a damn about me. She can have Dusty, too. That's all she want anyway...another boy like J'Rick. I miss my big brother so much. But I think when I leave here, I'mma miss Dustin the most.

My baby gone be alright though. He such a tiny little thing. He so sweet and funny when he smile and laugh at me...make my heart...well...it don't matter right now. I'll make it up to him when I come back rich and famous. I'm a be somebody he can be proud to call his momma. So proud he won't even care who his daddy is, or ain't. Mamma's baby...

CHAPTER 35
REDBIRD MUSINGS

Sojourn to His Motherland

To witness, with eyes, the beginning,
I slipped between the murder and the deep blue sea.
Waves of wind encompassing, and waves of water beneath me.
Ancestral ground of Mother Dawn
Is the drumbeating heart of Africa.
But it was not home for me.
To Uweyv did I return—surrendering alas to Peace.

~ WindRider TwoSquirrels

    We carry the blood of our ancestors, and sometimes the spirit. With every passing generation, the blood and the spirits pile up until you don't know what to expect from a newborn baby. You never know what you'll get; like Forrest Gump's box of chocolates. Karma could have looked like me, but she did not. She could have been a warrior like Dusty, but she was not. She could have had the patience of Doany, the perseverance of Sue, or the gentle kindness of EulaLee. She had none of these.

    We are all represented in the blood coursing through her veins; but other natures are there as well. Karma had the restless legs of Baptise; the leave-a-baby-motherless syndrome that plagued Philomena; the cowardice of Charlie III—who hung himself from a chandelier; the fighting rage of her father, Ricco; the devil may care attitude, toward family, Gwendolyn possessed—writing off an entire clan in Tennessee. A foremother in her ancestry had been an Irish whore; while another delighted in the deaths of five pox-inflicted children. Ricco's Dominican father, I later discovered, was a murderer, who was himself, murdered in return. Aaron's mother was first sold to a slave trader by her very own uncle. That uncle hides in the blood, noticeable perhaps at the base of the fingernails...minimal in scope, but there still; alongside my pappa, Fil Jr. and every crow in the storytelling that follows her journey. And then too, her mother is Blame...daughter of Ethel. They are all Philomena's girls. And Mine.

I don't reference these ancestors to provide excuse for Karma's behavior. I cannot even blame Mr. Perkins, her rapist, for all of it. We are individually responsible for our actions. We all have the power to choose. I remember her as a little girl, living in the Great Witch's capital city, called Washington D.C. She played with her dolls and books, and tried not to cry when she was hungry. She loved her brother and her mother and the dotsua, which shadowed her childhood, very much. There were no stone engravings saying she had to become this way. There were only paths opened before her—she chose her own way. As did I.

I ran into red dust and left my mother with devils. Maybe I could have helped my mother someway in her old age. I threw my daughter Dusty from the window of a burning house, and into a hell that burned much hotter. I uncovered hidden rabbits for Sue's supper; and the hiding rabbits—like Tuppie beating Jezzy—were merely thinking of clever ways to survive. So I do not judge, lest I be judged by the same merit. I will leave that sublime task to the Great Spirit. I only say that, like the rest of us, Karma, daughter of Blame, had the power to choose. I only wish she would have chosen Life.

CHAPTER 36
SWEET CHARIOT

2012

Breast cancer? Are they sure, I wanted to ask. And so I did. Abraham and J'Rick asked again, as well. But the oncologist kept nodding his head, saying "yes". Without hesitation I told him to remove it; cut them both off...right now. Dustin dropped his pacifier. Another doctor on the team advised us—I say us, because she was looking at Abraham and would not look at me—that it had spread. Spread where? My critical-thinking husband asked.

"*Everywhere,*" was her answer.

I knelt down and picked up the pacifier. I was about to hand it to J'Rick, so he could rinse it off in the hospital room sink, but I stuffed it into the pocket of my bathrobe, instead. Some irrational part of my thinking needed to hear Dusty cry. If Dusty cries, I thought, this will be real. If he doesn't cry, it is only a dream—vivid, like the dream where I was a flower in GranSue's hair—but a dream nonetheless. I hoped he wouldn't cry.

I held my breath and was oblivious to anything else the doctors said. I only remember Abraham nodding his head to their speeches and explanations. J'Rick was looking out the window, focused I believe, on three birds praying in a dogwood tree. He was trying to fight back the tears...mamma's brave boy. A machine was beeping, measuring one of my vital functions, I suppose. A sunray lingered across my son's shoulder and time stood still, for just a little while.

Then Dustin cried.

He pitched and screamed until his little face turned red. J'Rick rocked him and walked him and hummed him a tune—looking around for the pacifier. Dusty eventually calmed down.

But I could not calm my racing mind. I could not feel. I could not breathe. I could not cry, scream or move. And the ground shifted.

I looked around the room for my mother and father, and not seeing them, I fell out of the chair. My husband, my rock, fell to his knees and lifted me off the floor. J'Rick asked the team of doctors to excuse us. He walked them to the door, with Dusty still in his arms. Abraham laid me in the bed, and he collapsed in the chair beside me and wept. Abraham wept. J'Rick sat on the edge of the bed and stroked my ankle. I looked at it...surprised to see that I had an ankle, and unable to remember if I'd ever noticed it before. What else had I failed to notice? I thought, feeling time slipping away.

Dustin looked at his Grandma and laughed.

Because he's beautiful, especially when he laughs, I laughed too. I tried to block the words "breast cancer" and "spread everywhere" out of my mind...pretended I hadn't heard them. I attempted to be business as usual, pushing back my cuticles, changing the subject to forecasted weather. J'Rick looked dumbfounded. Abe took up the gauntlet—stiff upper lip, and all—and began leafing through my medical chart. He'd navigate this typhoon, for sure.

I even checked the messages on my cell phone, as if I had not just received a death sentence. There was only one message...from a detective in Newark. They'd found the body of a girl. My number was in her cell phone, under "Mamma". According to her ID, her name was Karma Rane. He was very sorry. If I knew this young lady, I needed to catch a flight and come identify the body. The police department could arrange travel.

Dustin was still laughing, gurgling and cooing, really.

I choked on my own saliva, which tasted like a post-it note I'd once eaten. I searched the room again for my parents—and there they were. My father's glasses were on fire and my mother's hair was aflame. The earth was shifting for sure now...rocking back and forth. I dropped the cell phone in my lap and started pressing the buttons to my right.

I kept looking for the right button, there amongst the other buttons on my hospital bed. I imagine the medication had me delirious. Death and dying coming to greet me in one hour brought out my insanity. I was searching for the rewind button. I was going to back it all up. Make the doctors come back in the room, take back their fatal news, and walk out again backwards. Watch the pacifier leap from the floor and fly back into Dustin's sweet mouth. Make the detective on the recorder swallow his words...and never leave a message...make him never utter the name Karma Rane...and take back his fucking lie! Lie! Lie! Lie!

I couldn't find the rewind button. I clawed at the metal railing; the button to erase what I could not bear *had* to be there. I became aware of a shrill noise that I wished someone would turn off. Dustin stopped laughing and started crying, trying to match the hideous screech resounding in my head. I realized, at some point, it was the sound of my own screaming. I was cutting my fingers, tearing at the metal bedrail...looking for that damned button...the one that would bring my daughter back...my life back.

My knuckles were bleeding. J'Rick and Abraham were trying to arrest my hands. Daddy was crying and mamma was laughing at me. But where was Dusty? And could someone please silence my screams?! Then a nurse, who looked like Karma, or was it Karma? Karma, baby? ...came to sedate me.

The storytelling of crow swooped down to catch the bird that had fallen from their flock. Poor Tuppie Rane had fainted. Gwendolyn cried bitterly; and WindRider trembled mightily, like the thunder of heaven, feeling absolute and perfect pain.

CIRCLES
WindRider TwoSquirrels

The saddest thing about it all is; before she met her demise in New Jersey, Karma Rane was on her way home. I know because I was there. I couldn't help following my little girl—lover of the dotsua. So I was the only witness to that crime as well—the murder of yet more of my flesh. I guess you know her assailant was left with one eye. But I didn't carry that one with me. I abandoned it at the crime scene, under one of her thick brown braids, so the guilty party could be identified by his DNA.

He was a Jewish fellow named Isaac Cohen. The same boy she'd met on the internet, who said he knew people in the music industry and was going to make her a "star". But my Karma was already a star. He didn't mean to do it. The papers described it as a passion-killing; but he'd done it just the same. He was sentenced to seven years in prison. Seven years for my Karma.

His great-great-on-and-on Jewish grandfather, I learned, had come to this country when it was still raw and new (to the Europeans). That grandfather was the owner of two indentured servants—children really, a red-headed boy and girl—whom he'd purchased from a debtors prison in Ireland. The little Irish boy had a clubbed foot. The little girl would die with a groove in her forehead. They both died too young, like me.

Some centuries ago, Cohen's people relocated from the eastern United States to eastern Texas. They had a cotton plantation and once owned another little girl, named Sue, who would live to be 110 years old. His nearer kin relocated back east, to New Jersey, at the turn of the century.

Isaac was a spoiled boy; used to having his way. He had a fetish for robust black girls, who could sing like angels; and had fallen in love with a girl named Karma. He couldn't understand that his lover, still too young to understand love, might cheat on him. He couldn't control his woman. She was too headstrong. He didn't know what to do with the pain she brought; so he lashed out, with a knife in in his hand.

You could Blame her mother for not loving her right, but you might as well be blaming the rain. I (thinking at the time I was doing right) introduced my own daughter to hell. Finger-pointing won't change the Circle of Life.

It really is amazing, how life on this globe is a circle. Around and around we go. Look at me, living here on Uweyv...right back where I started from. Our job, I believe, is to learn to spiral, upward.

CHAPTER 37
KHADIJA

I sit here on my throne and quietly watch them all. I was the daughter of a King and Queen before the Great Taking Away. I was just a little girl, nine years old, when BoBo (my uncle) sold me to an Arabian slave trader for eight bars of iron and twelve glass beads. Like my seed Dusty, I too was born free.

I travelled across the continent by foot. Lived in a pen on the island at Goree', and sailed across the wide Atlantic Sea in a ship bound for Haiti. From there, I was purchased again, put in a fresh set of chains and loaded onto another boat headed to the port in New Orleans. I lived and died in Louisiana...never escaping my bondage.

It's a wonder I survived at all, I could not stomach the diet of my peers. Slaves were kept alive on the least choice parts of the pig. I never ate the pig. I couldn't remember all the things my mama and baba taught me in Africa; but I remembered not to eat the pig. I remembered too, that God is one God; and I was born Queen.

I bore thirteen seeds. My son, Aaron, was the only seed I got to keep, raise up and teach...if only for a little while. My body was in chains, but my heart and my spirit remained free all the days of my life. I taught that freedom to my son. Aaron, being the only flesh of my flesh who I knew in life, is by default, my *special one*. He ran away to the freedom and Kingdom I preached when he was old enough and strong enough...brave and King enough. He got to be free, live free and love free, chart his own course...if only for a little while, in a place called Orange. He and his woman, the WindRider, taught freedom and

King/Queendom to their daughter, Dusty Awiyusti. The knowledge was lost with the next generation, little Sue. Though a good girl, she was simply too young to understand or realize her Queenhood before the Great Separation from her mother. My Aaron fared as men fare. It is the daughters whom my heart broke for, my womb knotted for, and my soul ached for.

My daughters, *all* of them were lost and confused, full of ignorance and pain. They had not the knowledge they were Queens. With the teaching of the Truth cut off at the root, who, but me, could have told them? The woman in my line, called Blame, seed of Aaron, is from a foolish lot—*my* ignorant lot; and the brood spawned from the pigeon and the crow. I watch the crow, here from my throne. I watch them all.

I watched her seed Baptise, too, saw him run away, like my Aaron. Baptise was 1 of the millions of Blacks who got swept up in the Great Migration...whole droves of Blacks running up north to escape the oppressive regime of the Jim Crow South. A couple of generations later, and the people forgot they ever lived on and off the bounty of the land. Poor fellow never knew freedom couldn't be found in a geographic location...his ancestors, raised up from babies by their masters, could not teach him true freedom is a state of mind.

I am pleased Blame has returned South—land of her ancestors. Truth is; we were never really city people at all. We have always been tied to the land...since the dawn of time, which I'm also able to see from this vantage point. We have sustained it, and it has sustained us. Blessings to the son of the pigeon for honoring his heir with land. Blessings to the daughter of the crow, for acquiring land for Blame. Blessing to their seeds, the ones called Rone and Doany, for sacrificing their lives to the bittersweet earth.

I should be saddened by the fate of my seed called Karma. But I have seen too much, understand too deeply for sadness to ever touch me here, upon my throne. There are things that are inevitable in these circles called Life. Like all my daughters before her, she was without a mother. Even when her mother was present in the flesh, she could not hear the music in her child's sweet voice, nor teach her what she knew not. So she was never *really* there. My daughters and their daughters are like feathers, blowing upon the wind. The knowledge and therefore opportunity to be Queens passed them by. The wisdom and the way (which should have been passed down through the generations), was stolen, in the Great Taking Away.

Karma was not taught wisdom...like the millions of little Black girls with absent or distant mothers. She became hardheaded and precocious. She was a heedless child, void of gratitude and shame. She did not seek out knowledge, wisdom or understanding in her lifetime, as her mother Blame had finally done. Better late than never, I have learned. Karma's fate was written on the wall...plain enough for Hezekiah to read. This is why the living must be wary of the Time...any day could be your last on the earth. There may be no second chance to go aright. If you have breath in your body; go aright *this* day.

I watch them all. I bear witness that: though she was a fool, Blame's intentions were never cruel. Blame did seek, until she found, the fountain...the narrow spring which gushes forth with knowledge, wisdom and understanding...even in the autumn of her life. In doing so, perhaps the cycle of death will be broken.

And the water can be poured now, giving my future seeds
Life...eternal freedom!

I am extra-terrestrial these days, no longer requiring the terra
firma to sustain me. I am pleased to cee the seeds of my flesh,
who still dwell upon the earth, are learning the significance of
the life-producing land. The boy, Dustin, tends the vegetable
garden, like his foremothers and fathers. The boy Dustin will
know a freedom which none before him had the pleasure to
enjoy. I believe, knowing what I know, he will enjoy it with
patience and grace. Aaron—called J'Rick, this time—is there to
guide him.

Dustin's grandmother, my daughter called Blame, has taught
and loved him well, bless her heart. Once she stopped passing
blame...once she got here feet out of concrete and put them in
the ground where she was originally planted, she grew.

Ah, Time flies. I must go now and put the stars out for you.
Look to these lights in the sky should you ever become lost. I
am Khadija, your mother, and I will light your way home.
APDTA.

CHAPTER 38
INDIAN SUMMER
October 27, 2015

We're enjoying an Indian summer here in Baylorton...the family and I. Birds included.

I'm not able to do too much anymore. I still sew some; mess around in the garden a bit. I get around pretty good, as long as I get my rest. So I walk every day; and that's good. Most of my time is spent in the amazing world of my four year old grandbaby. I swear every day is an all-out adventure for that little boy. Dusty makes me feel so alive!

One of his favorite pastimes is rummaging through my old memory box from Rose Lane. I told him it was my treasure chest, and he just loves that. I've added a few items along the way, like the gold cufflinks and two pieces of silver we found tucked back in the attic. Wilbur's medal is in there, along with a rusty thimble that had to be grandma Eula Lee's. There's a little book amongst the treasure, one his mommy had when she was his age, about a courageous train. Dusty made some airplanes from the yellow pages of Mrs. Douthit's legal pad. We keep those in the box, too.

He is a child, but I speak to him as if he is a full grown man. Time is of the essence. I teach him about the pits and snares that are laid out for him, how to think carefully and avoid them. I tell him about the feasts and vineyards that are laid out for him, how to strive and attain them.

Dustin loves discovery...always finding and learning something new. With thirty-nine acres, that's an easy goal to meet...we just follow the birds to wherever they lead us. With so many trees, flowers and rocks, squirrels frogs and rabbits, this place is a little boy's paradise. We pick apples off the apple tree, catch fish from the pond and pick supper from the vegetable garden. It's peace here; and I'm so glad I have it for him...this HomePlace...and glad, too, someone had it for me.

He'll be the first one of us, in a long time to grow up here. According to Uncle Mack, the historian, Dusty is like Doany—who was serious, like Rone. He is already locked to this land, Uncle Mack says. That is certainly music to my ears.

Uncle Mack described J'Rick, on his documentary, as something unseen—a Rane by blood, brought to manhood by Ismines. He said my firstborn was going to be a giant among men. He denies saying it; even though Monique captured it on film. He says "you have to be firm with boys so they grow straight." Yes, old Mack is still hard on my boy, but proud of him too. How could you not be?

J'Rick is finishing his MBA this year. I can't believe my baby is twenty-three years old. Time flies, don't it? He stays busy too, always traveling. Ismine Construction does business in three states, now, and J'Rick is the Project Manager, slash Accountant, slash Contract Specialist, slash... You should see what he's done to the corner of Rane Lane. He added some office space on to the shop. He handles his businesses out of one office, and his fiancé Rita Wynn, Erma's niece, sells insurance out of the other. She's such a blessing for my family, treats Dustin like her very own child. J'Rick tore down his old produce stand and built a regular little convenience store...does a brisk bit of business, too. Walking this land is still his favorite thing to do. He's my best....he is my sun.

Monique is a freshman at Winston-Salem State University, a college about an hour's drive from here; taking up nursing, like her mother. She comes to "mamma" her nephew every other weekend. Dusty eats her up. I'm so glad I took the time to get to know her; I wouldn't have a daughter in the world at all, if I hadn't. She still carries that camcorder everywhere she goes. Her current documentary is on the strange behavior of my three birds—a crow, a cardinal, and a pigeon. They nest together, believe it or not, and they don't mate or migrate. Monique has it all on film. She says most of their time is spent just sitting, watching this family. I believe her.

Her mother, my best girlfriend, Keisha, vacations on the farm as well. She's thinking about moving to Baylorton. Being a registered nurse, she can find work anywhere in the world. Abraham's always threatening to build her a house and find her a good country man. I told her we got thirty-nine acres; put your house wherever you want. Uncle Mack says, "She can come live in my house. I need a nurse pretty as you to give me one of them sponge baths." We have a good laugh about that.

Isabel Gutierrez handles the boutique for me, selling and sewing, too. She's teaching Dusty how to make earthenware, and other things about Honduran culture. For him, sculpting pottery is a chance to play in mud, so he adores his time with her. I have always been fond of her. She's Honduran, but she looks like she could be my sister. And really, she is only an American...a Black and White, Indian, like me. Honduras is just the label some Spaniard put on the land she comes from...just like some Englishman dubbed this place Carolina.

Isabel's husband, Marco, and a couple of other families from the trailer court, lease about twenty-five acres from me to farm tobacco—inspired by the Dick Noggin fiasco. So we have plenty of everything we need around here. Life is good, because God is great.

My Abraham finally harvested those loblolly pines, sparing no expense on my medical care. But after three rounds of chemo and radiation over the past three years, there's nothing else they can do. It is what it is...fucking cigarettes... The doctors are actually threatening me with Hospice, now. But I'm staying *right here*. I told my oncologist that my sister was a nurse, and she would care for me. Keisha even sent a certified letter with all her credentials to prove it. We laugh about that too.

There's a lot of laughter in my life these days. The only thing that aches, besides my cancer-riddled body, is the place in my heart and soul where Karma lives. God Almighty, I miss my baby girl! I dream about her all the time; and she's happy in my dreams. I take that to mean she's in a place where she doesn't hurt anymore. I wish I could have stopped her pain when she was living though...but I could never put my finger on what ailed her so. Truth is, I lost Karma in the storm of my life. I could have done more, tried harder to break through. I bear full responsibility for the part I played in the death of my poor baby girl.

We all have to pay the piper someday. And with the life I led, Lord knows I owed a serious debt. But my God the price was so great. I could have broken the cycle that's plagued my family for centuries—the curse of mothers not knowing their daughters and daughters not knowing their mothers. But I was too caught up in the struggle of survival to fight and win that battle...too busy living Life. I failed Karma Dominique Rane; period. I only wish she wouldn't have failed herself. It took some time; but I've finally learned to forgive myself. Alas, the Lord giveth and the Lord taketh away. I can certainly testify to that!

I remember telling Karma, once upon a time, to work at becoming a woman she could proud of. I've thought for a very long time about that. Could I, at the ripe old age of 45, say the same for myself? Can I be proud of the life I've led...proud of the person I've become? And the answer is a resounding, Yes! Oh, I've made my mistakes…more than most people could boast in ten lifetimes; but I've learned from them, too.

After my parents died, I developed a habit of looking at and touching things two and three times, to make sure they were still there. I guess because so much was taken from me overnight. Now, however, I have a habit of thinking about things two or three times, considering different angles and perspectives…not opening my mouth or making a move until I've weighed the outcome, the cost and consequences.

Back when I was hustling with Nick Gentry, there were times when I wanted to stop, call it quits. But I found out too late, everything that has a way in; doesn't necessarily have a way out. With some things, you can only exit by way of the penitentiary or the graveyard. I think my Karma found herself in such a situation. So to be on the safe side, I've learned to be very careful about what I enter and entertain. I'm trying desperately to teach Dustin the same.

On days like this, slightly breezy and 74 degrees…the leaves changing colors on the trees and not a cloud in the sky…I really wish I could stay here. But I know I cannot. I was angry, at first. So damned mad that just when I'd found the straight path, the right way…just when I'd finally gotten to the way things are supposed to be…and my life was…well, perfect; I was handed a death sentence. But I've decided to squeeze a lifetime of living out of every second the Good Lord gives me. I'm here **this** day, and that's enough for me. And I have so much Joy my heart can hardly contain it!

If I had it to do all over again, though, (other than the loss of my only daughter) I wouldn't change a damn day. One thing about my foolish years, I sure had a hell of a lot of fun! I

265

lived the fucking life of Riley. And I wouldn't be the woman I am today without those experiences—good, bad *and* ugly. I just sit back laughing sometimes, thinking back over my manic life.

Though there's a lot of laughter in my life these days, there are also a great many tears. I don't cry for myself anymore...it don't make no flowers grow. My tears, when they come, are for Abraham, Dusty and J'Rick. I don't want them to hurt. Lord I don't want them to feel the pain of my leaving. So I write things down...things I'm thinking, feeling. I've got little notes tucked all around this house and my husband's home, as well. They're in coat pockets, under the sink, behind the urns on the mantelpiece. Telling Dusty to always be honest...telling J'Rick he is the joy of my heart...telling Abraham thank you, for saving my life...sending each of them my love from afar.

I wish sometimes I could clone myself for Abraham. I don't know what my husband's going to do without me. If he's not taking care of his business, he's right here with me...morning, noon and night. We still switch houses every other day. I love that Abraham Ismine. He's so good to me...so damn good it really ain't no words to describe it. When his lips touch mine, I still think my heart's gonna stop from the pure passion. He is the King who allowed me to be Queen.

Abraham told me the picture of the woman, in the front of Doany's photo album, was named Tuppie Rane. I have a longing to meet Miss Tuppie. I want to see my mother and father and daughter again...find the first Dusty and GrandSue, too...Baptise, Wilbur and EulaLee. I know I'll be seeing them all someday soon and it gives me something to look forward to.

But I'm not rushing it. I'm gone sit here in the sun with these three wonderful men God has blessed me with, and these three beautiful birds that just refuse to leave my side. I'll keep saying my prayers, reading my books, finish knitting this blanket for Dusty, and enjoying this Indian summer.

God is Great! And He's been mighty good to me! When life wasn't good; it's because *I* made it bad. But I don't Blame Rane anymore; I know the Blame IsMine.

I used to tell my children, after I learned some sense, this life is about right, wrong and responsibility. That knowledge made me stronger, wiser...more understanding. I finally learned to stop blaming my misfortune on everybody else. When I learned to accept the fact that I was the responsible party; I was able to make better decisions. And better decisions resulted in a damn good life!

I am, at last, at Peace.

CHAPTER 39
JOY COMETH IN THE MORNING

April 3, 2016

Dustin Abraham Rane was born with a twinkle in his eye—like he was privy to some secret the rest of the world was clueless about. He couldn't wait to be born, and arrived a full three weeks early. He was the color of peaches in winter, roasted almonds in the summertime—like the first little Black boy who lived on his farm, named Rone. He wore WindRider's straight black Cherokee hair cut close to his scalp. He had the peculiar marble-like eyes of a little Anglo girl who grew up behind the walls of a fort, in the wild frontier or Tennessee. Philomena's dimple rested in his chin.

Little Dusty slept in the room Doany and Baptise used to share. The same room his mother, Karma, left him in, as a baby. It was next to his grandma Blame's room, which was his first destination *every* morning.

If she wasn't at Papa Abe's, then she would be sitting up in her bed, greeting him with open arms and a big smile. He loved to slide across the hardwood floors and dive into her loving arms. When he heard the preacher at church, say, "Joy cometh in the morning," he knew very well what that meant. It was his happiest time of day...just him and his grandmommy, laughing and tickling each other under the covers. She always had a good story to tell him—bursting with information he knew he would need someday—first rays of sunshine swimming across her beautiful face.

On the morning of April 3rd, in the year of our Lord, 2016, Dustin arose and ran to greet his grandmother, Blame. He couldn't tell time, but it had to be pretty early, because she was still sleeping. He could hear J'Rick outside, going to tend the fields before he left for the construction office. He could hear the clock ticking on the wall, and three little birds lamenting in the bird bath. He slid across the floor, beaming and laughing, shouting. "Good Morning GrandMommy!"

But she did not take him up in her arms. Blame was smiling. Dustin assumed she was playing possum, which he loved to play. He climbed into the high four-post bed and lay across her chest, but her warm bosom was frightfully cold. Her soft face, when he kissed her cheek, was hard like the smooth stones Papa Abe was teaching him to skip across the thin creek.

"Grandma?" he tried shaking her. "GrandMommy Blame?" Dusty tried lifting her arms, but she was frozen, like the snake he and J'Rick dug up last winter. He kissed her again, and cried.

He remembered Felicity, the cat, being this way, cold and stiff, before Uncle J'Rick wrapped her in a soft blanket and took her away. He cried because he missed his kitty. But Papa Abe said Felicity had gone to her heavenly home. He said she'd been ready to go for a long, long time, and she would be very happy there. Dustin still missed the cat, but he didn't cry anymore, knowing she was happy in her Heaven Home.

Rain clouds moved past the window and a light spring shower trickled from the sky. Dustin suddenly wanted his Papa Abe, but the man was in Fayetteville, securing a contract for construction of a nursing home. Dustin kissed his Blame again, slid down from the high bed and walked solemnly down the hall, and down the steps, quiet as a mouse.

He walked out in the drizzling rain, barefoot and crying. His uncle J'Rick scooped him up off the damp earth and kissed his warm forehead. "What's the matter little man?" he asked his five year old nephew.

Dusty didn't answer. The tears ran down his face in rivulets. His momma was dead, two-fold now. He wrapped his arms tight around his uncle's neck. Riding J'Rick's hip had always been the safest place he'd ever known. He nuzzled his nose into the groove above J'Rick's collarbone and wept like the baby he was.

Dustin Abraham Rane—more American than apple pie or baseball could ever dare to be—stood in the morning rain and pressed his lips against the thick vein, pumping Rane blood, on his uncle's strong, brown neck, and whispered softly, "Grandmommy Blame in heavenhome."

Dusty watched longingly, as an odd quartet of winged creatures flew into the glow of the rising sun...a crow, cardinal and pigeon...with a small brown sparrow, in tow.

Ethel's Song

"One bright morning, when this life is over, I'll fly away…"

~Albert E. Brumley

BLAME'S PRISON READING LIST:

Torah, Gospel, Qur'an
When & Where I Enter
The Destruction of the Black Civilization
Willie Lynch Letter and the Making of a Slave
Their Eyes Were Watching God
Message to the Blackman
Beloved
The Wretched of the Earth
The Color Purple
Without Sanctuary
The Secret Relationship Between Blacks and Jews
Langston, Morrison, Walker, Baldwin, Cooper,
Tademy, Shange, Hill, Obama, Wright, Brooks, Wilson,
McFadden, Angelou, Haley, Welsing and Muhammad,
Giovanni, Zinn...
Four Hours in Bondage
The Book of Enoch
A House for Mr. Biswas
Say You're One of Them
Behold the Pale Horse
Making of the White Man
Slavery By Another Name: The Re-Enslavement of Black
Americans From the Civil War to World War II
Lies My Teacher Told Me, etc, etc, etc....

Special Thanks to: the Creator, for Everything; Grandma Eva, for instilling in me an unshakeable love for God and family; my daughter, Cydney (Reason), without whom this journey would not have been possible; my son , Nicholas (Forever) for laughter and being; Cyllana Nichole (Gwanny's Girl!), my inspiration, joy, and most favorite little girl in the whole wide world; mamma and daddy, Johnnie and Kennard, for life itself; William Welch III, for the lessons; Toni and Alice, (my personal favorites) for the food; Akmir, for the Book; the ancestors, for existing, surviving and guiding; the storytellers and prophets (pbut), for sharing; my family and friends; Manataka.org for the Tsalagi; D. Wooten, for the picture; Wikipedia.org; readers worldwide; the believers; the artists who create; Joanie, for listening; Michelle; and the three little birds which have *always* nested outside my window. **Thank you.**

ABOUT THE AUTHOR:

Rene' O'Shea is a social activist and successful entrepreneur. She is also Editor of Black Girl Green World, a monthly online magazine.

Rene' has two other published works of fiction, a novella and book of poetry. **Blame Rane** is O'Shea's debut novel.

Rene' O'Shea lives on the historic Welch Farm in North Carolina with her husband, William Welch III. She is currently working on her second novel.

R O'Shea